"We have no reason to believe anything untoward has happened," Aubrey added in a hurry. She should've left this to Calvin. She pushed back from the desk and stood up. "What was your decision on the coffee?"

"Yes, please," Leo replied. Leaning forward in the chair, he rested his elbows on his knees, hands hanging loose.

She was almost overcome with the need to soothe, to massage the tension from his neck and make him foolish promises about his finding his sister safe and happy. What a dumb reaction considering she hadn't even run a background check on him yet.

She deliberately turned away to find some coffee for him. Her compassionate streak would be the death of her career. Given the chance, her coworkers would put those rose-colored sunglasses on her face at her funeral.

She would take his statement and finish her shift and, most likely, they'd never see each other again.

Unless she found his sister.

Dear Reader,

It's a joy to return to Philadelphia, PA, for another Escape Club adventure. Although the club itself took heavy damage in *Braving the Heat*, the commitment to community and the dedication of local heroes are as strong as ever.

That is great news for Leo Butler when his younger sister, a college sophomore, disappears from her campus. Though the police are polite, filing a missing person report doesn't leave him with much confidence. He turns to the freelance investigators at the Escape Club for help.

Aubrey Rawlins adores her role as a Philly police officer. Sympathizing with Leo's desperation, she soon finds herself caught between trying to help him and protecting him from his risky choices.

As Aubrey and Leo continue to search, they stumble onto a bigger threat to the community. I hope you'll enjoy their crash course in learning to trust, falling in love and their courageous fight for a happy future.

Live the adventure,

Regan Black

HER UNLIKELY PROTECTOR

Regan Black

H HARLEQUIN

ROMANTIC SUSPENSE

Recycling programs
for this product may
not exist in your area.

ISBN-13: 978-1-335-62895-4

Her Unlikely Protector

Copyright © 2021 by Regan Black

This edition published by arrangement with Harlequin Books S.A.

For questions and comments about the quality of this book, please contact us at CustomerService@Harlequin.com.

Harlequin Enterprises ULC
22 Adelaide St. West, 40th Floor
Toronto, Ontario M5H 4E3, Canada
www.Harlequin.com

Printed in U.S.A.

Regan Black, a *USA TODAY* bestselling author, writes award-winning action-packed novels featuring kick-butt heroines and the sexy heroes who fall in love with them. Raised in the Midwest and California, she and her family, along with their adopted greyhound, two arrogant cats and a quirky finch, reside in the South Carolina Lowcountry, where the rich blend of legend, romance and history fuels her imagination.

For Mark and the countless ways you make me feel loved every single day of our happily-ever-after.

Chapter 1

Take a deep breath. Keep an open mind. This was a mix-up, not a crisis. But by the dull thud of his heartbeat and the persistent prickle at the back of his neck, he knew his body wasn't buying in to the theory. Leo Butler would have an easier time believing there had been a mistake if his sister, Lara, would just answer her phone.

When the restlessness grew too big, he dialed her cell. Better to try again than stride up to the campus security information desk to ask how long he was expected to sit here doing *nothing*. In his ear, the call went to voice mail. The same result he'd had every day for the past eight days. He'd lost count of how many text messages he'd sent, but the last one—an hour old—was still unanswered.

He shoved his phone into his jacket pocket. Right now he knew he personified the accepted definition of insanity, doing the same thing over and over and expecting a different outcome.

There were times, like this one, when the nine-year age difference between him and his sister seemed as wide as a generational gap. Sure, he remembered what it was like to get caught up in the freedom and fun of college life and, yes, occasionally she'd ignored his messages before. This was different. Lara had never gone this long without so much as an emoji reply in the text message thread.

The age gap and a thoroughly disinterested mother had created a stronger bond between them. They supported each other and were open about everything. Concerned, he'd used his access and checked her bank account and credit card. He paid the bills that her scholarships didn't cover and the lack of activity was as out of character as her extended silence. That was the factor he couldn't dismiss, the one that had had him hopping on a plane to knock on her dorm door.

She hadn't even placed an order for books—electronic or paperback—for the semester. This was the start of spring semester of her junior year. She was a political science major. There had to be some required books for her heavy class schedule.

He'd been desperate enough, baffled enough, that he'd reached out to their mother. She had been courteous enough to tell him she hadn't heard anything from Lara before ending the call.

Naturally, Lenore Butler wasn't concerned about Lara. The moment her daughter moved into her dorm for her first year of college, Lenore had considered motherhood a task fulfilled. She'd sold the house they'd grown up in, sending Leo scrambling to recover and store anything he and Lara were sentimental about. Gliding into the role of moderately wealthy widow unencumbered by parental duties, their mother moved to a condo on the Gulf Coast of Florida. Leo had only seen the pictures she'd sent to Lara.

On breaks and holidays, Lara came to his house in Cincinnati, where they were both happier without the strain of old family drama and threadbare emotional baggage. They had new traditions now and built cheerful memories with friends gathered around the table for good food and pleasant conversation.

What else could he have done but come pound on Lara's dorm room door when she had gone silent for so long? In the midst of the ruckus, a pajama-clad girl from across the hall informed him that Lara, the residence assistant on the floor, hadn't been around much since winter break.

Much wasn't real, actionable information. Granted, classes had only been back in session for a week, but his sister never ghosted him. Stalking up and down the dorm halls, on each of the floors in her building, he tried to find someone who could tell him more. Plenty of people recognized her name or the picture he showed around. Not one of them had seen her lately.

He needed facts and timelines. He needed *something* to go on, something to give him a direction. What he didn't need was this current intervention.

Apparently, in Philadelphia, the city of brotherly love, a man couldn't search a school for his sister without drawing the ire of campus security. Their assertive and competent response would have been more reassuring under different circumstances. If, say, she'd been mugged. Instead, he rushed to show his identification and explain his fear that something worse had happened to her.

Reluctant to test the patience of the responding team or endure a jolt from the Tasers they carried, Leo allowed them to walk him here, to the main office. He would've stopped here first if he'd known he was walking into a crisis. The administration building was a fine example of classic architecture. He vaguely recalled being impressed when he'd accompanied Lara for her college visit and tour.

The glossy grandeur she'd been thrilled with had dulled significantly in Leo's view. Today he caught the stale whiff of mustiness under the polished marble, high-tech upgrades and museum-quality displays.

He supposed it was a courtesy, allowing him to sit here, pretending he was a normal visitor, but he just wanted to get back out there and find his sister. Talk to the police, chat with the few friends he knew by name. She had to be *somewhere* on the campus.

And if she wasn't?

He couldn't dwell there.

As an operations officer at the Cincinnati/Northern Kentucky International Airport, he worked to find solutions. He and his team persistently searched for ways to improve the everyday processes and ways to overcome any crisis. He excelled at problem solving, even in the worst-case scenarios. Given a chance, he knew he could track down Lara. Admittedly, a lead would help.

A whiny hinge protested from the hallway beyond the waiting area. Rubber-soled shoes squeaked on the polished floors, coming his way. A tall, barrel-chested man wearing the campus security uniform appeared and stopped at the desk. Completely bald, the guard had ebony skin, marred by one thin scar that started at his cheekbone and curled around behind his ear. He exuded authority, though Leo couldn't pick out any obvious differences in this man's uniform and that of the team that hauled him in here.

They were less than twenty feet from him but all Leo could hear was a low murmur. The uniformed receptionist nodded and handed the man a few papers stapled together.

He read through each page, his lips pursed. After rolling up the pages, he tapped them on the desktop as he turned toward Leo.

"Mr. Butler?"

The deep voice filled the waiting room with measured authority. This man knew his job, his role and his effect on others. Leo appreciated that. He was sure this man would help him find Lara. The cramped muscles of his shoulders eased as he stood and crossed the room.

His extended hand was gripped firmly and released. "Campus Security Chief Jones," the other man said by way of introduction. "The incident report states you caused a disruption in one of our dorms."

"My apologies for that." Leo smothered the surge of desperation stinging the back of his throat. "I was looking for my sister."

"Come on back and let's talk about it." Jones and his squeaking shoes led the way down the hall to his office. He gestured to a chair in front of the desk and closed the door. "Mr. Butler, you upset several students."

"Again, I apologize," Leo repeated in the weighty silence that followed. He sank into the chair. "I only want to find my sister." Didn't anyone else care that she hadn't been around *much* or *lately*?

Jones set the papers on his desktop. "This is only a cursory report," he said, taking his seat behind the desk. "From what we've gathered so far, I don't believe your sister is currently on our campus."

"She wouldn't move out of the dorm." She wouldn't have made a drastic decision like that without talking to him. "She was an RA," Leo added. Surely, the housing and security departments had some overlap or cooperation. "Is it possible for me to speak with her professors?"

Jones tapped the paperwork with his blunt fingertips. "Mr. Butler, your sister withdrew from all of her classes last week."

What? No. That wasn't possible. He saw the chief's lips moving but he couldn't make out any more words with his pulse pounding in his ears. He couldn't swallow, his throat dry as sand. There had to be another Lara Butler. It was a common name.

"A—a mix-up," Leo managed. "Her tuition was paid."

Jones slid the papers across his desk, nodding for Leo to take a look. "Yes, it was. At her request, the money will be held as a credit on her account until next semester. As I said, she'll need to make a final decision about her future here at that time."

No. Leo's mind latched on to the one thing he could. No way he was letting that kind of money just sit in the school's account. "And what is the interest rate you're offering to keep her money for all that time?"

Jones's black eyebrows lifted and then settled back into place. "She is welcome to make alternate arrangements with the finance office."

"If she was *here*," Leo said through gritted teeth, "I'd feel better about the prospect of that conversation."

"Your sister is an adult, Mr. Butler. A quick look at

her campus employment history shows she's a valued member of the residence life staff."

At the end of last year, though, Lara had been frustrated with her res life supervisor. Leo had reminded her she didn't need the tuition discount and housing perks that came with her role as an RA. Leo had been helping her search for off-campus housing until she decided to keep her RA post for one more academic year. *This* year.

Another two semesters. What had changed? Why the hell wouldn't she talk to him about it? "Chief Jones, may I please have a list of the classes she took last semester?"

Jones reached out and tapped the papers in front of Leo. "I'm afraid not. Your sister did not update the release of information authorization. Officially, her business with the school is just that—*her* business."

Leo couldn't have heard him correctly. The knot of temper in his throat turned hot and oily, burning a trail down past his heart and deep into his belly. He dried his palms on his jeans.

"An oversight," he said, jaw clenched. "Her behavior has changed. All of the family support materials say I should seek help if I'm concerned for her."

Jones linked his hands, his thumbs tapping slowly. "I do understand your concerns, Mr. Butler. Unfortunately, there isn't much I can do. She is not on campus and my records show she made that choice on her own. It happens," he finished, not unkindly.

A picture of Lara's freshman move-in day flashed through his mind. At eighteen, she had been so bright and eager to dive into this new chapter of her life. "She had plans." Leo didn't recognize the rasping sound as his voice. "This isn't right."

"In my experience, Mr. Butler, a withdrawal for a semester can clarify a student's goals and ambition."

"She didn't leave because she was struggling with the coursework or clarity."

"I agree with you there," Jones allowed. "She had excellent grades."

"Then what do you think happened?" Lara had not run off or walked away from her carefully constructed plans without good reason. The finances were in order and the coursework and grades were fine, leaving Leo with a big pile of questions no one seemed inclined to answer.

The big man studied Leo. Coming to some conclusion, he reached into the top drawer of his desk and pulled out a book of matches. "Your sister is not on this campus. At least not legally, if she's crashing with a friend. I will talk with my staff and keep an eye out for her."

"Thank you."

Jones's dark gaze intensified. "I assume you intend to keep looking for her?"

"Of course." His next stop would be the police department. He couldn't go back home without answers. She was the most important person in his world. When tragedy tore their family apart, they leaned on each other. He knew her. When either of them needed space, they asked for it. None of this made any sense. Lara would not willingly stop communicating without warning. "I still have access to her bank records. She hasn't bought a ticket for a plane, bus, or train. She hasn't rented a car or taken out any cash. In the past week there hasn't been any activity at all."

Jones pushed the matchbook across the desk. "You

should file a report with the police, but I doubt you'll make much headway there."

"Because I'm the only person who gives a damn about Lara," Leo snapped.

"I'm sure it feels that way." Jones shook his head. "Though it isn't true," he countered gently. "Like many police departments these days, they don't have the manpower to track down every adult who decides to behave out of character."

Leo wanted help finding just *one* missing adult. Was that such a big demand? He picked up the matchbook, turning it over in his fingers. *Escape Club* was emblazoned on the front in bold, neon letters. Inside the flap was one word. A name: *Alexander*.

"What's this?"

"That nightclub is owned by a former cop. He's a good man and he has a reputation for helping resolve cases that slip through the cracks in the system. The club is on the pier at the Delaware River. They had some trouble a while back, but I've heard they plan to reopen soon."

"They'll help me find Lara?"

Jones nodded slowly. "If the police don't have a better idea, it's worth the cab fare to go out and ask."

Not much to go on, but more than he had a few hours ago. "What can you tell me about the area around the campus?" Leo asked.

A pained expression crossed Jones's face. "We keep our space as safe as possible. You've noticed we don't live in a bubble. There are pockets of trouble that try to encroach and occasionally succeed." He swiveled around and pulled a printed map of the campus from a pad on the low filing cabinet behind his desk. With a highlighter he outlined two areas that abutted its borders.

"Nothing I've found indicates that your sister was ever mixed up with the kind of activity that occurs in these pockets. We encourage our students to avoid these areas. Drugs and homelessness are peak issues here and here." He tapped the highlighted circles on the map. "I wouldn't recommend walking into these areas alone, Mr. Butler."

Leo folded the map, tucking it and the matchbook into an inside pocket of his leather bomber jacket. "I'm not as helpless as I must look."

"Of course not," Jones said.

Leo didn't bother to address the older man's skepticism. No matter how Leo blustered or tried to defend himself, the man had a point. Leo didn't know Philly like Jones. Or Lara.

He only knew he had to find his sister.

Released with what amounted to a slap on the wrist and encouragement to let the proper authorities find Lara, Leo left the building. Out on the street, he turned up the collar on his coat, though it offered little protection against the biting wind funneled between the tall buildings. When he found Lara he'd use his airline benefits and take them both to Jamaica for a week. That should thaw them out and give her time and space to explain herself. He wanted to know what had prompted this erratic departure from her plans.

Only three semesters from graduating, Lara wouldn't throw away all that hard work without a good reason. Or ten. He checked the map and headed for the college library, where Lara had worked during her freshman year. She still preferred to study there. He knew the names of her closest friends and professors. Surely, someone there would have more insight than campus security.

They might even have an idea of what had been on her mind before she withdrew.

Lara had spoken with him about every big decision in the past. Why shut him out of this one?

Leo had listened to her long list of insecurities when she wanted to join the debate team in middle school. Later, it was concerns over whether or not drama club showed the right balance of interests for her senior year and college applications. He helped her prep for her SAT and together they'd evaluated collegiate programs and reputations when she'd decided to major in political science. Leo had joined her for all but one college visit. Their mother had only shown enthusiasm for Lara's visit to the University of Kentucky, the place where their parents had met.

He couldn't simply go back to Cincinnati and hope she called when she was ready. They'd been a team for her entire life and more than half of his, to compensate for their less-than-reliable parent. Lara had stood by him, too, time and again, when things between him and their mother turned ugly at school events, the grocery store, or even the dinner table.

There was no way to convince a stranger just how out of character this lack of communication and withdrawal decision were for his sister.

At the mat just inside the library doors, Leo knocked the slush from his shoes. His feet were freezing in the thin leather dress shoes. He should've taken the time to check the weather and pack smarter before he'd hopped on the first flight out here.

At the checkout desk, he introduced himself to Amy, a fresh-faced sophomore who was familiar with Lara.

"She, um…" Amy looked around. "I overheard her talking about leaving the RA position."

Leo nodded. "Did she mention why?"

Amy shook her head. "Just said it was just too much." The girl chewed on her thumbnail. "I'm told third year can be the worst workload in some programs. Professor Whitten is her department mentor. He's got a reputation as a real hard-ass."

That was progress. "Thanks for your time, Amy." Leo nearly gave the girl a high five. He pulled out a business card and circled his cell phone number. "If you see her or think of anything else, will you give me a call?"

She took the card as if he'd offered a priceless treasure. "I will."

With another thank-you, he went back out into the weather and traced Lara's most likely path between the library and the dorm he didn't dare approach again. The entire route was within campus limits.

No, there wasn't a protective wall or bubble keeping the outside world away from the students. Anyone could cut across the campus or hang out in the areas between buildings. It had been one of his concerns when they visited. Lara's common sense and conviction about the program had made it worth the potential risk. She'd reminded him the world wasn't always a safe place. A lesson they had both learned early in life. But he'd wanted her college life, her first solo foray into the world, to be different than the home they'd survived.

Leo would never believe she'd toss away this kind of opportunity for something like drugs or a guy. He stamped his feet and blew into his cold hands. He should go back to his hotel and regroup before filing a report with the police. It would give him time to warm up a bit, too.

He ignored the sting in his fingertips and pulled out his phone to send Lara another text message as he walked. Before he could hit Send, the device rang. He picked up even though he didn't recognize the number. "Hello?"

"Mr. Butler? This is Amy."

The girl had done some fast thinking. "Hi, Amy."

"You probably know this already, but just in case. Lara volunteered a lot last semester over at the Good Samaritan soup kitchen."

He'd known his sister participated in outreach and charity work, but not where she'd done either. "That's a big help. Thanks, Amy."

"It's not a great part of town," she said. "Be careful."

"Thanks." Ending the call, he vowed to get back to the gym, maybe start on vitamins. He had to do something if everyone in this town thought he couldn't handle himself.

He looked up the address and noticed three Good Samaritan locations around the city. The nearest was only a few blocks away, dead center in one of those unsavory pockets Jones had highlighted on the campus map.

With hope in his stride, Leo headed straight for it.

Aubrey Rawlins *loved* Philly. She thrived on the pulse and energy. It was far, far from perfect, but it was home and, therefore, as much a part of her as blood and bone. There were plenty of reasons to love the city, reasons that were easier to recall when her feet were warm and she wasn't trudging through gray slush in the middle of a bitter cold snap.

She'd been born and raised here, in a city that often got a bad rap in any weather. It was why she stayed, right in the heart of it; why she'd gone through the academy and joined the Philadelphia Police Department. Her efforts as a cop made a difference. A small one to be sure, but the subsequent ripples had the potential to become big improvements.

Lousy weather aside, she enjoyed being out here and taking action. Walking these streets day in and day out with her partner, Calvin Rice, she'd come to know the people on her beat, building trust and creating a stronger community and healthier neighborhood for everyone involved and invested.

This neighborhood ran the gamut from college students and staff to hospital professionals and business owners to homeless communities wedged in between. Aubrey and her partner dealt with their share of criminal activity, as well, though she was convinced they were making a dent in those statistics just by being more visible and engaged.

While Calvin chatted with someone on the corner, she ducked into the deli for her afternoon pick-me-up smoothie and a coffee for her partner. She checked in with the staff and regular customers while she waited. Everyone in the department gave her grief for being too nice and believing the best about people when she should be more pragmatic. Calvin had given her a pair of rose-colored sunglasses after her first month on the job.

The gift hadn't been a complimentary gesture or to mark the milestone. No, the glasses were meant to remind her that she'd screwed up and let misplaced trust and affection blind her to trouble brewing right under her nose at home. Before her boyfriend had become her ex.

Still, she kept those sunglasses taped to the inside of her locker door where she could see them every day. Everyone thought it was because she could handle an inside joke. Not even close. Whenever she opened her locker, she remembered to be herself and keep believing in others without broadcasting her softer side all over the place.

Smoothie in hand, she walked out to give Calvin his coffee. Applying the professional, friendly nod of acknowledgment to others out in the weather, they headed back to the precinct to thaw out for a few minutes.

Aubrey didn't believe a police officer had to be aloof or appear heartless. The whole point of walking a beat was to know people, the good and the up-to-no-good. Whether or not anyone else hopped on, this was the bandwagon she was driving. She didn't know how to live any differently and she wasn't interested in letting circumstances change her. Things happened, with or without a reason. According to her grandmother, Aubrey had been born with this perpetually sunny disposition. Everyone on the planet suffered at some point. She'd taken her share of hard knocks, made plenty of mistakes. Still, she made a daily choice to focus on the positives. It wasn't always easy, but she did it. If that made her overly compassionate, that was fine.

She and Calvin were at the precinct door when their radios crackled with a request from the dispatcher. A disturbance at a soup kitchen two blocks away. They exchanged a look and moved in that direction at a quick pace.

The soup kitchen was located in an older building, but the sidewalks were clear and the door and window glass gleamed behind protective ironwork. As Aubrey and Calvin approached, people slipped outside, one by one, skirting by and darting away into the shadows. She didn't care for the furtive expressions or the way they hunched into their coats as if by hiding their faces it would make the trouble disappear. Calvin tried to ask for information but no one replied.

"I'll head around back," Calvin said, his dark eyebrows flexed into a frown under the brim of his hat.

Aubrey nodded.

By tacit agreement, the notoriously rough neighborhood had designated the soup kitchen as a safe place. Off-limits to drug dealing and most other kinds of trouble, although many of the city's homeless were unpredictable. The shouting carried to her as she stepped inside. Following the noise, she hurried down the hallway that should have been crowded with people waiting for a hot meal. It was empty.

The ruckus was coming from the dining room.

A man she'd never seen in the neighborhood dominated the space. Not by size in particular, but by his presence. His voice, loaded with authority, filled the room as he demanded help.

The tight band across her shoulders eased a little. She never enjoyed hauling in someone whose internal trouble or rough day spilled out onto others. So often those situations were exacerbated by people who lacked control over themselves or their circumstances. This situation felt different. Clearly, this person wasn't having a great day, but he seemed in control as he thrust a cell phone at every person in sight.

She pegged him at six feet, average build. His dark blond hair was neat and trim and his face clean-shaven. The leather bomber jacket, unzipped, was fashionably distressed and his shoes were polished, though damp from the weather. He should be on a magazine cover or front and center of a movie poster, not here in the Good Samaritan dining room.

Mentally, she shook off the reaction. He was causing a scene and upsetting the people in the neighborhood she was sworn to protect. She set her smoothie down on the nearest table.

"He's new," Aubrey observed as the manager joined her. In the hallway, Calvin blocked the rear exit. "What's the problem?"

"He came in asking questions about his sister." The manager frowned, aiming her sharp chin in the man's direction. "He's convinced all of us know the girl and just aren't talking."

"Did he give you a name?"

At her question, the man turned, his eyes locked on to Aubrey. "Great, the cops are here." The sincerity in his words startled her. "*You* can help me, Officer. Make them tell me where my sister is."

Right. As if she'd side with a bully, even if he was the well-dressed and handsome type. "Sir, you're causing a scene," she said, approaching slowly. "Our neighbors come in for a hot meal and they like to eat it in peace."

"They can eat." He turned a circle. "They can eat while they tell me where my sister is. I know they recognize her." His voice cracked. "Someone has to know her."

"Come on over here." Aubrey motioned him closer, away from the center of the room. "Show me your sister's picture. Does she live in the neighborhood? Maybe I've seen her."

Behind him the manager mouthed her thanks and returned to the kitchen to get her staff and volunteers back on track. The crowd would undoubtedly be lighter than expected after this. Rumors and warnings spread quickly within this community. Aubrey smothered her irritation so she wouldn't escalate the situation. Whoever this man was, she had an obligation to protect him, as well, even from himself.

"This is my sister, Lara Butler." The man held out his phone and showed Aubrey a picture of a lovely young woman. The sibling resemblance was strong. They shared the same dark blond hair and deep brown eyes. In the picture, her eyes sparkled and her lips were tipped up as if she was about to burst into laughter. She looked like a very happy person.

"She's been here," he said. "They recognized her." He swiveled around, pointing at a cluster of people hunched over bowls of hot stew.

Aubrey knew the two men and one woman he'd indicated. The trio was usually a stabilizing force in the community, inside the shelters and out. If they weren't talking, there was a good reason for their silence. Most likely, they'd been stringing the stranger along to keep him away from others.

The dispatcher's voice came over her radio, asking for an update. A few regulars nearby flinched and Aubrey let Calvin answer. "Let's talk over here." Aubrey led the man into the hallway between the kitchen and delivery door.

Calvin moved back a few paces, giving her room and making sure they had the man cornered. "Your sister— Lara, you said?"

He nodded.

"She lives in this area?" she asked.

"She's a student," he replied. "Well, she *was* a student

according to the school. Third year." Worry creased his brow as he corrected himself. "She's not on campus."

"Could you show me your identification, please?"

He handed over an Ohio driver's license. Leo Butler, twenty-nine years old, Cincinnati address. "Spring semester just started, right?"

He nodded.

"If she's a third year, I'm assuming your sister is over eighteen."

"She's twenty-one." He pushed a hand through his short hair, mussing it so bits of gold caught in the overhead light. "I'm aware she's an adult and all that implies. I'm also one hundred percent sure she's in trouble."

And Aubrey was one hundred percent sure she needed to get her mind off Mr. Butler's looks and deal with the situation properly. "What makes you so sure?"

"Because she hasn't spoken to me since she came back to school. It's been eight days of silence. I know she got off the plane safely here in Philly and I thought she was all set, but according to the school, she suddenly withdrew from classes."

"Sounds like the two of you are close."

He nodded, morose. "Someone in there has to know something," he said. "One of her coworkers told me she volunteered here."

"Someone in there very well might know her," Aubrey allowed. "They're not cooperating because they don't know *you*. It takes time to earn their trust. Even then, it's no guarantee they have the information you need."

"I'm sorry." He leaned back and thumped his head against the cinderblock wall lightly. "I was out of line. I'm really sorry."

The apology made her want to comfort him. She resisted. "You said Lara volunteered here. Do you know when or how often?"

He shook his head.

"Did you speak with the staff?"

"I tried." His eyes narrowed and he slid a glare in the direction of the kitchen. "They all denied knowing her, too."

Irritation returned with a vengeance, prickling across the nape of her neck. The staff here did wonderful, thankless work. "And you assume they're lying." She returned his identification. "There is a high turnover rate for volunteers in these facilities. Some people come in once and call it a job well-done."

"I offered to pitch in," he said. "To work while they talked."

That surprised her. "What happened?"

He scrubbed the back of his neck. "The lady with the ladle said I was a distraction."

He was certainly distracting her. Her fingertips tingled as she studied his strong jawline and the subtle cleft in his chin. *Down, girl.* She didn't have any business getting tangled up with a stranger in town willing to raise havoc in a soup kitchen.

"This was supposed to be a lead," he said. Again, his head thumped the wall. The man couldn't seem to stand still. "I didn't mean to lose my temper," he said. "It doesn't happen. Hasn't. Not in years. But she's my little sister. I have to find her."

It took every ounce of willpower not to wrap him in a hug and tell him they'd get out there and look until they found Lara. "We all have our breaking point," she managed.

Losing track of a sister was clearly that point for Mr.

Butler. She couldn't find much fault in that, having dealt frequently with people who'd done far worse for much weaker reasons.

Aubrey waved Calvin over and introduced him. "Tell us about your sister," she said.

"She's of legal age." He dropped his head back against the wall, staring up at the flat, fluorescent lights creating dash marks on the ceiling the length of the hallway. He rattled off stats about his sister and her goals and efforts in a glum tone that squeezed her heart. As a cop, compassion was part of the job, though she wasn't supposed to get sucked in by every sob story.

Mr. Butler's story rang true for her, maybe because his sister reportedly shared Aubrey's concern over the city's homeless community.

It was no hardship to study his striking features while he spoke. Not the point. She chalked up her fascination with him to underused hormones. She hadn't bothered dating much after the disaster with her ex. "Come with us to the station, Mr. Butler, and we can get that missing person report filed."

"Will that do anything?"

"Yes." It would get her out of this hallway and help her regain her professional perspective. She eyed his bomber jacket. "Do you have a heavier coat? Gloves?"

"No."

"What about a car?"

"I walked from the campus," he replied. "Don't you have a car?"

"We walk as much as possible on shift," she said, tipping her head toward Calvin. "It isn't far."

The three of them started for the front door, pausing at the kitchen where she introduced Mr. Butler to the manager, Rosie Marlowe. "She's been a manager here for several years and she knows the regular customers and volunteers quite well."

Rosie wiped her hands on her apron, kept a firm grip on the fabric while she gave Mr. Butler a long stare.

"Ms. Marlowe, I am very sorry for the disturbance I created," he said.

"You're distraught," Rosie replied. She evidently hadn't expected him to apologize so graciously. "Many people here have struggles." She released her apron and beckoned with her hand. "Show me the picture of your sister again."

The poor guy scrambled for his phone as if he was sure the offer would expire in ten seconds or less.

Rosie studied the picture closely. "She is quite pretty. You said her name is Lara?"

"Yes," he whispered.

Aubrey watched the muscle in his jaw twitch. In his place, she'd want to point fingers and call Rosie a liar, too.

Rosie returned the phone. Her gaze darted from Aubrey, to Calvin and then settled on Mr. Butler. "She brought in several students to help us the week before Thanksgiving. Again at Christmastime, before her school closed for the winter break."

"Why didn't you say that earlier?" Aubrey queried.

"I don't know this man," Rosie replied. "What if he wanted to harass or harm Lara? She is a good girl."

Aubrey exchanged a look with Calvin, but her partner only shrugged. She made a mental note to come back and speak with Rosie again after her shift.

"Have you seen her?" Mr. Butler stood a bit straighter, hope lighting his face.

Rosie shook her head and returned his phone. "I am sorry, no. Not since the new term began."

All of the hope of a moment ago leached from Mr. Butler's body. Aubrey half expected him to collapse in a puddle of misery on the floor.

Calvin spoke up. "Rosie, did Lara say anything the last time she was here that stands out now?"

"No." Rosie's eyes were full of sympathy and she patted Mr. Butler's shoulder. "I am sorry I cannot be of more help."

In a perfect world Aubrey would ask for Calvin to escort Mr. Butler out and give her a minute to question Rosie privately. She had the feeling that would only get Mr. Butler spun up again. She'd come back alone.

"Thank you for your time, Rosie." She shot the other woman a meaningful glance over her shoulder as they guided Mr. Butler out.

"She did lie to me," he said.

"Didn't give her much choice," Calvin pointed out.

Aubrey chose not to argue the obvious. "You might have noticed this isn't the nicest street in the neighborhood," she said. "The people here have learned to be cautious."

Neither Calvin nor Mr. Butler spoke on the remainder of their walk to the precinct. Aubrey was grateful for the silence. Rosie might not know anything about Lara's disappearance, but she suspected something. Like Aubrey, the soup kitchen manager knew most of the regular faces in their community.

Someone who'd been in frequently to lend a hand and brought others along would be valued and appreciated. That person would have Rosie's loyalty. It wasn't much of a surprise that Rosie hadn't cooperated with Mr. Butler.

She wouldn't offer up answers about a trusted volunteer. In her shoes, Aubrey would have done the same thing.

Once they were finally back inside the precinct, the blast of heat was a welcome relief from the biting wind outside. Calvin went to write up a summary of their patrol, and Aubrey took Mr. Butler's official missing person report.

He shrugged off the bomber jacket, revealing a plain blue oxford shirt unbuttoned at the collar, and sat down in the plastic chair next to the desk. Had he removed a tie or just never put one on today? That really wasn't the point. He wasn't dressed for the current cold snap. The man needed a thermal layer, warmer shoes and outerwear.

None of which fell in the category of her responsibilities.

She focused on the report, taking down the basics from Lara's birthdate to her approximate height and weight. She retrieved the most recent photo of Lara from Mr. Butler's cell phone and sent a request to the school for a copy of Lara's student ID photo.

Mr. Butler struggled to explain when he'd last seen Lara. He obviously knew the facts, but the process of stating those facts tripped him up and made him emotional.

"Would you like a coffee or hot chocolate, Mr. Butler?" she offered. He needed a break.

"Please call me Leo," he replied. "Lara would drink half and half," he continued. "Half coffee and half hot chocolate. She'd put on this silly French accent when she called it 'café and cocoa'. I can't do it the way she did."

"You'll hear her say it again," Aubrey assured him.

"Will I?"

An alarm clanged in her head, similar to the alarm when a delivery truck shifted into Reverse. "I can't make any promises, of course. I'm just encouraging you to keep up a positive outlook."

He cocked an eyebrow, that dark gold arch a clear challenge.

"We have no reason to believe anything untoward has happened," Aubrey added in a hurry. She should've left this to Calvin. She pushed back from the desk and stood up. "What was your decision on the coffee?"

"Yes, please," he replied. Leaning forward in the chair, he rested his elbows on his knees, hands hanging loose.

She was almost overcome with the need to soothe, to massage the tension from his neck and make him foolish promises about his finding his sister safe and happy. What a dumb reaction, considering she hadn't even run a background check on him yet.

She deliberately turned away to find some coffee for him. Her compassionate streak would be the death of her career. Given the chance, her coworkers would put those rose-colored sunglasses on her face at her funeral.

She would take his statement and finish her shift and, most likely, they'd never see each other again.

Unless she found his sister.

Chapter 2

Leo appreciated Officer Rawlins's effort and dedication. She seemed to be making an attempt to help. Still, Jones was right. He didn't see how this report would do much good.

He found solutions on a daily basis, a job requirement that utilized his natural analytical tendencies. Translating those skills to his personal life was never as simple or effective as he hoped.

Here in the police station bustling with action, Lara's disappearance and continued silence was too real. His behavior in the soup kitchen shamed him. The manager had been right not to cooperate based on the way he stormed in and lost his cool.

Leo sat up straight and let his one leg bounce. He needed to move, preferably in the right direction this time. Whatever they said about the general futility of missing person cases, maybe he could convince Officer Rawlins to help him search the area for some sign of Lara. She obviously knew her beat and the neighborhood well. And if the manager at the soup kitchen was any indicator, people trusted her.

With her bright blond hair and earnest, clear blue eyes, she was a ray of sunshine in a wintry gray landscape. She crossed the noisy room, a paper cup in each hand, an angel in a PPD uniform.

"How do you do that?" he asked, taking the cup she offered.

"Do what?" She peeled back the little tab on the lid of her cup and the rich aroma of hot chocolate filled the space between them.

"You seem to just hover somewhere above all of this." He circled his finger, indicating the room at large.

She watched him as she took a sip of her hot beverage. The heat must have stung her lips. She pressed them together and then her tongue slid across, soothing the burn. His pulse kicked. If he'd ever had a more inappropriate reaction, he couldn't recall it.

"What's your office like?" she asked.

"Busy," he replied. "Not so noisy." The constant flux of sharp sounds and voices running the gamut from deep to shrill made his ears ring.

She leaned in as if worried she might be overheard. "The noise in here is why I like walking the neighborhood in any weather."

He could smell the sweet chocolate on her breath and he wanted a taste. What was wrong with him? He was here to track down his sister, not flirt with a cute cop who'd been nice to him when she probably should have arrested him.

He carefully opened the lid on his coffee. "Smart."

Thankfully, she returned to the business at hand and though it pained him, he gave her everything he knew about Lara's return to Philly and her subsequent withdrawal from the school.

When the report was in the system, Leo knew it was time to go, but he was rooted to the seat. He couldn't walk out without some sort of action plan. Would the PPD *do* anything? "Being realistic, what do you expect to come from this report?" he asked. *Please, let her opinion contradict Chief Jones's.*

"You've given us a lot to go on. The pictures are great and it helps that the timeline is tight."

"But?" Leo prompted when she didn't say more.

"Your sister is an adult. She has resources at her disposal and is capable of caring for herself."

"Resources she isn't using," Leo reminded her.

Officer Rawlins nodded. "I understand. We will keep an eye out for her, I promise. Personally, I'll be asking around whenever I'm on shift." She pressed her lips into a hard line. "If you're expecting an organized search, that won't happen."

The statement wasn't a surprise and still a protest burned in his throat, unspoken. The coffee turned bitter in his stomach and the buzzing in his ears returned with a vengeance.

"Mr. Butler? Leo? Are you all right?"

"I'll manage," he lied. He'd never be all right again if something happened to Lara. The only goodness, the only happiness in his life after his tenth birthday, was because of his little sister. She'd been the warmth and acceptance his mother withheld. Even as a toddler she'd seemed to sense how much he needed her, showering him with laughter and unconditional love.

"She's all I have." He spoke carefully, determined not to shout just so he could hear himself. Everyone else could probably hear just fine.

"Where are you staying?" Officer Rawlins asked.

He gave her the name of his hotel.

"Breathe," she ordered, kindly. "I'll have a shuttle pick you up here. Just breathe through it."

Breathe through what? He didn't understand what was happening, why it felt as if the police station was shrinking around him and crushing him in the process.

It wasn't as if she'd told him Lara was dead.

Except that was exactly his fear. She'd made a bizarre life change and no one had seen her since. She hadn't accessed her money. What was he supposed to think? He rubbed a hand over the unbearable ache behind his sternum. "I promised to protect her," he said.

Officer Rawlins tucked the phone between her ear and shoulder and wrapped his free hand in both of hers. "Breathe," she mouthed silently, making exaggerated movements to demonstrate the process.

His gaze locked on the tight circle of her lips as she mimed a slow exhale. Her smaller hands were strong and steady on his. Eventually, the pressure in his chest eased.

Her eyes on his, she finished her brief call. At least he thought it was brief. Everything around him felt disjointed and slightly out of sync.

"Better?" she asked, her blue eyes filled with worry. "The shuttle will be here in ten minutes."

He couldn't sit still that long. Not here where people were working, coming and going with purpose while he didn't even have a plan. Drawing back, he missed her touch immediately. He was losing any semblance of common sense or logic. He pushed to his feet, grateful his knees held. "I'll walk." Or better yet, run like a madman.

"All right. I'll walk with you."

That was ridiculous. They'd both freeze out there in the wind and slush. "Are you afraid I'll go stir up more trouble?"

"It's crossed my mind," she said.

"You aren't a normal cop," he observed.

"Probably not," she agreed. "But I don't plan on changing."

He admired that self-awareness and confidence. Hopefully, the job wouldn't alter her, harden her.

She grabbed her coat, and his, falling into step as he walked toward the front door.

"Don't leave without this." She held his jacket out for him.

He grabbed it and shoved his arms into the sleeves, zipped it up. "I can't stand here and wait on a shuttle," he blurted.

"Why not?"

He stared down at her, searching for an answer. The woman looked far too innocent, too untested, to protect and serve a rough urban neighborhood. What was the department thinking, putting her here?

"Because." *Oh, strong start, man.* He quickly launched into a second attempt. "Because someone should be out there looking for a lead on my sister."

"Where do you plan on looking?" Officer Rawlins asked.

"The school," he blurted. Campus security wouldn't be happy with that choice, but Amy had been helpful.

Maybe he could track down one of Lara's friends and pick up another piece of this dreadful puzzle.

"Someone there led you to the soup kitchen?"

"Yes," he replied. "I don't plan to go off on anyone again. Rookie mistake."

Clouds rolled into her clear blue gaze. "We all make them," she said.

"How long have you been on the force?"

"Almost four years. Take my card." Her smile radiated pride as she handed it to him. "Here in this precinct from day one."

And she still looked fresh and friendly. Impressive. "I know you've done all you can and I appreciate it." Had he said that already? Didn't matter. As a cop she probably didn't get compliments often enough. "I'm just—" He couldn't explain this persistent urge to move. Sitting still had been a problem for him since he was a kid. At nearly thirty, he remained the king of fidgeting. He could *think* better on the move, and standing still when Lara was who-knew-where wasn't working for him.

He pushed through the front door of the precinct just as the hotel shuttle pulled to a stop. Guess he wouldn't walk after all.

Leo looked back over his shoulder to see Officer Rawlins watching him. Her arms were folded, her hands bare. She should put her gloves on. He could feel the sympathy rolling off her and see it in the gentle curve of her mouth.

"I'll be in touch, Leo."

"Thanks," he repeated, boosting himself into the shuttle and closing the door.

How had she done that? No one kept him in one place when he needed to move. As the shuttle pulled away from the police station, the view passing by the windows settled his frazzled nerves. Watching the buildings glide by and people hurrying along on sidewalks hemmed by slushy, gray-tinged snow loosened the knots in his neck.

Was *he* doing all he could to find Lara? On the surface, his answer would be a resounding "yes." He'd filed a police report and followed a lead and created a spectacle, scaring good people in the process.

He couldn't be expected to maintain any cool detachment when his sister was missing. Leo closed his eyes, ashamed all over again. If one of his subordinates at work offered a similar excuse for poor behavior, Leo wouldn't let it slide. He would do something, make some kind of gesture to earn the manager's forgiveness.

At the hotel, he gave the driver a tip and headed upstairs to his room. Locking the door, he set his phone on the top of the dresser near the television. He set the business cards from Officer Rawlins and Chief Jones side by side, adding the Escape Club matchbook to the row.

The PPD, or Officer Rawlins at least, would keep an eye out for Lara in the neighborhood. What else could *he* do?

Leo retrieved the paperwork Jones had given him, pacing in front of the window as he read each page over and over. This disappearing act was unlike Lara, but apparently typical enough that the school and police weren't troubled. The only ray of hope was that nothing pointed to foul play. He was just getting started, but no one had mentioned an aggravated boyfriend or infatuated student. Financially, his sister was sound. What else could have prompted this stunt?

Officer Rawlins seemed sincere enough, but what could one cop really do? Sympathetic to his worries, she hadn't rallied the other officers and organized a search. Had he really expected that?

He leaned his head against the cool glass of the window, recalling the day he'd chaperoned Lara's fifth grade field trip to the zoo. He'd been the cool brother and most of her classmates seemed determined to hang on to his group rather than stay with their own chaperones.

Preparing for lunch, they discovered one boy—not in Leo's group, thankfully—was missing. Teachers, chaperones and zoo security dropped everything, searching until they'd found that kid. Silly as it sounded even in his head, that was the response Leo had expected today.

If being a certain age meant no one had to care about your whereabouts, someone needed to implement a better plan. He hadn't stopped caring for Lara when she turned eighteen or twenty-one any more than she'd written off his support and love at those same milestones.

There was no way to convince law enforcement professionals, though. They'd heard it all, seen it all at the school and the police station. There was no reason to make Lara a priority.

"Come on." Leo marched across the empty room, speaking aloud. "I know you. You had a good reason for doing this. Why didn't you talk to me?"

This time when worry stole his breath and made his pulse race, he didn't have Officer Rawlins to help. He slumped onto the bench at the foot of the bed and fought through the desperation by ticking through the short list of facts.

Chief Jones had told him Lara had put her belongings into storage, but there was no record of a transaction with a self-storage business in her banking or credit card statements. Charges like that would've shown up by now. Unless she'd prepaid in cash. Or used a different name.

Avoiding another panic onset, Leo grabbed his phone and logged in to her back account. Though he scrolled back through two months of activity, there was no sign of a cash withdrawal large enough to prepay for a unit.

In fact, there weren't even any charges that might be related to packing or moving supplies. She hadn't just shoved her belongings away haphazardly. Lara was too conscientious. He guessed she could have found boxes from local stores or around campus. That didn't answer where those items might be right now.

She might have donated her possessions and let people assume she'd stored them. Whatever she'd done, it had to be close. Lara didn't have a car in town, so moving her belongings from her dorm to wherever meant she'd had to enlist the help of a friend or a car service.

A few minutes later Leo hit another dead end on transactions that might be traceable. He leaned back in the chair and stared up at the ceiling. He only knew her friends by first names. He'd never be able to track them down without a lot more information.

He covered his face with his hands and muffled a string of curses. It shouldn't be this hard to find the one person in the world he knew better than anyone else.

Pacing again, he knew Jones and even Officer Rawlins believed he was overreacting. But he wasn't. As well as he knew Lara, she knew him, too. She knew the silent treatment wouldn't work, so he had no other conclusion to draw than the obvious. Whatever she'd intended when she'd left school, something had gone wrong.

Otherwise, she would've told him she was fine just to keep him off her trail.

* * *

After confirming Lara Butler's information and picture were in the system, Aubrey created the standard flyer for a missing person and printed out a dozen. She uploaded the same report to the PPD website, asking that they share the information on the public pages.

Fixating on one particular case wasn't her job. That was best left to the detectives. Her role was to keep the peace from the ground up, by staying visible and present in the community.

At her last performance review, she'd been asked if she aspired to move up the ranks. It had felt like a trick question. Yes, she wanted to advance in her career. Yes, being a woman in a male-dominated field meant navigating a few more potholes and pitfalls on that path.

And yes, the major screwup with her ex early in her career eroded her enthusiasm about advancement. She wasn't the first officer to be fooled by a close friend, but her error in judgment had been broadcast in front of the entire department and made for weeks of embarrassing media headlines. Any step up the PPD ladder would come with more scrutiny as well as more skepticism about whether or not she'd earned it.

If she'd wanted an easy career, she should've chosen differently. It wasn't too late to shift gears, but when she imagined attempting anything other than police work, she practically broke out in hives. Mistakes or not, this was where she belonged.

At the bulletin board across from the desk sergeant, she found a space and posted Lara's missing person flyer. The officer on the desk was one of her favorite people in the precinct. Sergeant Hulbert was a third-generation cop near the end of his career. His bright red hair had faded to silver long before Aubrey graduated the police academy. Built like a bull, he could move as quick as a whip and he was generous about sharing his wealth of experience on the streets of Philadelphia.

"What are you still doing in here?" Hulbert asked, his voice booming across the lobby. "Too cold on the street for your wee bones?"

She grinned at the jibe. Of all the ribbing she took in a week, Hulbert's teasing came from the heart. He was a grandfather, a supervisor and a mentor all rolled into one. With her parents retired in Florida to avoid bitter winters, she felt like she still had family in town, thanks to Hulbert. He invited her over for hockey games and cookouts and she'd spent three of the past four Thanks-givings with his ever-growing brood.

"My bones can take it," she said. "I'd be out there already if you hadn't stopped me."

"My knee says we're getting more snow tonight."

"Your knee is exaggerating as usual," she teased. "We'll only get a dusting tonight. Just enough to keep us humble before that big front moves in."

"That big front can move right on," Hulbert rumbled.

"I hope it does," she agreed, thinking about Rosie and all the people who relied on the shelters and soup kitchens to survive.

"What's that you posted?" Hulbert queried.

She handed him a flyer from her stack. "Missing person. Best guess is she's been out of contact for seven to ten days. Her brother is desperate to find her."

Hulbert shook his head, his blue eyes sad. "I bet." He pulled out his phone and took a picture of the flyer, then gave it back to her. "One of the saddest parts of the job. Was she sick or in a bad relationship?"

Aubrey agreed with him one hundred percent. "By all accounts she was healthy and single. She's a college student. Her brother found out earlier she also volunteered at Rosie's soup kitchen."

Hulbert snorted. Everyone in the precinct knew Rosie. "What does she say?"

Aubrey stared at the picture of Lara's smiling face. "Rosie confirmed the brother's assessment. Says the girl is kind and reliable and healthy."

Hulbert released a gusty sigh. "Officer Rawlins, tell me you didn't?"

Caught by his scolding tone, Aubrey looked up, met his gaze. "Didn't what?"

"Did you promise the brother you'd find her?" He *tsked* at her. "Girl, that soft heart will get you into more trouble. What will it take to toughen you up?"

"Almost," she admitted. "He was so sad. But I did *not* make him any promises aside from telling him we'd do our best." Though she'd been gentle with the facts, she'd been straight enough with him that he freaked out. She should get responsible cop points for that.

The sergeant harrumphed this time. "You sure?"

"Yes," she replied, reining in her frustration. "My heart may be soft, but I know the job and I do it well."

"That's the spirit. Keep that soft heart behind body armor and you'll be just fine."

With a smile and a wave that weren't as sincere as they should've been, Aubrey left the station. The soft heart issue didn't bother her quite as much from Hulbert, but it sure would be nice to shake off that reputation.

Apparently, two and a half years wasn't enough time for the department to forget she'd been fooled by her boyfriend in her own home. The whole mess underscored the rose-colored sunglasses in her locker. It shouldn't matter what her peers thought of her. As long as she remained her chipper self and refused to believe the worst of every person who crossed her path, the skeptics and doubters would consider her an easy target.

Neil Crowder hadn't actually been living with her when she'd arrested him for dealing drugs. That had been the logical next step in their relationship, a milestone she happily anticipated until she'd caught him in the act of making a sale. Appalled, she'd seized the drugs, cuffed him and called for backup to handle the evidence and make the arrest.

Her soft heart had been blamed for not seeing the signs of his criminal activity sooner. For letting it slide when she'd discovered he occasionally smoked pot. But the pot had been the only infraction he'd revealed to her. Still, her judgment had been questioned in a thousand little ways for months. The Internal Affairs investigation was arduous, but the unofficial reckoning among her co-workers had stung more. The pressure cracked her pride as everyone felt compelled to share an opinion of the way she'd ignored and then ratted out her dealer-boyfriend.

Ex-boyfriend.

She'd handled everything by the book when she'd caught Neil. Not that it mattered. She hadn't given her ex an opening to request any favors, discretion or leniency. She didn't expect a commendation, but she'd assumed IA would stop looking over her shoulder. Two and a half years and they didn't seem to have anything better to do than keep tabs on her and dig into anyone who asked her out on a second date. Did they think "criminal tendencies" were something she actively sought in a partner?

Though guilt still prickled along the back of her neck

occasionally, she believed time would smooth it over. Her parents and Hulbert and even Calvin reminded her of that when she'd been in the thick of it, when she was sure IA would force her off the PPD. Yet, that one mistake continued to haunt her. Her biggest fear of a promotion was the possibility of media finding out and dredging up the old story.

At the end of her shift, Aubrey picked up the flyers. Her building was only a few blocks away and she could post the flyers on the way home. She stepped outside, into the teeth of a gust of cold air. Lousy winter conditions wouldn't deter her from posting it at the shelter or the soup kitchen. There were several stores between Lara's college campus and the soup kitchen Rosie managed. Aubrey would check with the staff in each of those locations, as well. As she'd told Leo, there wasn't much anyone could do unless Lara wanted to be found.

He'd presented a fair argument, assuming he was as close to his sister as he claimed. Why would a girl with seemingly everything going her way disappear?

She popped into the deli where she'd ordered her smoothie and spoke with the manager on duty. Lara wasn't a regular customer, but Aubrey tacked a flyer to the community board anyway.

When she returned to the soup kitchen, normalcy had been restored. Rosie and her staff were settled, chatting away in the kitchen. Everyone in the dining room seemed content, savoring the hot food and the break from the weather.

She posted the flyer of Lara on the bulletin board, alongside several other faces of people who were missing. Yes, her soft heart gave a pang of distress. These flyers rarely came down due to a happy resolution. Most

of the faces were runaways or addicts. It hurt to contemplate how many families would never find closure.

Not Leo, if he had his way. He was determined to have
answers. Either the man was too compelling, or she was
as soft as everyone believed. Aubrey couldn't ignore the
instinctive nudge that Lara's disappearance was different, though. At some point she had to start trusting her
intuition again. The odds of Leo being a criminal, someone like a handsome and manipulative drug dealer, were
ridiculously low. Still, she couldn't toss out PPD protocol
because of one distraught and persuasive brother. She'd
do her job, add in some extra effort and let the system
work the way it should.

She found Rosie in the kitchen and asked to speak
privately. Rosie led the way to the office, which doubled
as an overstuffed supply closet. A battered metal desk
wedged up against one wall had just enough space left
for a laptop. Aubrey didn't envy the administrator who
had to work in here.

Rosie unfolded a chair and sat down with a sigh.
"How is the brother?"

Aubrey closed the door and unfolded a chair for herself. "Distraught," Aubrey replied candidly. "He's sure
something terrible happened."

Rosie's lips thinned and worry pleated her eyebrows.
"He might be right."

Aubrey's intuition snapped to attention. "I knew you
were holding back. Spill it." They were friendly and
shared a mutual respect and concern for the people who
utilized Good Samaritan services. If Rosie was reluctant
to share, there was a good reason.

"Lara has a heart of gold. She treats everyone with
equal compassion." Rosie twisted a towel in her hands.

"It's a rare gift, beautiful to watch and oh-so-necessary in places like this."

Aubrey agreed wholeheartedly, wondering if Leo had ever given Lara a pair of rose-colored glasses. "People like her, like you, make a world of difference."

"Thank you. But Lara. She wanted to do more."

"How so?"

Rosie pressed her towel-clinging hands over her mouth, then dropped them again. "She sometimes talked to me about going out, living on the street. Just to understand the situation and where, um…where the assistance broke down." She shook her head, frowning. "Something like that."

"Why didn't you say anything about this earlier?"

"She asked me not to say anything at all." Rosie swallowed a small sob. "She wants to do this. To feel what the others feel." She pressed her lips together. "What she is doing is important."

There was more to it. Had to be more than curiosity for a girl to withdraw from classes and attempt life on the streets in the dead of winter. "The others feel cold and hunger because they have no other choice." Aubrey was inexplicably angry. "Her brother feels miserable." It seemed like a heartless experiment for a compassionate woman to conduct. "Is she checking in with anyone? Is there a time limit?" she asked. "I can keep her brother out of her way if she'll give him some sort of assurance."

Rosie shook her head again, lips clamped together as if she couldn't risk uttering even a simple "no".

"You realize I have to work this as a missing person case, since he filed the report. The flyers go up, we'll ask questions and be on the lookout for her."

"You can't shuffle it to the side?"

Insulted, Aubrey had to take a deep breath. "No." She let Rosie feel the full pressure of her silence.

The woman didn't crack. "Is there anything else, Officer Aubrey?"

Aubrey had encouraged people on her beat to call her by her first name in an effort to be more approachable. This was the first time she regretted it. Wanting to shake the woman, Aubrey stuffed her hands into her pockets. There was no way to hide the clenched teeth. "If you hear she's in trouble, you'll let me know?"

The small dip of the chin wasn't a resounding confirmation, but Aubrey took it as an affirmative anyway. If Lara was so valuable and such a good person, surely Rosie wouldn't want her to freeze to death. Or worse.

She wouldn't get anything more out of Rosie today. Summoning the self-control to walk out of the office without slamming the door, Aubrey aimed for the dining room. She had no evidence of any wrongdoing and these people needed the relief provided by the soup kitchen.

She chatted about nothing in particular with a few of the regulars, just to make Rosie nervous. Shuffle this to the side? That rankled.

Leaving the flyer in place, Aubrey headed toward the next shelter. Lara was welcome to conduct what sounded like a poverty experiment. This was a free country after all. But if Aubrey could reel her in just long enough to convince her brother everything would work out, that would be perfect.

From his perspective the siblings were close, and a decision like this wouldn't have been made without a discussion and plan. Granted, Lara might well have had an opposing view of her and Leo's relationship and the effect her abrupt choice would have on her brother. An only child, Aubrey had no personal frame of reference on sibling dynamics.

"Officer Aubrey?"

Hearing her name, she turned toward the voice and spotted the woman everyone called Mary-Tea in the delivery alley behind the shelter.

Aubrey had no idea if Mary's last name began with a *t* or if her real name was Mary at all. She'd been living in and out of shelters since before Aubrey had joined the local precinct. Everyone knew the woman preferred tea over coffee and that was likely the reason for her name. Impossible to know for sure as Mary never discussed her past or her plans. Mary did, however, have a good line on the happenings of the homeless community and she cautiously shared information with the PPD from time to time.

Most days she simply greeted Aubrey and went on about her business. Today she motioned Aubrey closer, skulking in the shadows between the buildings.

"How are you doing, Mary? Staying warm?"

"Warm enough." The older woman bobbed her chin behind the faded scarf wrapped around her head and neck. The ends were tucked into the collar of the military surplus peacoat. "The young woman you're looking for. She's out here with us."

"You've seen her?" Aubrey managed to keep her voice casual. It was a bigger fight to hold back the avalanche of questions that would send Mary-Tea scrambling away.

"I have." She studied her mittens. "She's nice."

Yes, by all accounts, Lara Butler was the nicest woman in the city, possibly on the planet. Her brother wanted more than that. He needed to know his wonderfully nice sister was safe and secure. And pressing

Mary-Tea for details and more information before she
was ready would backfire.

"I'm glad to hear it, thank you. Are you going in for
dinner?"

"I will."

"Good." Aubrey worried about the older woman. "If
you need anything, or if she does, you find me, okay?"

"She says the same thing," Mary-Tea mumbled
through her scarf. "Says she's out here with us to find
what *we* need."

"That's good." Aubrey's intuition leaped. "That's
good for everyone." This could be a lead to follow from
another angle. If compassion and research had pushed
Lara to leave school and live on the streets, there had to
be a catalyst. She needed Mary-Tea on her side, needed
the older woman to bring her tidbits on Lara.

"It is." Mary-Tea pulled a crumpled flyer from her
pocket and pushed it toward Aubrey. "So stop this."

"I have to hang them up," she explained gently. "It's
my job."

"I don't think you should." Mary-Tea shrank back.

Aubrey inched closer. "Why not?"

"She's safe, Officer Aubrey."

"And you think the flyers will make her unsafe?"

Mary-Tea nodded furtively and then scurried backward.

Aubrey resisted the urge to give chase. Mary-Tea had
a mother-hen tendency to nurture those who let her. Impossible to know for sure if she considered Lara her new-
est chick in the nest, but it seemed likely.

How could a search for Lara put her at additional
risk? Maybe she hadn't come out here simply to figure
out where the system broke down, as Rosie suggested.

But what else could have driven Lara into hiding on the street? Worse, searching for a woman who didn't want to be found was pretty much an exercise in futility, regardless of who suffered from her absence.

Aubrey moved back onto the street, second-guessing herself as she continued tacking up flyers and asking if Lara had been seen. This *was* her job. Without any evidence to back up Mary-Tea's assertion that they would create trouble for Lara, she had to continue.

Flyers for the missing went up and were taken down every day. Or so it seemed. More than a little bummed out by the low success rate, Aubrey finished the task and headed to her apartment for a much-needed break from the weather and city.

Her building, classic red brick with arched windows, was centered in a block of refurbished properties converted to apartments. Her street was doing its best to return to its heyday as a family-friendly neighborhood. She lived with a core of stable residents plus several that transitioned through the year. Grad students came and went with each academic term and occasionally a new professor would move in before realizing it was better to have more distance from the campus. In the building next door, someone frequently rented space to tourists, which kept them all entertained.

She loved the job, loved walking the beat with Calvin and talking with permanent residents and business owners as well as the college students passing through each semester. There was an upbeat vibe to the area that she happily cultivated.

Nothing wrong with being happy. Not even when there was someone like Leo Butler out there miserable and worried. There were highs and lows in every shift and if she could find his sister with a snap of her fingers, she would've done so.

Planning to stay in for the night, Aubrey traded her uniform for her comfy sweatpants, thick socks, a silk undershirt and a chunky sweater. She poured leftover stew into a pan, reheating it on the stovetop while she turned on the television and flipped through channels for some lighthearted background noise.

Finding a local weather report, she paused, thinking of Hulbert's knee. It sure looked like the notoriously achy joint was right again. Flurries tonight would make the city sparkle in the morning and brighten her walk to work. Scanning forward, she looked for something more interesting. Finding an old favorite movie, a romantic comedy with an edge of suspense, she turned up the volume, listening to the familiar lines while she poured her stew into a bowl. Tucked into the couch, she enjoyed the simple meal and tried to forget her day, or more precisely, the overwrought brother who continued to dominate her thoughts.

She couldn't do any more for him tonight, yet she couldn't seem to let it go. She picked up her cell phone to check in with the precinct and jumped when it rang in her hand. Answering, she winced and pulled the phone away from her ear when clanging sounds poured through the speaker.

"Aubrey? Hey, it's Jason."

"Hi." She'd met Jason during a CPR recertification course. After a brief stint as an active firefighter, he seemed happier in his new role as manager for a nightclub owned and operated by a former cop down at the riverside pier. Except the club had burned down months ago and wasn't yet rebuilt. "Is this your grand reopening night or something?"

"No. Hang on." The background noise faded away. "Sorry. I'm in the office now. I'm pulling taps at Pomeroy's."

The neighborhood pub was about halfway between Lara's former campus and Aubrey's apartment. "Sounds like a busy night."

"Busy enough. You know how people get when they're gearing up to be snowed in. I've got a guy in here roaming around, asking questions about the Butler girl on that flyer you posted today."

Smothering a sigh, Aubrey offered up Leo's description. She wasn't done working tonight after all.

"No, that's not him," Jason said. "This guy isn't upset—he's slick. Or trying to be. Black hair with too much product and he's a smoker. In and out twice for a cigarette in the last hour."

She immediately pictured a young John Travolta in the role of a mob enforcer. "Age?"

"I'd put him at midthirties or better," Jason said. "I just added a second Citywide Special for him and one for the girl he's chatting up to his tab. He'll be here for a bit if you have time to come take a look at him."

"On my way," she said, hoping the words went through before she ended the call. Anyone asking about Lara could be a lead.

Swapping the comfy sweats for a pair of jeans, she figured the sweater would fit in well enough with the normal Pomeroy crowd. Still, she took a minute to brush her hair, added mascara and lip gloss to sell the idea that she was a neighbor out to meet friends instead of an off-duty cop eager for information.

She should've asked Jason to sneak a picture of the guy asking about Lara. Jason had probably thought of that on his own. And the bar probably had a camera angle that would give her a good view of the man's face if he left before she arrived.

Pulling on her coat and gloves, she looped her scarf around her neck as she dashed down the stairs. Naturally, the temperature had dropped significantly after sunset and as she neared the popular little pub, the foot traffic increased. She wound her way through the pedestrians who weren't in such a hurry and finally reached Pomeroy's front door. The bouncer recognized her and insisted on checking her ID. They both knew the PPD could ticket him and the bar if he didn't. "Good job," she joked as she put away her identification and stuffed her gloves into her pockets.

Undoing her coat, she glanced around as if she really expected to see friends on her way to the bar. The crowd wasn't too bad, though the music was cranked up to a volume designed to prevent all but the most determined conversation.

She didn't see anyone she knew other than Jason at the taps, taking care of customers. The man he'd described to her wasn't in sight, either. "Good crowd," she said, squeezing into an empty space at the bar.

"It's a good night for Pomeroy's," Jason agreed. "I'll be glad when Grant reopens his place."

Aubrey gave herself a mental high five for letting that go without so much as a raised eyebrow. Grant Sullivan had served with the PPD for several years before he was forced into early retirement after being shot in the line of duty. His second career, opening the Escape

Club down at the pier, had proved an immense success until an arsonist torched the place.

For all that Sullivan had invested, he hadn't retired his instincts or desire to help. She'd heard about several occasions when Grant or members of his staff, like Jason, helped out victims—real or potential—rather than let the PPD handle those cases.

Most of her coworkers on the force admired Grant for his ongoing commitment to community. And with the rise of assaults during dates, all club owners needed to be aware and alert. In her opinion, Sullivan took things a step too far. Aubrey kept that to herself rather than open herself to criticism or argument with her peers.

She agreed that Sullivan was a great guy, but dishing out his own form of justice? That wasn't a philosophy she could support. The legal system wasn't perfect, but it was far more reliable than one man's interpretation of right and wrong.

"You look gloomy," Jason observed, sliding a beer in front of her. "That's not like you."

"Gee, thanks." She did try and adjust her expression to something friendlier. "I don't see the guy you described."

"He stepped out a few minutes ago, with the girl he was hitting on. He'll be back."

"You're sure?"

"He didn't strike me as the sort to be done for the night."

"What did he want to know about Lara Butler?" she asked while she could.

"He tried the casual approach with me and a few of the customers, but he's actively looking for her," Jason replied.

That didn't bode well. Jason had more practice than

she did reading people in social settings. "All right, I'll wait." It had been a few weeks since she'd let herself just hang out and relax. The music wasn't her favorite, but it hardly mattered. She sipped her beer, watching the crowd ebb and flow.

The faces were mostly young and most of them were newly legal by her estimation. Several were possibly pushing the boundary with fake IDs, although the bouncer was usually up on all the tricks and trends with that. She endured a brief internal debate and pushed the idea of spot-checking aside.

The pub had a good reputation and Jason was a stickler for the rules. If someone had gotten a fake ID past the bouncer and Jason, she probably wouldn't catch it, either. Besides, in this neighborhood, because of the strict penalties for serving underage, those under twenty-one usually reserved their illegal drinking for house parties.

She was here for the man Jason described and throwing her weight around as a cop wouldn't make observing or questioning him any easier.

Over the course of the next hour, she nursed her drink, courteously dissuaded two advances and still saw no sign of the man Jason had overheard asking about Lara. She finished off her beer, asked for a glass of water and gave herself five more minutes to observe.

The front door opened and, recognizing the new arrival, she nearly ordered a shot of tequila. Leo Butler was the last person she needed around while she was trying to do her job undercover. A zippy hum of awareness slid through her system and her sweater suddenly felt scratchy against her skin.

She checked her hair in the mirror behind the bar and scowled at her reflection. She didn't need perfect hair or flawless makeup to impress anyone when she was off the clock. Her skills as a cop and her character as a person were top-notch on or off duty. So why primp for him? He was the face of one of her cases, not the man of her dreams.

His gaze roamed the pub as if he was intent on finding a familiar face. Not hers, clearly, as his attention skimmed over her, zeroing in on tables and groups of people.

Leo was here and the other man asking about Lara was gone. That couldn't be coincidence. Had he hired an investigator after he'd left the police station? Not an outrageous possibility. He was justifiably desperate to find his sister.

Aubrey noticed when his gaze landed on someone and held in recognition. He stopped short at the end of a booth in the corner. She assumed he introduced himself. He wasn't shouting or waving his phone around; she gave him points for composure this time, though he wasn't invited to sit down.

When Aubrey had arrived, there had been three girls and two guys in the booth. They struck her as the right age to know Lara. She watched Leo shake hands, saw his lips curve in a weak smile. Interpreting body language was a skill she was working on. It wasn't a perfect science and she still made a few errors, but overall, her track record was getting better.

As the conversation continued, Leo's stance changed. His shoulders tensed up, his fingers curled into his palm, then flattened again to tap his leg and curled again. Over and over. He was getting agitated. They must be stonewalling him.

She'd done the same for her girlfriends in the past,

dodging questions or withholding information from an overprotective brother or too-curious ex. Until right now she hadn't wasted much time worrying about how the boyfriend or brother had felt.

He was doing an admirable job of staying calm, and his effort touched her soft heart. She was off the bar stool and crossing the room before she thought it through. "Leo? Hi," she said a little too loudly.

His brow flexed into a frown as if he couldn't place her out of uniform. A moment later his expression cleared. "Officer Rawlins."

"Off duty, it's just Aubrey," she said with a smile. "Are you guys having a good time?" she asked the table at large.

No one flinched or squirmed, so she assumed they were all over twenty-one. All five of them answered in the affirmative. The only one who came across remotely uncomfortable was the man standing beside her. Why was that? She assumed this was a group of Lara's friends. Had she misread the situation? "Well, I won't intrude," she said. "I just wanted to say hello."

As she hoped, Leo followed her to the bar, away from the group at the table. "What are you doing here?" he demanded, leaning close.

She caught the scent of winter on his clothing and something warmer that must have been solely him. A quiver of anticipation swirled low in her belly. She really had to get a handle on her runaway senses. Striving to keep her cool, she nodded toward Jason. "My friend is tending bar and he invited me down. It's a happy coincidence."

"Nothing happy about it on my end."

The words stung a little, though she had no true reason to be offended. "Why not, Mr. Butler?" she asked in a cool, polite tone.

He shoved his hands into his pockets. "Please, call me Leo."

The name truly suited him. He was growly and protective, lean and—*enough of that.* "I assume that group knew Lara," she said, tipping her head toward the booth. The five coeds were there, taking turns peeking at her and Leo.

If they were hoping for a scene, they were doomed to disappointment. She wasn't about to create a stir or give IA any cause for worry.

"They are," he admitted.

"What happened to letting me and the PPD handle it?"

He glared at her, then turned that glare on the rest of the crowd as he leaned back against the bar. "You can't expect me to sit still and wait."

"I can," she said. "You gave me your word you would do just that."

He had the grace to look embarrassed. "I was in the hotel, thinking."

Overthinking this was his first mistake, though she could hardly blame him. If she had a sibling who'd gone off and done something so out of character, she'd be equally consumed with finding information. Still, he wasn't making her job any easier. "And?"

The despair in his dark brown eyes hit her hard. "You don't understand."

She pressed her lips together to hold back the long list of things she *did* understand. "Explain it. I'm listening."

"You see my sister as an adult. I understand that she *is* an adult. But the two of us talk about everything. We're close. She must have had a good reason for leaving school and not discussing it." He aimed another laser-hot glare at the group in the booth. "They have some idea, but they won't tell me anything if she asked them to keep quiet. People are loyal to Lara like that."

Aubrey thought of Mary-Tea and silently agreed with him.

"Something is wrong," he continued, urgently. "However this started, she wouldn't let me worry. If she can't reach out, she must be in trouble."

Aubrey wouldn't dismiss his intuition as swiftly as she might doubt her own. "You'll get yourself or someone else hurt if you don't let the police handle this."

"Are you telling me the PPD will do more than post a few flyers?"

She started to answer, but he cut her off.

"Be honest, *Officer*."

The way he exaggerated her title annoyed her. Still, he was not at his best right now. He was hurting and worried and— She snipped off that line of thinking like a loose thread. It was not her job to comfort him, not even while she was off duty and hanging out in a crowded bar.

"The police won't do enough," she began. "The general consensus seems to be that the police never do enough to protect our communities or prevent problems."

Leo's eyes rounded. "All right. Well, not all right, but the candor is refreshing."

She angled herself to block his view of Lara's friends in the booth. "Just because we don't have any new information within a few hours of filing the report doesn't mean the PPD is ignoring you or your concerns." She was half tempted to tell him what really brought her to Pomeroy's. Imagining a dozen ways that would backfire, she kept her mouth shut.

Leo stared at his feet. "I want to believe you."

"Then believe me," she urged.

"Will you please go speak with them?" Leo asked.

She'd known the request was coming. It was an inevitable culmination of everything Leo had seen and done today. A smart woman—a smart cop—would've refused and walked out of the bar, headed for the peace and quiet of home. Too late for that now.

She scanned the bar for any sign of the man Jason had initially called about. Nothing. Annoyed with herself as much as the situation, she grabbed her coat and turned on her heel. At the booth she paused, offering a professional smile. "Leo is worried about his sister."

"We noticed." The young woman who'd spoken was gorgeous, with light brown skin, wide, nearly black eyes and straight black hair that flowed to the middle of her back. "We'd help him if we could, Officer."

Aubrey decided to assume the best and buy into the sincerity shining in the younger woman's eyes. "I'm glad to hear that. If there's any insight you could give about where or why Lara left school, it would help the investigation tremendously." She made eye contact with each of them, but only the first replied.

"He's not going home, is he?"

"I doubt it," Aubrey replied. "At least not anytime soon. I've been asked to keep a confidence, so I do understand your reluctance to share if Lara asked the same of you."

The designated spokeswoman glanced at her companions. Poker faces all around. This group wasn't moved by Leo and they weren't moved by Aubrey. "One quick question," she said, changing tactics. "Do any of you know of a reason Leo should be worried about his sister?"

"No." The answer came from all five of them.

"We're confident she's fine," the spokeswoman added.

It was more than she had. "Good. I'll pass that along. If your confidence wavers for any reason, please reach out to me or someone on the PPD." She reached into her pocket, but she didn't have any business cards in this coat.

Each of the five nodded an agreement and that would have to be enough for tonight. As satisfied as she could be with the conversation, Aubrey headed for the door, eager to get home.

Her path through the pub was momentarily blocked by a bigger man in a black leather coat. He reeked of cigarette smoke. A quick visual inventory matched this man with the description Jason had given her. *Great.* She couldn't do anything to figure out why he'd been asking about Lara, not with Leo watching her like a hawk.

She mumbled an "excuse me" and did a little side to side until he brushed past her with a curse. The man was a real charmer. As he passed her, she noticed the unmistakable bulge of a shoulder holster under his coat.

She dismissed all but one of the options that rushed through her mind. Outside, she texted Jason, warning him about the gun. Odds were good he'd picked up on the guy's concealed weapon already. His training as both a first responder and bartender would have covered how to spot that kind of trouble.

Her mind on how best to follow up with Jason tomorrow, she didn't pay any attention to the rush of footsteps behind her until it was too late.

A hard grip caught her elbow, arresting her momentum. Her first instinct was to jerk around and go on the offensive, but she hesitated. The last thing her personnel record needed was a misguided assault charge if she struck out when she wasn't actually in any danger.

"Leo." She was tempted to shove him just to release some of this pent-up energy that seemed to go from simmer to boil whenever he was near. "Release me."

"What did they say?"

"Nothing," she admitted. "If they had given me anything helpful, I would've walked back and shared it with you."

"I'm supposed to believe you? Just take your word on that?"

A passerby jostled her shoulder and Leo scowled. Clearly, he, too, was bucking for a way to burn off this restless sense of helplessness. "Go back to your hotel," she said.

He focused all that desperate attention at her, nudging her out of the path of others and moving his body to shelter her. His coat was open and she caught a whiff of the crisp, woodsy scent of his soap or cologne.

The fragrance punched through her and she locked her hands at her sides when she wanted to reach out and pull him closer. She was a professional, damn it. This wasn't how a cop should feel about anyone linked to a case.

"You need to step back." Her voice quavered. She pulled herself together and raised her gaze to his only to find him staring at her mouth.

Her tongue slipped over her chilled lips before she could stop herself. "Leo, did you hear me?"

"I did." He didn't step back. He leaned closer, his arm

braced against the wall, over her head. How was it they weren't already touching?

The street noise faded away. She'd never felt so removed from the city she loved. Tucked under the shelter of his body she found warmth, a place where the bleakness of winter could give way to the hope of spring.

He was going to kiss her. Or try. Unless she kissed him first. She was caught in the middle of that harsh internal debate when at last he dragged his gaze from her mouth to her eyes. Something in those warm brown depths shifted and snapped, breaking the delicious anticipation.

No, no, no. Not delicious. Foolish. Inappropriate. She could *not* afford to see him as a man. He was a *case*. A stranger in town on a quest that probably wouldn't end well.

He pushed away from the wall, far too late for her to consider the movement obedient or cooperative. Eyes still locked on her, he shoved his hands into his coat pockets.

A cold blast of air filled the now-respectable distance between them while a voice in her head screamed about lost opportunities. The only missed opportunity that mattered was that she hadn't found a way to interview the slick guy with the concealed weapon asking about Lara.

"I'll walk you back to your hotel," she said.

"I don't need a babysitter," he grumbled, stalking away.

She fell into step beside him. "Prove it."

He trudged on, shoulders hunched against the wind, in the general direction of the hotel.

"You can't convince me that the flyers will pay off."

"Then I won't try." Unless they'd already brought out a possible lead she'd left behind in the pub. If she tried to explain that to Leo, he'd turn around and confront the man himself. "Tell me about her."

He shot her a hard look. "I already gave you a description. Her habits and everything I know about her life here."

He hadn't mentioned her friends or knowing that she visited Pomeroy's. Pointing out the obvious felt petty. He was hurting enough already. "Come on," she coaxed. They had blocks to go on a cold night and he didn't seem inclined to call for a ride or grab a taxi. "Does she love to read or go rock climbing? Is she dating anyone? What about a secret passion for knitting?"

"If she knits in secret, how would I know?"

"So you do have a sense of humor."

"Not much of one lately." He moved to block her from a sudden gust of wind. She trembled again, but not because of the weather. "We should find a car. You're cold."

She was. Just like every other person silly enough to walk on a wintry night. "I'll survive." She had every intention of calling for a ride from his hotel to her apartment.

"Lara is a complete and total bookworm," he said suddenly. "Always has been. I would read to her at night when she was little and I'd replace the batteries in her flashlight when she would burn them out from reading past her bedtime."

"That sounds…" Sweet and warm. All the things she'd want an older sibling to be if she'd been lucky enough to have one. "You're a good brother," she said.

He scowled, apparently uncomfortable with the compliment. "Did you read past your bedtime?" he asked.

"I did. Before I was old enough to change the batteries in my flashlight, I'd swap out the dead one with the flashlight in the kitchen drawer. That's how Mom caught me. Though I'm pretty sure she knew what was happening all along."

"No siblings to blame?"

She shook her head. "And the dog slept in their room, so they knew it wasn't him."

His low, rusty chuckle made her feel like a heavyweight champion throwing a winning knockout punch in round one.

Her cheeks were nearly frozen and his were windchapped by the time they reached his hotel. "Will you stay put for tonight?" she asked when they were inside the warmth of the lobby.

"I will. I promise," he said.

"Good. Because I'm off duty. If you raise a ruckus again and drag an officer out of the warm station and into this weather, that officer will not be patient with you."

His lips twitched as if he was trying not to smile. "Noted."

"What?" She could see him losing the battle with that smile and couldn't think of a reason for the change. Though it would be nice to see that striking face at ease and happy rather than tense and worried.

"Nothing," he insisted.

She waited, a duel of wills.

"Fine." He choked back a laugh. "You look like Rudolph with the red nose and everything."

The comment was so unexpectedly flirtatious, she was left speechless. This glimpse into the man behind the anxiety only attracted her more.

"You made me say it," he pointed out.

"I did. Go get warm," she ordered. "Get some sleep, too. I have a few things to run down in the morning and then I'll touch base."

"Let me come with you," he said eagerly. "Assuming those things pertain to Lara."

The things she wanted to follow up on did pertain to Lara's case. "No." Having Leo around would complicate her attempts to find a lead on his sister…and with her personally.

"Please."

"No." She said it more firmly because she wanted to cave to his pleading gaze. "I'd get slammed for allowing you to tag along. My partner and I can handle it. If I find anything, I'll come straight over and fill you in."

"That's just a sneaky way of trying to keep me in the hotel."

"I'm trying to do my job and keep my pocket of the city safe."

He snorted. "I'm no threat to your city."

"Not from where I'm standing," she said. "I know it isn't easy to be patient but interfering with the standard protocol won't help anything." Especially not his sister or Aubrey's own reputation at the precinct.

She folded her arms, waiting for him to leave the lobby.

"You plan to stand guard down here?"

"No," she fibbed. "Just humor me and go up to your room so I can more easily convince myself that you'll keep your word."

"I won't go out looking for her anymore tonight."

"Mm-hmm." She shooed him away.

With a shake of his head, he stalked toward the elevators. She waited a few minutes before moving to the front desk and asking to speak with their head of security.

She hadn't had much cause to work directly with hotel security, but there was respect and cooperation on both sides of the tourism industry and the PPD. After a quick explanation, she asked for an assist, requesting a text message if the staff noticed Leo leaving. It was no guarantee that they'd spot him, and she didn't want him to *feel* watched. But a warning if he decided to go back out would sure be nice.

Chapter 3

After a restless night, Leo woke up as weary and frustrated as when he'd fallen asleep. His dreams had flipped incongruently between worst-case scenarios for Lara and snow-melting kisses with the lovely Officer Rawlins. She'd seemed so different out of uniform last night in the pub. Softer, warmer and even more tempting. The sweater had been rather shapeless, but the snug jeans had hugged her lean legs perfectly, giving his imagination plenty of fuel.

Since she was his best hope for finding Lara, he couldn't allow his misguided hormones to impede her motivation to help. He blamed the outrageous dreamscape on stress and went down to the hotel gym to burn it off. But an hour of weights and a hard run on the treadmill underscored by the morning news did nothing to improve his mood or outlook.

Back in his room, he showered and dressed for the day, downing the two available cups of coffee while he debated his best move today. Still no action on Lara's bank accounts. No replies to his voice messages or texts. The walls closed in on him, the weight of failure impossible to ignore.

What would Lara need to hide from him?

He bolted from the room and got as far as the front desk before a burst of guilt had him turning back to the restaurant. He'd promised to stay put. A meal would keep him in place as Officer Rawlins had asked. He might not like the waiting game, but she knew her city far better than he did. He could eat, make some calls, check in at work and pretend to be whole.

Technically, he didn't owe Officer Rawlins an explanation for his behavior. Sure, the scene he'd made at the soup kitchen had crossed a line and he'd made a nuisance of himself, but he hadn't broken any laws. Last night in the bar he'd behaved while talking to Lara's friends.

Well, he'd behaved until he was outside on the street with Aubrey. He still regretted stepping back when every fiber of his being had wanted to close the distance and learn the taste of her lips. He was sure it would've been an excellent diversion from the situation of his missing sister.

Part of him kept expecting Aubrey to pop out from behind a potted palm or stroll casually into view. He couldn't decide if he was happy or disappointed when she didn't. Was he missing a woman he just met or simply relieved that she trusted him to keep his word?

He was sleep-deprived and his thoughts were bugging him. Maybe it was best to stay here rather than attempt any direct search efforts today. As scrambled as his thoughts were, he was likely to make matters worse.

Hoping a good breakfast and more coffee would straighten him out, he chose a table near the window and tried not to think about where Lara might be or what Aubrey was doing to find her.

More than anything, he wanted to get back over to the campus and find this Professor Whitten Amy from the library had mentioned. If not today, definitely tomorrow. He didn't recall Lara mentioning Whitten by name, though she had expressed frustration with her program curriculum occasionally. He'd chalked up those complaints as a typical student desire to get through prerequisites to the more relevant classwork.

Despite Aubrey's wishes, Leo couldn't sit here twiddling his thumbs indefinitely. It was one thing to take time off work to actively search for his sister. Staying in Philly just to enjoy the hotel's amenities in the dead of winter wasn't his idea of time well spent.

The waitress brought him a pot of coffee and he opted for the buffet. As he loaded his plate with savory hash browns, eggs, bacon and a slice of toast, he wondered what Lara was eating. Where she was eating. The thought nearly felled him, turning his knees weak. He couldn't bear not knowing if she was safe or not, alive or dead. The longer he went without any word, the more he feared the worst.

Taking a minute to pull himself together, Leo used his cell phone for a quick search on the professor. The sites where students posted ratings gave him a mixed view of the man. Overall, the ratings were positive, though there were frequent comments about the way he challenged his students. Leo got the impression he encouraged his pupils to get involved with the community and to step outside their comfort zones, taking action for the things they believed in.

That sounded like a positive approach to Leo. While he ate, he kept digging. He read a few articles Whitten had written for campus publications and a city newspaper. Whitten was lauded as a man who developed people to become leaders in both small and far-reaching endeavors. The man had a track record as well as what appeared to be a full speaking schedule.

Leo agreed that making real change in a community involved more than throwing money at a problem. Time and effort stretched monetary donations to make the maximum difference. Lara had a heart of gold, often too big for practical purposes.

Their relationship, her persistent affection and care for him was evidence of that. She wanted to make an impact, to create positive changes, and she'd chosen her college and poli-sci major for that express purpose.

Walking away from those soul-deep, heartfelt goals, even for a semester, didn't add up. She'd been applying for internships and researching various opportunities over the winter break. He'd proofed another round of cover letters for her. How could he believe she'd simply changed her mind when she was only three semesters from graduating?

Leo poked at his breakfast without tasting much of it. His first stay here had been for Lara's college visit. They'd sat at the table near the window, watching Philly wake up and move by on the street. He smiled, recalling how she'd been too excited to eat much on touring day, but she'd made up for it on the day after.

Once she'd moved in for her first semester, all of Cincinnati had felt empty. His work was great, his house was great, even with her stuff wedged into the second bedroom and half the basement. But he only felt balanced when she was home on breaks.

She was his little sister and his best friend. He realized that would naturally change as she stretched toward her goals and needed him less for advice or a sounding board. Preparing for that day, he'd been forcing himself out of his shell, expanding his circle of friends and dating more. It remained a work in progress. Some emotional and geographical distance was healthy for them, but this sudden silence cut to the quick. She'd trusted him with everything in the past. Why not whatever she was going through now?

He stared at his nearly full plate, his appetite long gone. He knew there wasn't really anything more he could do here to find Lara except wander and nag the police. But the idea of going back to Cincinnati without any word, without answers, tested the steel spine and rigid independence he thought he'd forged so long ago.

Lara shouldn't love him at all after what happened. His mother had cut him loose after the disaster, but not his baby sister. Nothing, not even the brutal facts when she'd been old enough to understand them, fazed Lara. She just kept on loving him as if he really was the greatest big brother in the world.

He still had the silly gold plastic trophy with the "greatest big brother" title stamped onto the false wood base on his bookshelf at home. A Christmas gift from Lara when she'd been in fourth grade. He kept it out, a daily reminder that he was more than one epic mistake, at least to her.

He wouldn't rest until he knew his sister was all right.

Campus security might not get it, the police might label him grief-stricken or obsessed, but he didn't have any other choice. Without Lara he wasn't sure about the man he faced in the mirror every morning. People waxed poetic about love making life full and worthwhile and Leo knew those people were right. His memories of a happy, loving home burned bright against the years that followed when his only light had been Lara's unrelenting joy despite the cloud of grief.

Yes, he'd made his own way, had a good life and career, but he couldn't give up. Not yet. There were still people to talk to. A coworker or friend might remember something else. Lara might actually answer one of his text messages.

"Mr. Butler?"

With a start, he glanced up into the friendly face of the woman who'd checked him in the day he'd arrived. He glanced at her name tag, Carrie from Illinois. "Yes, Carrie?"

"A note was left for you early this morning."

He stared at the small square envelope embossed with the hotel logo. Fear curdled the bits of breakfast he'd managed to eat, his stomach clenching. "Who left it?"

"I'm sorry, sir, I don't know. I wasn't the one who accepted it."

"No problem." He reached for his coffee, inexplicably unwilling to take the note. "Thank you for bringing it over." He hoped the smile he gave her was the friendly variety and not an expression that would give her nightmares later.

"You're welcome." She placed the envelope on the table. "I'll leave it here for you."

"Great." What was wrong with him? He acted as if

she'd offered him poison rather than possible information. "Thank you," he repeated as she walked away. His coffee cup rattled as he lowered it to the saucer.

The small white square taunted him. It could be from Lara or Aubrey or someone from the soup kitchen. He didn't recognize the writing on the outside of the envelope, but that didn't mean anything. Someone from the front desk probably labeled it for the sender. He only had to man up and open the damn thing to find out, yet still, he hesitated.

Would it be relief to learn his sister was safe or his worst nightmare come true? He should take it upstairs and deal with this in the privacy of his room. Or he could just deal with it and ignore the potential for another public spectacle.

Irritated with his cowardice, he plucked the note from the table and slid a finger under the flap. The paper inside was a scrap, a partial page from a spiral-bound notebook, not the quality stationery of the hotel. The sketchy penmanship was smudged and ragged, as if the person's hand had been dirty or shaking. The message itself sent a chill over his skin.

"Leave Lara alone. We need her. You don't."

The message left him reeling. She was *his* sister. Of course *he* needed her.

He lurched to his feet and his chair toppled back with a crash. Muttering apologies, he clung to the note while he righted his chair and hurried out of the restaurant to the front desk. He needed more information, a look at the security cameras maybe. If they wouldn't cooperate with him, he'd call Officer Rawlins.

It wasn't his worst nightmare, but it was close. Another lead he couldn't quite see clearly. Who would need

Lara more than he did? And how did that person know where to find him?

The rush of questions left him deflated and he veered away from the front desk toward a grouping of chairs on the opposite side of the lobby. There, in front of the windows that overlooked the street, he read the note again, forcing himself to analyze and assess.

It could be a prank. Mean and insensitive, but effective. A way to get even for his disruptions yesterday. It could also be another attempt to get him to stay out of whatever Lara was into. He couldn't believe his sister would ask a friend to do this. She knew him better than that. This sort of vague threat would only keep him right here in Philly, hounding the police or her friends until he got some real answers.

Real or fake, the note was evidence that Lara was still close and someone knew more than they were sharing. He would hand this over to the PPD, specifically Officer Rawlins. With luck, the note would be enough to prompt a more active search for Lara.

He took a picture of the note with his phone and carefully tucked it back into the envelope as he walked to the front desk. Carrie looked up, smiling as he approached. "How can I help you, Mr. Butler?"

This was a longshot. "Is it possible to sit with your security team and look for the person who dropped off this note?"

"I can pass on your request," she said, already making a note.

Leo knew she'd been trained to handle every guest request in a positive way, even those that couldn't be fulfilled. "Thanks," he replied, in kind. "You have my cell number if it works out?" No sense pushing the issue without even giving Aubrey a chance. Everyone but him would be happier if such a request came through the official PPD channels.

"Yes, sir."

"Great, thanks."

He almost headed right out of the hotel before he realized he didn't even have his coat. Officer Rawlins would likely force him to sit down and have coffee if she caught him without it. He didn't need that kind of delay, now that he knew for sure Lara was close. Too impatient to wait for the elevator, he took the stairs up to his room. Although it would be fantastic if the person who had delivered the note was also the author, Leo wouldn't hold his breath waiting for helpful information from the security cameras. He would, however, keep looking for clues to Lara's abrupt decision, starting with her mentor, Professor Whitten.

Tempting as it was to go to the campus first, he headed for the police station. The sergeant at the desk informed him that Aubrey and her partner were out on their beat. When the man offered to take a message, Leo opted to handle it directly, sending her a text along with a picture of the note. After a brief skirmish with his conscience, he decided *not* to let her know where he was going or why.

Back out in the elements, Leo noticed every detail and nuance of the weather around him. Faint shadows cast by the clouds scudding overhead, the nip of the wind across his neck and the gray-black slush gathered at the edges of the streets and sidewalks. As bad as his home life had been, he'd always had good food and a sturdy roof over his head. He couldn't imagine how those who had neither fared on these streets through the winter.

It was all too easy to see Lara diving in to help at the soup kitchen or any other way she could to make life better for someone else. He thought about the brief, cryptic note in his pocket. Was the author someone Lara had helped? Someone who worried that Leo would interfere with a particular effort Lara was involved in now?

Lost in those thoughts, Leo almost walked right past the building that housed Professor Whitten's office. Fortunately, when he did get inside and find the right floor, the door was open. A trim man dressed in jeans and a button-down was at the filing cabinet, his back to the door.

Leo knocked. "Pardon me. I'm looking for Professor Whitten."

"You found him." The man closed the file drawer and turned around. "How can I help?"

Leo was momentarily dumbstruck. Based on Lara's description of Whitten, the man was a font of wisdom and insight. Leo had expected white hair, a suit with a bow tie and thick glasses. Dowdy. Scholarly. Old. This guy, young and fit, didn't even have a tweed jacket with patches at the elbows. How did a man without a wrinkle or crease on his face have any life-changing wisdom to share with students?

"You're Professor Whitten? Dean of the poli-sci department?"

"That's me." The man's smile was flawless, the close-trimmed beard on trend and the knowing sparkle in his eyes suddenly irritating. "Not what you expected?"

Leo was starting to think maybe his sister didn't talk much about Whitten for reasons completely unrelated to the curriculum. As a big brother, he would've fought to keep this guy away from his sister. "No."

"Happens all the time. Poli-sci profs don't have to be stuffy. It's my mission to make politics sexy again. Only way to keep students engaged."

"Uh-huh." Brotherly urges to put a fist through the professor's arrow-straight nose were hard to suppress. He finally recovered his manners. "Pardon me." He stepped forward and extended a hand. "I'm Leo Butler." At Whitten's quizzical expression, he added, "Lara Butler is one of your students. More accurately, she *was* one of your mentees."

The professor frowned. "Was? I'm not sure I follow." He gestured to the chair. "Please have a seat."

Leo sat. Either the guy was also an asset to the drama department or he didn't know what was going on. "You didn't know Lara withdrew from all of her classes for the semester?"

"I did not." The professor took the chair next to Leo rather than the one behind his desk. "She's an excellent student and a good mentor to others in the department. I was counting on her. What happened?"

While the compliments were appreciated, Leo was here to get answers, not give them. "I was hoping you could tell me. Several days ago she stopped answering my calls and texts, she's moved out of her dorm room—"

"But isn't she an RA?"

"Yes." Leo didn't need another recitation of Lara's contributions to life on campus. "From what she told me during previous semesters, she enjoyed her work in the dorms, in the library before that and in her classes."

"I'd agree with that assessment. As I said she's an asset. She was on my short list for teaching assistants this semester."

For the first time Whitten sounded like the stuffy professor Leo had expected to meet. And a potential TA post was news to Leo. Just how much had Lara been keeping from him? Yes, part of college was personal growth and increasing independence, but she'd never hidden anything before—that he knew of.

"Is there a reason you didn't hire her?"

Whitten fidgeted in the chair. "Well. Several, really." He cleared his throat. "In the end it came down to someone else being better for the job and needing it for the résumé as well as the work-study benefit."

Leo didn't like the way the man shifted, his gaze skittering around the office. Maybe the professor had hired someone willing to go above and beyond the job parameters. He reeled in that ridiculous leap of something other than logic. He could practically hear Lara accusing him of being an overprotective big brother. There was a difference between wanting to interfere and actual interference. In Leo's mind he usually stayed on the right side of that line and let Lara live her life.

"Her tuition was covered," Leo said. "So she didn't withdraw over finances. I'm sure a post as your TA would have looked good on her résumé, too."

The professor nodded. "I always have more qualified candidates than openings." His gaze fell to his hands. "She and I had discussed her joining me on a research project here this summer."

Again, news to Leo. "I take it you're having second thoughts about that?"

"If she's no longer a student, it's a moot point." He gave a halfhearted shrug.

Leo bristled. Whatever was going on, he wouldn't let a lapse in judgment cost Lara a good opportunity. "According to the enrollment office, she's only taking a semester off." Hell, they were still holding her tuition hostage, though it wasn't any of Whitten's business.

"Then I guess I'll remain hopeful."

The reply, along with the slanted smile, grated against Leo's frayed and raw nerves like gravel imbedded in a scraped-up knee. He couldn't point to any one detail or reaction, but he was sure the professor was holding back. Of course, he'd been sure the people in the soup kitchen were holding back and that assumption had ended poorly. He pulled himself together.

"Well, give her my best," the professor said, standing. "I'll look forward to her return in the fall."

Leo didn't budge. Wasn't this guy listening? "I thought you might know where to find her. As I said, she isn't returning my calls or text messages. Her things are gone from her dorm room. She has, effectively, vanished."

The professor slowly sank back into his seat. "If she withdrew from classes, wouldn't she go home?"

Leo felt sorry for the entire department if this guy was the anchor. He wasn't seeing anything to back up the famed wisdom, insight, or hard-ass reputation. "If she'd gone home, I wouldn't be *here*," Leo said, pointing out the obvious. "Do you have any idea where she might have gone in the city?"

Whitten folded his arms over his chest. "Girls—I mean, young women—her age can be headstrong."

The change in tone made Leo edgy. He assessed and recalculated. This might be his only chance to speak with the professor; better to go all in. "She spoke with you before deciding to withdraw," Leo accused.

The declaration hovered between them.

The professor's mouth pulled into an imposing frown,

framed by his beard. After several tense moments, his expression eased. "She did. I encouraged her to think it over during the winter break. I expected her to talk with you about her choices before she made a decision."

What choices? "She didn't mention anything other than how well things were going here and how eager she was to come back."

The professor dropped his arms, his hands landing on his knees as he leaned forward. "I encourage all of my students to think for themselves. Your sister has an excellent, limber and creative mind."

Leo's fingers curled into his palms. Something about those adjectives, or the way Whitten said them, didn't seem wholly academic. The professor knew more than he was saying. Hell, he might just know more about Lara than Leo wanted to contemplate.

"Lara has a gift for analysis and problem solving. Something she claims she learned from you," Whitten said.

When would Lara have cause to share anything like that with her professor? Leo held his tongue, preferring to give the man enough rope to verbally hang himself.

"If she decides to withdraw—"

"She *has* withdrawn," Leo snapped.

"Right. I don't know her like you do, of course, but I know she wouldn't make such a decision lightly. Whatever her reasons for taking such a drastic action, I'll respect her choice. I'm sure she believes you'll do the same."

"I'm sure she knows me well enough to know I require a full explanation," Leo said. None of this was adding up. There was something far more personal than student and mentor going on here. "Did you seduce my sister?" Leo demanded. "Is that why she withdrew?"

Whitten reared back as if he'd been struck. "That's absurd. You're out of line," he said in the stuffy voice. "She is a student I value." He stood, glaring down at Leo. "Whatever reasons she had for withdrawing, I hope she returns to complete her program."

"Nice speech." He gave a slow, unimpressed round of applause. "I assume you've practiced that." Leo came to his feet. "You know something. Better to tell me now."

"I know you've overstayed your welcome." He moved toward the door, gestured for Leo to walk out.

At the door, Leo held his ground. "When you hear from her, tell her I'm worried."

Whitten shook his head. "You're mistaken. Please go."

Leo stepped into the hallway. "I'm going to look up your track record with undergrads," he said, allowing his voice to carry. He pulled a business card from his pocket. "I suggest you put my number in your contacts list because you and I are far from done."

The professor tried to close the door, but Leo was quicker, shoving his foot into the gap. "Holding out on me isn't smart. Think that through."

"Mr. Butler?"

The office door closed behind him with a hard snap as the voice of Officer Rawlins caught his full attention. She had a tone that blended authority and compassion in a way that smoothed out his rough edges.

He turned, enjoying the view as she approached. In uniform, her winter coat open, she looked boxy and official. The part of his brain—or rather his anatomy—eager to be distracted overlaid the current view with the memory of her in civilian clothes last night. She hadn't exactly been softer last night. More accessible, maybe. More relaxed. Something about the contrast made him think he could be more open, more at ease around her.

"What are you doing here?" she asked. "My next stop was your hotel." Her clear blue eyes turned wary. "For information about the note you received," she added quickly.

Had she heard her words the way he had or had she noticed his immediate reaction? Leo dialed down the interest and desire that wanted to take a more personal and inappropriate angle to this relationship. This was some misplaced loneliness in search of a connection that wasn't Lara. Attraction or not, he needed this woman— this police officer—to help him find his sister.

"I could ask you the same question." He didn't want to, though. No, he wanted to take her hand in his and walk away from the worry in his heart and the noise in his head. Away from questions no one would answer clearly. Guilt swelled, crashed over him. How unfair was it for him to long for a respite when he didn't even know where his sister was? "Did campus security call you?"

"No." She stepped away from the office door. "Calvin and I were working the search for Lara into our daily routine."

Leo rolled his shoulders, but it didn't help to release the tension. "One of Lara's friends mentioned Professor Whitten. I guess he was her academic mentor." Had Lara been crushing on him? Leo shoved the thought aside. He couldn't dwell on anything more personal. "I'd hoped she'd talked with him about taking the semester off since she apparently didn't talk to me."

Aubrey's gaze softened. "Did she?"

"Yes."

Her golden eyebrows rose at the curt response, but she didn't press for more details. "Does he know where she is?"

"He claims he doesn't," Leo admitted. Implying otherwise would only backfire and he'd made enough missteps with the one person who seemed to sympathize with him. "You want to take a crack at him?"

She pursed her lips, gaze on the door as she considered. "I heard him slam the door. It didn't seem to end well." Her long fingers reached for her radio, but she didn't use it. "My partner might be able to get through."

"Go for it." He shrugged and shoved his hands into his coat pockets. "The professor and I could only agree that we don't like each other."

Aubrey rocked back on her heels. "Any chance you'd wait out here if we tried to talk to him?" Leo snorted. "That's what I thought. I'll just give him time to cool down."

"There was one patch of common ground," Leo said grudgingly. "Both of us think the world of Lara."

"That's good." Her smile sparkled with hope.

"I suppose." Restless, he cracked his knuckles as the only available outlet. "So why doesn't he care that she disappeared?"

"You're suspicious of everyone," Aubrey said.

"Everyone but you," he admitted without thinking. He cleared his throat. "Have you found out anything helpful this morning?" If she had, she would've told him already. In his pocket, his fingers found the outline of the matchbook from the Escape Club. It couldn't hurt to head out to the pier and ask for more help searching for his sister.

"Not so far," she replied. "It would help to have the

actual note instead of just a picture." She reached out and pushed the call button for the elevator.

He hadn't noticed her leading him away from Whitten's office. That strange prickling of need slid along his skin. "I'd rather take the stairs," he said, heading toward the door in the corner.

Being in a small space with her would be too tempting. He couldn't sort out why he was so drawn to her. Wasn't sure knowing would make him feel any better about himself. Last night he'd seen her as a woman separate from the officer who'd filed his missing person case. Yes, in a normal social setting, he would've asked her out without any concern about motives. He might even have tried to make a few dates into something more lasting, if she'd felt the same way. Now there was no way for him to separate why they met from why he wanted her.

"Leo, wait."

He kept moving. Edgy, his thoughts a tangle, this wasn't the best time to test his self-control or resolve. Her footsteps followed him down the stairs and she caught up to him on the second landing.

"We are working the case, Leo."

He paused, sighed. "Do you want to see the note?"

"Yes," she said. "Preferably at the station."

"As evidence." Her nod should have made him feel better. Instead, he feared losing the only scrap of proof he had that Lara was still in town. He continued down the stairs, Aubrey beside him. "Do you have anywhere else to check for Lara?" he asked, thinking of the Escape Club again.

"Not yet. Calvin and I are talking with people around campus who interacted with her." She held out a printout of Lara's class schedule and official activities.

"Campus security plays favorites," he muttered. It made sense, but he didn't like it. He stopped abruptly and turned. She halted on the last step, her lips parted as if she'd been about to ask him a question.

Her mouth was right there within reach and he couldn't drag his gaze away from that full lower lip, the sexy bow of the upper. He could close the distance and finally know the taste of her. Why did he keep putting himself in this position? In the past he'd had no problem focusing on Lara's needs. During his senior year of college, she'd broken her arm and he'd cancelled a spring break trip with his girlfriend to help his sister through the surgery and recovery. This was an all-new level of trouble and the worst time for him to be distracted.

Aubrey was a cop who had the misfortune of being on duty when he'd gone off the rails. She was stuck with him and he was being pulled like taffy, the search for his sister all twisted up with his attraction to the woman assigned to help him.

"We won't find her, will we?" He yanked his gaze back to her clear blue eyes just in time to catch her staring at his mouth. His lips tingled. "Will we?"

"I…" She swallowed. "I want to tell you yes," she finished in a whisper.

But she couldn't. The raw honesty blasted through him as cold and unrelenting as the wind outside. As much as he wanted to hear those comforting words, he knew the truth was better. "I'm not giving up." He marched out of the stairwell and back onto the street.

Chapter 4

On quaking knees, Aubrey watched him go, her thoughts jumbled up with emotions that had to take a backseat to logic and procedure. Cold air flooded the stairwell, doing nothing for the heat that had gathered when they were eye to eye and nearly lip to lip. Again.

She had to stop thinking about kissing that man.

Using her radio to let Calvin know where they were, she rushed after Leo. Aubrey ordered her heart to return to its rightful place in her chest. She could not let herself get knotted up over the new guy in town.

Those seconds left her nerves sizzling and proved last night hadn't been a fluke. Why couldn't the man be a toad, rather than a walking temptation who wore the caring, determined big-brother role to an advantage?

She tried once more to blame her only-child issues. If she'd had a sibling of the older variety, she would've wanted one like Leo. "Lara is lucky to have you," she said, catching up to him. She had to do something to keep her mind on the job rather than those long legs and that great jawline.

"Drop it," he said. "I know you think this is a lost cause."

"I don't," she insisted. The note he'd received had ramped up both her concern and her optimism. "Someone will come forward if she's in town." Aubrey was confident Mary-Tea would share more information soon. Part of her wondered, based on the tone of the note, if the older woman had written it.

"Now you don't even think she's in town?" He stopped at the edge of the courtyard and stared her down. "Should I remind you her bank accounts and credit cards haven't been touched?"

Her heart fluttered, the foolish, uncooperative organ. "No." She squared her shoulders, relieved to see Calvin hustling up the walk. "We're out here, gathering information as quickly as possible."

"We need a bigger team," he snapped. "A search party."

"She isn't a five-year-old lost in the woods," Aubrey countered. Her patience was fraying and it had nothing to do with the case. Deep inside, where all of her secret hopes and doubts lived, she sighed. There had to be a better place for her to meet people than work. "Let me take the note to the station and get it processed."

Leo seemed to deflate and she worried he'd drop.

"Everything good?" Calvin aimed an irritated look at Leo that went completely unnoticed.

"I'm running out of places to look," Leo said.

"We're just getting started." She reached out and patted his shoulder, ignoring Calvin's silent assessment. "We'll retrace her steps and keep asking questions. We'll scour social media for any insight into her associations or recent activity. Every business on the block has her picture posted." Despite Mary-Tea's warning. "Something will break our way."

"Great." He clutched his chest and winced. "I'll just wait here."

Calvin moved first, guiding Leo to a bench. "You're too young for a heart attack." He shot her another look and she was braced to call an ambulance. "Just breathe a minute," he said.

"I'm all right."

He still looked too pale. "Just take your time," she encouraged.

Leo scrubbed some color into his cheeks. "Here." He reached into his coat and pulled out an envelope. "Take it. I hope it helps." He leaned back and stared up at the sky. "I asked the hotel if I could see the security feed, but they won't let me."

"I'm not surprised," Calvin said. "We're more likely to get approval for that."

"And you might actually recognize someone," Leo said.

That worried her more than it should. She took the small envelope, tapping it gently against her palm. He'd sent her a picture of the note by text and she knew what she'd find inside. Still, she opened it to confirm. "We'll take this, handle it the right way and update her file."

He rolled his eyes. "Right. Will you tell me if you discover who dropped it off?"

"We'll keep you informed about every development," Calvin said, his sobering voice ending further discussion.

She was grateful for that, despite the sympathy for him that wound through her chest. "You can get back to your hotel?" she asked.

Leo nodded. "I'll behave."

Calvin snorted and Aubrey shot him a quelling look. "Officer Rawlins?"

"Yes?"

"You know this city," Leo said. "Who would possibly need my sister more than me?"

Calvin urged her along, but Aubrey couldn't leave him without an answer. She considered what Mary-Tea had told her about the flyers making Lara, a helpful person, unsafe. Doubt niggled at her for keeping the information from Leo.

Until she remembered he would leap into action and stir up more trouble.

"You know who sent it," Leo said, rising from the bench.

She held up a hand, thankful Calvin didn't move between her and Leo. She might get ribbed from her peers about her soft heart and trusting outlook, but Calvin did trust her to handle herself as a professional.

"The picture we're getting is that Lara was compassionate and a willing volunteer. Lots of people would benefit from her assistance."

"That's not an answer," Leo challenged.

Aubrey couldn't imagine the older woman going close enough to a busy hotel to deliver that note, but that didn't mean she wouldn't ask someone else to do it for her. "It's the best I have right now. Give us time to investigate thoroughly."

She tipped her head, urging him to come along with them. Leaving him out here in the elements, even if he wasn't as distressed as yesterday, still didn't feel right. At last, he fell into step with them.

"For what it's worth, it sounds like you hit the jackpot when it comes to sisters," Calvin said.

"You have no idea," Leo said.

When they arrived at the precinct, he paused as Calvin walked through the doors. "Aren't you coming in?" she asked.

"No. I've decided to visit the Escape Club."

She flinched and felt her cheeks go hot with frustration.

"You shouldn't play poker." Leo's mouth slanted. "Why are you so against me talking with them? I was told they often helped with stuff the police couldn't tackle head-on."

An army of ants marched up and down her spine at the pure hope in his voice. She guided him away from the front door of the station. "This isn't the place to have this conversation."

"Then let's not have it," Leo said. "You work on the note and I'll go out to the club and see if they're willing to help me search."

"We're doing all we can, Leo."

"But is it enough?"

She met the challenge in his eyes with some grit of her own. "I believe in the system and the rapport I've built in this neighborhood. If your sister is out here in the area or anywhere else in my city, we *will* find her. You have to give us time to work."

"Take all the time you need," he said. "I don't see the problem calling on this Escape Club."

She was sure he would hear her teeth grinding. "Grant Sullivan and the people who helped him are not legally authorized to get involved in an active case. Do you understand?"

"I'm still going."

Mentally, she stomped her foot and cuffed him to the nearest building. Then the cuff idea sent her overactive imagination in the wrong direction. "Why are you being so stubborn?"

"Because she's all I have!"

His outburst bulleted through the air and ricocheted off the stonework. It couldn't be true, unless he was this obnoxious about everything in life and pushed everyone except his family away. No. If he was this unbearable as a general rule, something else would've popped on the background check. Instead, he was clean.

"Fine. I'll go with you." She couldn't believe she'd said that, but she wouldn't take the words back. Better to be there than to wonder.

"You'd do that?" He stared at her for a long moment. "No. You only want to go along to disrupt the meeting."

"Not true. I'd appreciate it if you waited until after my shift." Going in uniform would only make an errand she was already dreading that much worse. "Calvin and I need to be out here and visible."

"I understand," he said, studying her closely.

"Then you'll wait?"

He shook his head. "I'll call you when I'm done."

"Leo!" Once more she was chasing him, if only for a few steps. "You're making it exceedingly difficult to help you. What will it take for you to believe I'm on your side?"

His frown said it all. Nothing shy of her raising a citywide search party would be enough. "Come on," she said. "I'm not letting you out of my sight."

"Is seeking help a crime now?"

"No." Many of her peers disagreed with her about the value of the Escape Club and Sullivan's approach. She found the independent methods too risky, but grudgingly admitted its success rate spoke volumes. "You've proven you can get into trouble," she replied. "Let's go." She took a step toward the precinct and waited for him to make his decision. "Don't push me. I will cuff you if necessary."

One eyebrow arched, creating an interesting swirl low in her belly, but he eventually followed her. The precinct was humming and everyone around her seemed way too distracted to notice Leo was with her two days running.

She sat him down and found a coffee for him while she added the information about the note to the file on Lara. Calvin had spoken with the security team at the hotel and the two of them were welcome anytime.

"See," she said to Leo when Calvin walked off. "Progress."

He raised his coffee cup. "To progress."

If only he'd shown a bit of enthusiasm. "The club isn't even open yet," she said in another attempt to discourage his plan.

"The number works." He raised his cell phone. "I've been texting with someone."

She pinched the bridge of her nose and counted to ten. Twice. The effort futile, she met Leo's gaze. "About Lara?"

"Not yet. Not specifically. Apparently, the man I should speak with won't be available until closer to four."

Inside, she did a little happy dance over the reprieve. Based on the scowl, Leo wasn't nearly as pleased. "That gives us plenty of time to visit with hotel security," she said. She'd also be able to complete her shift and handle what seemed to be an inevitable meeting with Grant Sullivan off duty.

"I suppose you're right. I'll wait and you can join me."

It would be rude to rub it in. "It's all progress," she said quietly. "Not as fast as you hoped, but it *is* progress."

Leo shrugged. His phone lit up with an incoming call and he muttered something about work as he stepped away to answer. She kept an eye on him throughout the afternoon, half expecting him to leave. He didn't. Though he wasn't in the way and didn't interfere with her or any fellow officers, he distracted her, constantly present at the edge of her vision. Of course, he was front and center of her awareness as she and Calvin worked their shift and the search for Lara.

Once they arrived at the hotel, Leo went to his room. She was grateful he hadn't pushed to sit in on the meeting with hotel security. The review of the security camera footage wasn't as helpful as she'd hoped. The person who'd dropped off the note was bundled up into a nondescript blob of old coat and hunched shoulders.

The overnight attendant for the hotel's front desk who had accepted the note and put it into an envelope for Leo claimed it had been a man in his midtwenties under the layers. Aubrey let Calvin ask a few more questions while she reviewed the grainy black-and-white images over and over.

Her hopes of making any kind of identification faded. It had been a longshot to start with, but whoever had left the note had taken every precaution, deftly evading revealing camera angles. Someone had walked into the hotel with full awareness of the security setup. Someone knew Leo by name. Progress, she reminded herself.

She sent a text message to Leo that they were done and promised to meet him in front of the hotel as soon as her shift was over. Meeting Sullivan in civilian clothing seemed better in her mind than going in uniform. He had cops and first responders in and out of the club all the time and no one gave it a second thought. Her situation was different, with IA judging her every move.

"All good?" Calvin asked.

"Yes." She tucked her phone away and pulled on her gloves as they walked out.

"Hot date tonight?"

She nearly tripped over her feet. "What? No. Why would you ask?"

Calvin gave her an arch look. "I'd rather assume it's a hot date rather than Butler that puts that look on your face. He's part of the case. You can't go there."

"Stop," she said. "There's no date and no look." Curiosity, maybe, but that was it. "Leo is insisting on a visit to the Escape Club. I made him agree to let me go along."

Calvin's dark eyebrows snapped together. "Then I really don't get the expression."

Her partner was the only person in the precinct who knew just how little Aubrey cared for Sullivan and his self-appointed role of helping people outside normal legal channels. Successes aside, she believed working within the system was better for the community as a whole. "I'm just happy to finish the shift and I'm looking forward to changing clothes, especially my socks. My feet have been cold all day."

"Uh-huh."

"Seriously, stop now." She didn't need him teasing her. "You misread my face."

They walked another block in comfortable silence.

"Maybe I did," he allowed. "Only because I want you to be happy. On duty and off."

"I am," she assured him. She enjoyed her quiet off-duty hours, needing the time alone to recharge. She had friends to hang out with occasionally and until someone worthy of the scrutiny came along, she didn't worry about dating. Her career fulfilled her. Even on days when a shift was monopolized by good people struggling with hard circumstances, like Leo Butler's search for his sister. "I'd really hoped one of us would recognize the person who left him that note."

Calvin nodded as they rounded the corner and the station came into view. "At least Butler can take comfort that his sister's alive."

"Would you tell him to go see Sullivan?"

"Yes," he replied with zero hesitation. "We're doing all we can. If Butler wants more action, he'll need help from Sullivan or someone like him."

Sullivan was one of a kind, thankfully. Everyone touted his experience and dedication to community, but Aubrey still felt he posed more of a danger than a benefit. "You think he should hire a private investigator." That would fly in the face of Mary-Tea's warning, as well.

"It's the only non-Sullivan option," Calvin said as they entered the building. "Aubrey, you know as well as I do that if she doesn't want to be found, if she is helping out the way the note implies, there isn't a damn thing we or her brother can do about it."

"True."

"Maybe Sullivan helps, maybe he doesn't, but it can't hurt." Calvin bent his head close, speaking low. "You shouldn't make him wait. Go on."

"Right now? In uniform?" Calvin knew if she got

caught actively enlisting Sullivan's help, it opened her up to more hassles from IA.

"Yes. The longer he's in town, the more trouble he's likely to raise."

"Fair point."

"I'll cover for you through the end of the shift."

Her partner's words followed her as she hurried back to Leo's hotel. Calvin had tried to convince her more than once that Sullivan's efforts were generally helpful. Maybe Sullivan could shake loose a better lead.

Something about Leo's desperation and the raw grief in his eyes grabbed her by the throat. It wasn't pity or her soft heart. Not just that anyway. She couldn't stomach the idea of sending him on his way with only her best professional platitudes.

She couldn't call the minimal effort good enough because she believed Leo's depiction of his relationship with Lara. She also believed his take on the disappearance, despite the lack of evidence of foul play. There were dozens of ways to help the homeless without living on the street. Why wouldn't Lara give her brother a reply, if only to keep him from interfering and worrying?

When she reached the hotel, Leo was walking out of the main lobby. He didn't look any different from earlier, but the attraction punched her in the gut, left her momentarily breathless.

"The valet is bringing my rental around."

She managed a jerky nod. "Good."

"You look like you swallowed a lemon-flavored goldfish," he said. "Did something happen?"

The weird observation made her laugh, and the laughter seemed to restore order to her breathing. "Not in the past hour." All of this had been happening inside her since she first saw him.

His car arrived and she settled into the passenger seat and buckled up, adjusting the seat belt around her radio and equipment. When Leo was ready, they headed away from the streets she knew so well toward the river where Sullivan had transformed an old warehouse into one of the most popular music hotspots in the city. It wasn't a long drive, but traffic clogged the streets at this hour. It gave her too much time to revel in the spicy-clean scent of the man next to her and the heated memories of those two near-miss kisses.

When they reached the riverside pier, she noticed the building still wore a black scar near the roofline in the corner. Trucks and construction equipment created a loose barrier between the club and the rest of the city.

Leo parked as close to the construction personnel as possible. He leaned forward and peered through the windshield. Leo swore. "This is the place?"

"It is. A retired firefighter torched the place several months ago. Guess you'd say he went off the deep end during one of those situations people say Sullivan handles so well."

"You really don't like the guy."

She didn't care for the way Leo studied her. "He was an excellent cop," she allowed. "Experience or not, I think law enforcement should remain the job of professionals." Mary-Tea's request burned in the back of her mind. What if she was letting Leo make things worse?

"The PPD isn't perfect."

"I'm aware." She paused, collecting her thoughts. "The safe bet is Grant Sullivan isn't perfect, either."

Leo sighed. "Hard to argue with that. This must have been a bad fire."

"It was," Aubrey said. "Come on." She wanted to get this over with. It wasn't fair for her to hope Sullivan couldn't help find Lara, but she also wanted Leo to put his faith in the system she served. The police were capable of locating his sister, assuming Lara wanted to be found.

Despite his experience as a cop, in her opinion, Sullivan's actions amounted to meddling at best and vigilantism at worst. It was one thing to train his team to watch for predatory or risky behavior within the confines of the club. That was responsible. Sullivan had gone well beyond those logical limits through the years, assigning his staff to act as bodyguards or even investigators. It just didn't sit right with Aubrey. Yes, some cases slipped through the cracks of normal police work and those instances made everyone unhappy. Contrary to the urban myth, Sullivan couldn't fix everything. The law maintained rules and procedures to protect the innocent *and* the guilty. If one man started doling out justice, where did that leave the community at large?

Aubrey wanted to help Leo as much as she wanted him to respect the uniform and her role in the community. She wanted him to respect *her*. Her assessment, her ability and her effort.

Well, wasn't that a revelation? One that made her feel awkward and small. What Leo thought of her didn't make any difference in how she proceeded to search for Lara, and it shouldn't make any difference in any other aspect of her life.

Somehow, it did. Why? He was a stranger in her city. A temporary fixture, whether they found his sister or not. Maybe that was the draw. Leo was attractive and enticing and he wouldn't be around long enough for IA to pester her about him.

Leo reached for the door and it swung open. Jason nearly knocked them down. "Excuse me," he said. "Oh, hey, Aubrey." His gaze raked over her uniform. "What brings you by?"

"Leo would like to speak with your boss." She hated the stiffness in her voice. To Leo she said, "This is Jason. He's the manager here. Jason, Leo Butler."

"That title will sure feel better when we're back in business," Jason said. He shook Leo's hand. "Good to see you again."

"Again?" Leo asked, his brow furrowed.

"Jason was tending bar at the pub last night," Aubrey explained. Her pulse sped up as she relived the moment outside when Leo had sheltered her from passersby and the weather.

"I'm picking up shifts all over town until we reopen. Come on in," Jason said. "Mind your step."

Inside, construction dust swirled in the air, mingling with the scents of materials and sweat.

"I have a problem the police can't solve," Leo began.

"That's not true," Aubrey interjected. "We only disagree on how to proceed. His sister is the missing girl whose picture I just posted."

"I figured," Jason said. "The more eyes, the better?" he asked.

"Always," Aubrey allowed.

Jason's eyebrows arched and he turned to Leo. "And you convinced her to come here?" He whistled. "That's no small feat." He stretched an arm toward a wide, unfinished doorway. "This way. It's always better to tell the story once and be done."

Unless you needed to verify an eyewitness account or test a suspect's story. Then you needed to hear it more than once. But that was police work. She managed to keep those thoughts to herself as she followed Jason and Leo across what would be a nightclub again soon.

Walking through the noisy construction zone, she was happily distracted by the work going on. Leo was curious, as well, since he stopped beside her and tipped his head to the new roof support overhead. "What are you doing about acoustics?"

Jason, realizing they weren't behind him, came back. "Pardon?" he shouted over the clanging of tools and tunes blaring from a radio.

"The acoustics?" Leo pointed to the ceiling. "I read online that this club was all about the live music."

"We are. Grant is a drummer at heart." Jason pointed toward the far end of the big room. "When the stage goes in, it gets all sorted out. Grant can explain it better, if you want the science behind it all. There will be a bigger dance floor and they're reworking the bar," he added when they were in the service hallway.

Jason took a few swift strides, paused and turned back. "Door's closed. Wait here until he wraps things up." He'd opened his mouth as if to say something more, when a door at the end of the hallway opened and deep voices bounced around the unfinished space.

Aubrey recognized both men at once. Both Grant Sullivan and his guest, Councilman Benny Keller, had big reputations in Philly. Keller was often asked for his comments on various city issues, and Grant had done his share of appearances, as well, usually promoting a music event.

The councilman's lean frame looked even narrower next to Grant's stocky build. His perfect smile and gleaming white hair completed the contrast of old-money banker versus the working man.

"Looks like I'm keeping you," Keller said to Grant. "Thanks for your time." He shook hands vigorously with Grant and strode toward the new arrivals. He paused, his gaze skimming Jason and Leo to fix on her.

"Officer Rawlins." He stuck out his hand as he read her badge. She really should have changed clothes before this meeting. The councilman's campaign smile gave Aubrey an uncomfortable chill. Then he leaned back, murmuring her last name. "You and your partner were recently featured on the PPD website."

"Yes, sir." She'd forgotten about that article on the benefits of community engagement.

"Thank you for your service to our city, Officer."

"It's an honor, sir."

Keller greeted Jason and introduced himself to Leo, clearly assuming he had a potential voter in his grasp. Leo didn't have time to correct him, not that it mattered. The man had always struck her as a bit too slick, only hearing what he wanted to hear. As the councilman made his exit, Grant waved them closer, an amused twinkle in his brown eyes.

She was happy to trade the devil she sort of knew in Keller for the devil she didn't know as well in Sullivan.

"Grant," Jason began, "my friend, Aubrey Rawlins."

She in turn introduced Leo. "His sister has gone missing," she said. "No signs of foul play. Although the PPD is doing all we can, Mr. Butler has heard about Alexander and the extracurricular work you've done through your club."

Grant's salt-and-pepper eyebrows rose. Dang it, she hadn't meant to offend him. Though she didn't want the search for Lara getting twisted or blurred with an Escape Club assist, she didn't want Leo accusing her of sabotaging the meeting.

"Have a seat," Grant said, his voice kind and friendly. He reached into a glass-fronted refrigerator behind his desk and pulled out a bottle of water for each of them. "New upgrade," he explained. "When we decided to rebuild, it was an opportunity." He sat down, his desk chair squealing in protest. With a slightly guilty smile, he said, "The chair is next on the upgrade list. But it was about the only thing that survived the fire. How can I help you, Mr. Butler? I assume your sister is of legal age, since I haven't seen anything about her disappearance on the news."

"She is," Leo replied. "Dropping out of touch this way isn't like her. In fact, we've never gone so long without some sort of contact. Even after she moved to Philly for school, we talked or exchanged text messages daily. I haven't heard a peep from her for ten days now."

"So you came to town to track her down." Grant's fingertips started to tap on the battered arm of the chair.

"I'm sure I sound like an overprotective older brother," Leo explained. "And I suppose I am, but my gut tells me something is wrong. She's an intelligent adult and she knows me as well as I know her. If she was okay, she'd find a way to tell me so I wouldn't worry."

"Take it easy," Grant said. "I'm not judging, only gathering the background."

Leo sat forward in his seat. "The college told me she

withdrew. I have access to her activity on her bank account and credit cards. Nothing has been touched since she came back to school."

Aubrey listened as Leo related all the details, right up to this morning's note, impressed when he didn't downplay his mistakes at the soup kitchen or his frustration earlier with the professor. She'd thought she could listen dispassionately, maybe with only half an ear, but she'd been wrong. Leo's recitation of the events broke her heart all over again. If she could change this or fix it for him, she would without a second thought.

"And you think she's living on the street with the homeless community?" Grant queried when Leo subsided. "That's quite a fall for a college student with good grades, paid-up tuition and no known drug habit."

"Exactly my point." Leo bristled and reiterated his sister wasn't using. "She walked away from everything, including me. I'm absolutely certain the people at the soup kitchen recognized her."

Guilt prickled across her palms as she thought of Mary-Tea's warning. She should share the information, but the note would have to suffice while Leo was within hearing. Grant glanced at her. Was the guilt as obvious to him as it felt to her?

"Mr. Butler," Grant said, "I'm sure Officer Rawlins has told you the local homeless community is notoriously tight-lipped. Talking to outsiders usually brings trouble."

"Can you help me find her or not?" Leo tipped his head toward her. "Officer Rawlins tells me they're doing all they can."

"We are," Aubrey insisted. "Her college and the places Lara volunteered are within my precinct. We're posting flyers and asking about her everywhere. I'm sure someone has information, but surely you remember that this kind of thing takes time."

"I do." Grant pinned her with a serious, piercing gaze. His cop face. "Do you believe she's still in Philly, Officer Rawlins?"

Aubrey nodded. She wouldn't reveal Mary-Tea as a source in front of Leo, but she could cooperate right up to that point. "It's the logical assumption, based on her finances and the note Leo received. After asking around, and reviewing her social media, my partner and I have determined she's avoiding her typical friends and hangouts. It's hard to know where to look next but we're not giving up."

Grant's gaze narrowed on her. Aubrey's stomach cramped with this firsthand experience of what had made him such a good cop. The unflinching assessment, the expectant silence. Aubrey struggled against the urge to fill that quiet space with information she wasn't ready to share.

Eventually, Grant shifted his focus to Leo. "How did you hear about me?"

"The head of campus security gave me this." He fished the matchbook out of his pocket and held it up. "He said you might be able to do more than the police."

"Jones is a good guy," Grant said.

Aubrey pressed her lips together. Leo hadn't listened to her yet. Better if the hard truth came from Grant.

"I believe we can help you." Grant rapped his fists lightly on the desktop for emphasis. "And I believe we should."

"What?" Aubrey clapped a hand over her mouth, but it was no match for the outburst. "You can't pump him up with false hope," she said. This wasn't fair to Leo. She didn't like Grant, but she'd heard he was better than this. "She's an adult. Everyone agrees she left school on her own. No signs of coercion or foul play. Whatever she's doing, she doesn't want to be found."

"What do you think she's doing, Officer Rawlins?"

Aubrey surged to her feet. "Hell if I know. I'm papering the neighborhood with flyers, talking to everyone. Do you plan to muster a search party? We don't even know where to look."

"I can give you more manpower, reach out in other areas of the city, and possibly dig deeper into Miss Butler's motives."

"How?" Aubrey demanded.

She was ignored by both men.

"Yes, do that," Leo said. "Please, all of that. I just want to know she's safe. She doesn't do rash things like this. I'm sure she's in over her head."

Aubrey fumed at the way Grant played Leo. "How much will you charge him for the help?" It was an odd time to find her inner pessimist, but she wouldn't sit back and watch this quietly. Having been knee-deep in Leo's worry and grief, she wouldn't let anyone, not even the revered Grant Sullivan, take advantage of that.

"We don't charge a fee," Grant replied. "We just help out when and where we can. Sometimes that's here in the club. Sometimes it's out in the community. Lara—"

"You're raising a crew of vigilantes," she snapped.

"Sit down, Officer Rawlins," Grant said in a quiet voice that didn't hide the steel underneath. "You're testing my patience."

She sat, fingers laced together while she fought for cool, professional detachment. "Working outside the system might be successful in the short-term, but it's not sustainable. You were a cop. You know this."

"I know that protocols and rules should bend occasionally."

"This was such a mistake. I never should have come here," she muttered. Why had she? Oh, yeah, Leo. Leaving him unattended didn't seem to end well.

Leo reached over and covered her hands with his. The contact gave her a jolt that sent a sweet, enticing tingle through her body. His concern and commitment to his sister were admirable and gave her hope for people in general.

A voice in her head snorted. *Right.* Now she was lying to herself. Case or not, she didn't want to be too far from this man. Calvin would be rolling with laughter if he could see her now. She was ready to toss aside common sense, just to indulge some fluttery, feminine attraction.

Leo seemed to be her professional kryptonite. She couldn't maintain an appropriate distance. They hadn't crossed any lines yet, though her body set off a proximity alert whenever he was near.

In training, she'd learned certain calls and cases would be emotional triggers. A cop needed to be self-aware and remain calm when that happened. No one was expected to be superhuman, but when feeling reactive, she should look for ways to deescalate the situation.

She caught Leo's eye. "I know you need to find her through any means necessary." She faced Grant. "I'll go talk with Jason while the two of you work out the details."

Aubrey walked out on shaking knees. All the talking and wishing in the world wouldn't make the PPD's approach and effort enough for Leo. She didn't blame him for needing to explore every option. She just couldn't endorse this choice.

"She doesn't like you much," Leo observed. He wished Aubrey had stayed, yet he admired the way she stuck to her principles.

"Officer Rawlins has a strict code of ethics. I respect that," Grant said. "I'm sure she has an excellent record of service to the city."

"She's good at her job." She'd been persistent with Lara's case and her actions backed up her word. "And I appreciate her help. She could've arrested me for being a nuisance and disturbing the peace but didn't." A fact he appreciated more with every passing hour. Behind bars, with no hope of hearing from his sister, he would've lost his mind by now. "And she does have a connection with the people in her neighborhood." Leo rolled his shoulders. "I'm just not sure Lara's still in the neighborhood."

"That would be my concern, as well." Grant massaged the knuckles of one hand against the opposite palm.

Leo scooted to the edge of his seat, eager to hear Grant's plan. "What do you need to get started? I brought along a picture and a list of her friends."

Grant held up his hands in surrender. "Transparency," he said. "I've met your sister."

Leo couldn't have heard him correctly. "What? When?" It wasn't a stretch to think Lara had been to a nightclub. He knew she had a social life, though he didn't let himself dwell on the potential minefield of her going out on dates.

"Lara came to the club a few weeks ago," Grant began. "Just before she went home for the holiday break.

We were getting underway with the rebuild and she introduced herself. She'd brought along two other men who needed work."

"You know Lara." He glanced to the door, wishing Aubrey was hearing this. "Did you hire the men? Can I talk with them?"

"I did hire them," Grant replied. "They were down on their luck, but they had construction experience. Apparently, she'd met them while volunteering at the soup kitchen. I'll speak with both of them." His fingers flexed and curled into his palms. "Your sister's commitment to helping others impressed me."

"When she finds a cause, she sticks. That's why I'm so worried." Leo liked Grant already and felt real hope cool the hot streak of worry that had him by the throat. Here was a man who got things done.

"You think she got in over her head."

Leo nodded.

Sympathy warmed Grant's gaze. "I don't know your sister well, but she struck me as confident, smart. Not a pushover."

"That fits," Leo said. "Still, she knows me, knows how I'd react to her ignoring my messages."

"Is there anything you didn't mention in front of Officer Rawlins?" Grant pressed.

"What do you mean?" Leo had been running a little too wide open, emotions too close to the surface with Aubrey.

"Anything you can think of, past or present, that would compel your sister to wander away from her life," Grant clarified. "A new boyfriend. Or an old one. Trouble with a parent or a bad-news friend from high school? Maybe there are issues that came up in class and set her off."

Leo shook his head. "I was the problem child at home," he admitted. "Lara was everything good and right in our family. She has no history of mental illness, if that's what you're getting at."

"Any family history of that kind of thing?"

"No." Leo didn't count his mother's negligence as an illness. That was a choice. The grief he'd inflicted on her life had changed her, yes, but she was stable about her hatred of him and general "over it" attitude about motherhood.

"Lara has no ties to Philly beyond college?"

"No." Leo dried his palms on his jeans. He was the one with the persistent guilt that bit him at the worst times. This was one of those times. He'd thought this through, talked this through, time and again. He wanted to give Grant something that would make a difference and help them locate his sister. "Frankly, I was surprised she chose this particular school. Our mom pushed for her alma mater, where she'd met our dad. I was the only one hoping Lara would stay closer to home."

"What won her over?"

"I think the change of scenery. The dynamic urban landscape was a big piece of it. She wanted out of the suburbs," he replied. "And the program here had better marks and more significance after graduation."

"I see." Grant made a few more notes, then drummed his pen against the desktop. "In this instance, I'm going to put out a blanket alert. Most of my employees are or have been first responders. They can keep an eye out for Lara and much like Officer Rawlins is doing, they can ask around when they're out and about. A situation like this can take some time."

Leo's bubble of hope burst. "That's almost verbatim what Aubrey said."

Grant's eyebrows arched as though he'd been smacked with an epiphany. "She isn't wrong. We can't arrange a citywide search, but you'll have more eyes and ears out there. When we have a more definite location, we can get more aggressive. Will you stay in town or head back home?"

"I'm staying." At least until his leave ran out. He wrote down his hotel and room number on the back of his business card. "You have my cell number."

Grant nodded. "If we don't have a lead or better answers in a week, I'll reassess." He came around the desk and shook Leo's hand. "You're not in this alone."

"Thanks." Leo walked out of the office, spotting Aubrey chatting with Jason at the other end of the hallway. Whatever he was saying agreed with her. Her eyes were bright and a smile curved her lovely mouth. For a moment she looked like a model playing a cop. She was beautiful, inside and out, in any setting.

Leo had no idea why that suddenly annoyed him. His attraction to her gave him a break from worrying about Lara, even as she was inexorably tied to his search for his sister. Aubrey had shown him remarkable kindness. It wasn't her sibling that was missing, yet here she was, helping him explore all his options.

All that lovely brightness faded when she noticed his approach and a wary cloud came over her features. He owed her an apology, and not just for dragging her into a meeting she didn't want. What a jerk he'd been. Grief and worry weren't valid excuses for his outrageous behavior.

"Grant and I are done."

She cocked an eyebrow at him and then gave Jason a warm farewell. Leo fell in behind her as she stalked through the construction zone and out to the car in stony silence.

"I'm really sorry for making you come out here," he said as soon as they were driving away. "It was productive, if that helps."

"So you got the search party you needed?"

"Not exactly." Aubrey's outright anger stung more than it should. They were acquaintances, nothing more. Two random people shoved together by an awkward turn of fate. "He has a network of people from all corners of the city who will be keeping an eye out for Lara."

Aubrey folded her arms and stared straight ahead. "Good." She relaxed. "I do want you to find your sister."

He believed her. "He says if we don't have a lead in a week, he'll reassess."

"That's more than the PPD can offer you," she admitted. "He really isn't charging you a dime?"

"No." Leo had assumed there would be a fee. "Hiring an investigator was my next step."

"Last night I thought you already had," she said. "Jason called me to the bar because someone was there asking about your sister."

"Who was that?" He gripped the steering wheel, refusing to lose his temper. "I didn't cross paths with anyone willing to speak her name."

"I didn't have a chance to find out before you arrived."

Apparently, he'd botched up her search because he was too obsessed with his own. He really hadn't given her *enough* credit for what she was doing to help him.

She'd gone out on her own time to get a lead on Lara. "Sorry."

"You're worried." She tugged the seat belt away from her shoulder. "I have a description and I'm working with that."

Leo felt like a heel. He'd wedged himself into her work and in the process made an often-thankless job more difficult. "I don't know you that well."

She glanced at him while waiting for the stoplight overhead to turn green. "Same goes. What's your point?"

"Would you like to have dinner?" he asked quickly, before he could rationalize his way out of it.

"That's not a good idea," she replied. "Thanks for the invitation."

"You must think I'm irrevocably selfish," he said.

"No." She shifted to face him, sighing a little. "You're hurting and baffled by the actions of someone you love. I understand that well enough."

There was a wisp of old pain in her voice. Who'd put it there? The question he had no right to ask burned in the back of his throat. They weren't friends, though if they'd met on equal footing it would've been harder to ignore whatever simmered between them.

At least from his side of the equation. He was definitely attracted to her from those honest eyes to her candor to her principles. Not to mention the mouth he kept fantasizing about. But he couldn't act on that. Wouldn't take the chance on insulting her just in case what he felt was some crazy stress-coping mechanism. Once they found Lara, and he had to believe they would, that would be the time to ask out Aubrey. Except they didn't live in the same city.

"Are you saying that if you were in my shoes you'd

sit back and let someone else handle it?" He pulled into the line for the valet in front of the hotel.

She took a deep breath. "No. I'm sure I wouldn't. And I suppose it isn't fair, me being a cop. If I had a sister and she went missing, my peers might be more willing to actively search."

Might? Another red flag popped up in his mind. Who wouldn't help Aubrey if she needed it?

"I understand desperate," she continued. "Based on my experience and commitment to the job, I like to think I'd let the police handle the search properly."

"But?"

"But what do I know?" Her blue eyes were full of compassion. "I'm an only child from a stable home. I haven't taken a single step in your shoes."

No one but Lara had aimed a look like that at him since his dad and grandpa died. Leo watched her climb out of the car when the valet opened her door.

Aubrey might not have dealt with a missing sibling, but she'd logged plenty of miles walking alongside those less fortunate in her neighborhood. She knew her beat and showed respect to all of the people in her pocket of the city, residents and tourists alike.

"You're good at your job," he said, joining her on the sidewalk. And he'd forcibly pushed her out of her comfort zone dragging her over to the Escape Club. "Please let me take you to dinner tonight. It's the least I can do after…" He wasn't quite sure how to put it.

"After making me do something completely against my principles?"

Right. He shoved his hands into his pockets. "When you put it like that, I feel even worse." There had to be some way he could make it up to her.

"Good." Her lips twitched and her teeth caught on her full lower lip. "It's not as fun as I thought it would be, making you feel bad about going to see Sullivan."

He laughed. Couldn't help himself, she was sincerely contrite. "You are a special brand of cop, Officer Rawlins."

"Thanks for noticing." She stepped back and adjusted her scarf against the wind. "Stay in and stay warm tonight. That's an order."

"Hang on. I still don't have a confirmation on dinner."

"No, thank you." The smile of a moment ago faded along with the humor in her eyes. "I really can't," she added. "You're part of an active case. It's frowned on."

"Somewhere across town, then," he suggested. "Away from your precinct. If you're worried about being seen with me." They'd been in the same bar last night and left together; someone might have drawn the wrong conclusions. "Did someone see us together last night and give you grief about it?"

"No," she replied quickly.

He wasn't sure whether or not to believe her. "Please, let me make up for being a problem child."

"Best way to do that is to not be a problem child."

"I may be too old to break the habit," he admitted. "Aubrey, come on. It's one meal."

She was about to crack; he could see it. He closed the distance so his voice wouldn't carry. "You choose the place and let me know where and when."

"I'll think about it." Her gaze coasted over his face as warm as a touch. "If we split the check."

"That's not how an apology dinner works." He followed as she started to walk away, pausing at the corner of the hotel. "I'll be waiting for your call, Officer Rawlins," he said, using her title since they weren't alone out here on the street. With her face tilted up to his, all he could think of was stealing a kiss. No, he wouldn't cross another line today. She was in uniform. He was part of an active case. He stepped back.

"Of course you will."

She left him standing there on the corner wondering if that was a "yes." He sure hoped so because case or not, he wanted to see Aubrey again. Soon.

Chapter 5

Aubrey stewed as she walked back to the precinct. She took a circuitous route, just keeping an eye out for Mary-Tea, Lara, or any trouble. Not even the idea of picking up a fruit smoothie calmed her racing thoughts. Leo had asked her out. Part of her danced around doing fist pumps, and another part of her bemoaned what could only end with more questions from IA.

Maybe he called it an apology dinner, but the vibe hadn't matched up with something that innocuous. His gaze had been loaded. Intense and hot in a way that burned right through the cold winter weather and made her think of warm beaches and sunshine.

The idea of Leo Butler lounging on a beach was an image she didn't need in her head. Was he as hard and muscled under those layers as she thought? Bad enough she couldn't stop thinking of kissing him here in Philly during the icy grip of winter. With sun-baked sand under her toes and the soft lap of the ocean against the shore, she'd be helpless against the lust pulsing through her.

She couldn't go on a date with the man who'd reported his sister missing. Well, she *shouldn't*. Even if they called it an apology, it would probably look like a date to any casual observer. Calvin's voice sounded in her head like a gong, warning her off such a dumb move. Being recognized at the Escape Club by Councilman Keller was enough potential trouble for one week. One month, really, based on her scorecard.

Then again, Leo was temporary. He wouldn't be in town long enough for anyone to get the wrong idea. Why was she so inclined to throw aside her principles to help him? She must be overthinking it. He hadn't asked her to do anything outright illegal. Meeting with Sullivan, chatting with Jason in the middle of a construction zone, didn't come close to the line of questionable behavior.

For most PPD officers.

For her, everything seemed questionable. IA had proven itself a serious thorn in her side, always eager to make her bleed a little more. Although none of her friends on the force held her ex's crimes against her, she knew they saw her as the token softie. She was the one the managers of soup kitchens called whether they were dealing with a grief-stricken brother or a fistfight.

Since catching Neil dealing drugs, she'd learned there was a cycle to her moods and thought processes about her life and career. But now she was revisiting the point where she didn't give a damn what IA or anyone else thought. She had a right to live her life—legally—on her own terms, pursuing her own interests, including one particularly interesting man.

Why shouldn't she enjoy dinner out with Leo? Doing everything by the book hadn't earned her any less scrutiny. It wasn't as if they were planning to rob a bank. She'd done the background work on Leo Butler. He had a stable job and no priors in Cincinnati or anywhere else. No one with any common sense or compassion could blame him for losing his cool while searching for his sister.

Tired of waffling and acting as if she wasn't in control of her life, she pulled out her phone and sent Leo a text message that she'd meet him for dinner. He replied immediately with the restaurant and time, making her wonder if he'd been staring at his phone waiting.

That was a delightfully flattering image. Smiling, she had a bounce in her step as she contemplated what she'd wear tonight. Half a block from a chair and a break from winter's bluster, her radio crackled with an emergency. The smoothie shop was being robbed.

She called in her response as she broke into a brisk jog, darting between people on the sidewalks and cutting through an alley to get there faster. It took a brave or foolhardy soul to rob any of the businesses that clustered around the police station, but to hit one frequented by so many cops? The perp would have had to work to find a time when the place wasn't serving one of Philly's finest.

A few people were gathered across the street, watching the scene play out through the big front window of the shop. She urged them to stay back as she approached the front door. A man wearing a faded navy blue down coat over a black hoodie and black sweatpants held a gun at arm's length, aimed at the woman behind the counter. His tennis shoes were worn and a clown mask hid his face, but not the lanky brown hair pulled into a ponytail.

Carefully, Aubrey eased closer. The robber held his weapon on Tina, who trembled like a leaf as she emptied the cash drawer into a canvas bank bag. Most days Tina left by two so she could be home to meet her kids after school. Her husband worked at the nearby college. This job was something fun and lively that got her out of the house regularly and padded the family vacation fund.

All of those details flitted through Aubrey's mind as she pulled her service weapon and reached for the door. "Lower the gun," she said calmly, as the bells tinkled merrily over her head. "And let's figure this out."

The man held the gun steady on Tina as he glanced at her over his shoulder. "A lady cop?" He snorted.

"A police officer asking you to stand down," she said. "No one needs to get hurt."

"You're gonna need backup, lady cop."

Not her first rodeo with a belligerent or sexist perp. Most of the time, the perps she dealt with were struggling, physically or mentally, due to drugs or illness or circumstance. This guy didn't fit into any one of those boxes. His clothes had seen better days but they were clean. His shoes, too. Even his voice was clean, no sign of impairment.

She pegged him as a bully looking for a soft target. Tina definitely matched the soft target description. The young wife and mother was friendly and sweet to a fault and working alone in a small storefront that did a brisk business.

Aubrey did her best to talk down the robber, who was now demanding the bank bag from lunch. How had he even known there would be one? Despite Tina's protests and Aubrey's insistence, the man wouldn't be swayed, wouldn't lower the gun. She could fire, should fire at this point, but there were customers behind him huddled between the tables. She couldn't risk hitting a bystander by accident. One by one, the frightened customers were inching toward the restrooms at the rear of the shop. She shifted, drawing the criminal's attention as she sought a better firing angle. She was losing faith that she could end this without bullets flying.

He wagged the gun at Tina. "Hurry it up! I want those tips, too."

Tears glistening on her cheeks, Tina upended the tip jar into the bag and shoved it across the counter.

"Go get the rest of it," he demanded.

"That's all, I swear," Tina cried.

"What's your exit plan?" Aubrey asked.

For the first time, he really looked at her. Maybe he was high if he hadn't noticed she blocked the door.

He turned back to Tina. "You." He waved the gun. "Come here or I'll shoot you."

She shook her head, pressing back against the prep counter. He repeated the order and she refused again. Points to Tina for courage, though she continued to quiver like a leaf in a hurricane. The robber took aim at her. "I gave you a chance."

Hearing the perp's voice crack, Aubrey knew he'd made his decision. "Get down!" she shouted at Tina.

Lunging at the gunman, she caught him hard in the hip as he pulled the trigger. The bullet meant for Tina tore through the ceiling tile. The man dropped his gun and wrestled Aubrey for control of hers.

She prevailed, getting a hard knee into his gut and flipping him to his stomach while he gasped for air. Holstering her weapon, she pulled out her handcuffs.

Once his hands were secured behind his back, she read him his rights.

There was movement all around her as Calvin and two more officers came into the store.

"You okay?" Calvin asked as the others checked on the customers.

"Fine." She patted down the would-be robber and shoved up his sleeves in a search for any gang tattoos. When she removed his mask, Tina sucked in a breath.

"Wes?" Tina swore and hurried around the counter, fury on her face.

"You know him?" Aubrey asked, holding her back.

"Have mercy. He's my cousin," she said. She looked up at the hole in the ceiling. "A cousin we will write off for good now." She crouched down and yanked his hair, forcing him to look her in the eye. "You lousy excuse for a human, coming in here and pointing a gun at me."

"Blanks," he said.

She swore at him and turned his head so sharply Aubrey feared for his safety. "That doesn't look like the work of a blank to me. You lying, cheating ass. You're pathetic." She dropped him hard, his forehead bouncing off the tile. Standing, she dusted off her hands. "I'm going home to my children."

"We'll need a statement," Aubrey said, stalling her. They would have to investigate to be sure the robbery wasn't some botched team effort, though Aubrey was already ninety-nine percent certain Tina had nothing to do with it.

Tina gave her statement as swiftly as possible to Calvin, practically gleeful as she shared Wes's history of minor offenses and troublemaking. While she called her husband to let him know she was all right, Aubrey asked one of the responding officers to drive Tina home.

Outside, there was a cheer as Wes was hauled out to a waiting police car. Aubrey didn't follow, turning instead to the seating area where customers had witnessed the ordeal.

No one was there. She supposed they must have filed out while she and Calvin were talking with Tina. She walked between the rows of tables, noticing the items that had been left behind as people sought cover.

"Aubrey?"

She turned toward Calvin, showing him what she'd found. "The shop will need a bigger lost and found box. Why did so much get left behind?"

"Escape was the priority," he replied. "There's a line of folks asking to come back in for their stuff."

"Good." She looked at the array of cell phones, a small purse, a tablet and a handheld game. "Do we need any of this for evidence?" Calvin shook his head. "All right, let them in. We can keep them away from the counter area."

"Sure thing."

"How did anyone get out?"

Calvin tipped his head to the door between the employees-only area and the public space. "A couple of witnesses say they went through that door and out into the alley."

The door was protected by a deadbolt with a ten-button panel. It was her understanding those locks were automatic and on at all times. She tested the handle. Secure, just as it should be. Someone in the dining area must have known the code. Maybe this had been a team effort after all.

Hearing footsteps, she turned and saw Leo striding

up behind Calvin. "What are you doing here? Who let you in?"

"I did," Calvin said. He carried several of the abandoned items to a table near the front door.

Leo stared at her long enough that her pulse throbbed in her ears. "Are you all right?"

She rolled her shoulders back. "Absolutely. Situation resolved safely, perp in custody. Only one shot fired and no perp or bystander injuries. It's a good day."

"You don't look happy."

"I'm confused." Her gaze drifted back to the locked door. "How did the customers get out?"

"Enter 2-5-8-0," Leo said.

She punched each button in turn and heard the click as the lock released. "How do you know the code for this shop?"

"It's often a standard code programmed on locks like this one. Employees don't have to remember anything but to go right down the line if they're under duress."

"That seems like something I should know," she said. If they'd covered it in training at the academy, she didn't recall it now.

"I'm worried about you, Aubrey."

That wasn't something she wanted to hear and she sure didn't want any of her colleagues overhearing his concern. "I'm good. Just processing." She gave the lock another long look. One of the customers must have known the trick Leo mentioned. "At least I didn't have to fire my weapon."

"That is good news," he agreed.

"Saves me hours of paperwork," she said. Leaving her free to ponder what to wear to dinner. Did she still want to go? Did he? The adrenaline rush was fading and she needed something to soothe the rough patches left behind. Being well trained and professional didn't mean being unaffected by events.

"How much of your shift is left?" he asked.

"I'm done as soon as the initial report is in," she replied as they walked out of the shop.

"How about I pick you up?"

"That's him!" A voice soared over the general chatter and city noise surrounding them. Aubrey followed the sound to see a man pointing at Leo from across the street. He bounced a little girl on his hip and she clutched a smoothie cup to her chest with one hand, waving wildly at Leo with the other.

A cheer went up as others spotted him and Tina's boss, Ray, rushed toward them. "What did you do?" she asked under her breath.

Ray nearly tackled Leo, bypassing a typical handshake in favor of a bear hug. "Thank you! Thank you!" He stepped back, shaking his head. "I can't believe it." He met Aubrey's gaze. "This man needs a medal." He smacked Leo on the chest. "Whatever you give to citizens who go above and beyond, he deserves it. This man led everyone out the back door. He saved every last one of my customers today."

"That's wonderful," she managed. Beside her, Leo tried to step away from the attention. "You were in the shop?"

He nodded. "I was restless and went for a walk. They serve a half hot cocoa, half coffee blend Lara likes." He finished with a shrug.

Too many options to fill in the blank left by his unfinished thought. Had he been too restless after meeting with Grant, after asking her out or after she'd agreed to go on what couldn't be labeled as a date? More than likely he'd just been seeking a connection to his sister.

People pressed close, the customers who'd been caught up in the robbery attempt showering Leo with gratitude and praise. Pushed to the fringes by Leo's admirers, Aubrey sought comfort in the routine of crime-scene protocol. She and her fellow officers finished up and informed Ray of his options. Aubrey then hopped into one of the cruisers rather than walk back.

Not five minutes later Leo walked in, looking for her. "Officer Rawlins." His gaze locked with hers. "You slipped away while I wasn't looking."

"I'm sure you don't mean for that to sound as stalkerish as it does." She couldn't stop the smile that tugged at her lips. "Thanks for being a hero today."

"Just doing the right thing." He rocked back on his heels. "About— Oh." He didn't finish the thought, apparently realizing where they were and how many eyes and ears were nearby.

If they'd been somewhere private, she would've been delighted to be the object of his attention. She would've been happy to return that attention, as well. The man made her long for the feel of his hands on her skin, the tangible expression of that heat in his eyes.

"Your sister's case is still front of mind," Aubrey said quickly. "I will be in touch as soon as there is something to share."

"Right." His demeanor shifted to something more professional, less personal, and she scolded herself for inwardly bemoaning the change. "Take care out there," he said.

Then he was gone and she was missing his face, the

warmth that had been in his eyes and the masculine scent that was all Leo with a crisp layer of winter.

Were they on or off for dinner? She cursed the ordeal with her ex on principle. Without that black smudge on her record, no one would pay any attention to her speaking with a civilian, case or no case. But Leo was the hero of the moment and she had a reputation for being too trusting. Didn't matter that the rep was based on more rumor than fact; it was what she was stuck with.

Dealing with reports and processing for the attempted robbery kept Aubrey longer than she'd intended and when she finally left, darkness had fallen and she only had an hour before Leo was expecting her at the restaurant across town.

She checked her phone and scolded herself for being disappointed at the lack of any voice or text messages from Leo. Probably best to forget dinner tonight. Hopefully, he'd be willing to try again another evening. Like maybe to celebrate finding Lara when Grant's infallible super-network found her.

Little flurries of snow spun up whenever the wind zipped along the street as she hurried home. Though this wasn't the coldest of nights, she was chilled through when she reached her apartment.

She stripped out of her uniform and stepped into the shower, eager to wash off the day and dress for a date. She'd go to the restaurant, just in case. Visiting Grant made her feel slimy, though he was more sincere in person than she'd expected. The tremors and sticky sensation on her skin now were a direct result of nearly shooting a man who thought his gun was loaded with blanks.

If a reporter picked up the story, it would be interesting which side they plopped her on. Would it be the side where a female cop hesitated to use her weapon or the side of the argument where she'd demonstrated expertise in a crisis?

She wasn't holding her breath for the latter choice when another option occurred to her. The press coverage might just focus on Leo and the heroics of one special tourist. That would give the department some welcome relief. Feeling fresher and more settled after the shower, she dried her hair and left it down while she debated what to wear.

Leo, with his dogged persistence and heroic tendencies, wouldn't renege on a dinner invite. Especially when he considered it some kind of atonement. She checked her phone, almost ready to call and beg for a rain check. That was only giving in to the post-adrenaline crash.

She expected Leo would handle the cancellation graciously, but she'd feel like a coward. Her stomach rumbled. A hungry coward. She picked up her phone and started a text message asking about the dress code when the device rang in her hands.

The caller ID showed his hotel and she scrambled to answer, worried something had happened. "Hello?"

"Aubrey Rawlins?"

"This is she."

"Wonderful. I'm the concierge. Leo Butler has asked us to send a car for you and I wanted to confirm your address." The one he read out was correct, though she wasn't sure who had provided the information. "The pickup time I have listed is in thirty minutes. Is that sufficient?"

She arched a brow at her reflection. "Sure. Do you know the dress code?"

"Upscale and elegant." Aubrey could almost hear the woman on the other end of the phone smiling. "Do you have a little black dress?"

Thanks to her mother's rule that every woman should, "Yes."

"That will be perfect. I'll have the driver send you a text message when he arrives."

Aubrey ended the call and pulled out the dress, sliding into the silky material that made her feel powerfully feminine. She chose black heels and onyx earrings framed by marcasite for a subtle sparkle that would contrast with her blond hair.

She was just sweeping on lip color when she saw the driver's text message. She smiled at her reflection and dashed down the stairs, eager to see what the evening would bring.

Leo knew how to behave in public, how to be still and calm. His mother often said he'd been born restless, though. As a kid he was always on the move, unless he was fishing with his dad or grandpa. He'd driven his mom to distraction; his teachers, too. School had been an exercise in all that was tedious, though he craved the thrill of learning new things. He couldn't recall a time when he didn't want to move or go or do *something*. His clearest memory of the car accident that had killed his father and grandfather was trying to scramble out of the wreckage, desperate to help. Though he'd been too small to make a difference at the time, that need to try went bone deep. Tonight he felt like that restless little kid again, fighting to remain poised and use his best manners as each minute ticked by without Aubrey.

Being here, being a tourist in the city, made things

worse. Philadelphia, with its wealth of history and warrens of neighborhoods, kindled that dreaded sense of smallness in his mind and heart. How would he ever find Lara? His body was convinced he could outrun the feelings of loss and helplessness and futility if he just got moving.

He took a sip of water, rested his fingertips on the cool handle of the fork near his plate. Aubrey would be here. They'd have a nice dinner. The flyers were out there, and Grant was mobilizing his people. Leo only had to wait and trust. His two biggest weaknesses.

Another sip of water. Life couldn't be so cruel as to take Lara from him, too. Logic said this situation with Lara wasn't his fault, though he wondered time and again what she'd missed by growing up without their dad. Leo had enjoyed the benefits of all that paternal pride and protective instinct during his early childhood. Their mom had done her best by Lara, but knowing their father would surely have changed Lara's outlook as well as her view of herself and her talents.

"Am I interrupting?"

Leo looked up to see Aubrey standing by the table. "No. No." He shoved to his feet. How had he missed her walking in? "You look…" She wore a black dress that might have looked simple on the rack. The fabric skimmed her body, highlighting every curve to stunning effect. Would it be rude to ask her to go back and start over so he could enjoy her approach?

There was a sparkle at her ears, glittering in the soft waves of her hair. "Your hair is down." He pulled back her chair, breathing in the sunny fragrance of her shampoo as she took her seat.

"Did you expect me to show up in my uniform?"

"No." He wasn't sure he expected her to show up at all. "Of course not." He laughed, resuming his seat across from her. "I'm an idiot."

"Why?"

The amusement on her glossy lips sent a sizzle straight through his bloodstream. "Did you want that chronologically and how many years back should I go?"

She cocked an eyebrow. "You're not the first guy who's into the uniform. If that's what the shock and awe routine is."

Not the first? Well, he'd be the last. *Wait.* What was he thinking? "You're teasing me."

"A little bit, yes." She reached for her water glass, but only traced the stem with her fingertip.

Her hands, unadorned, suddenly seemed small and almost fragile. Mere hours ago, those hands had stopped a robbery. "I never gave much thought to uniforms," he said.

"What do you mean?"

"At the risk of sounding completely sexist, it's hard to imagine you taking down that criminal right now."

She laughed. "I should hope so." Her gaze cruised around the restaurant. "The concierge told me 'elegant and upscale,'" she said. "This is far more than I expected for an apology dinner."

"We both know I owe you far more than a cheese-steak or burger."

Her lips twitched at the corner. "You clean up nicely. I should have said that right off."

He smoothed a hand down the length of his tie, willing himself to stay calm when he wanted to taste the pale column of her throat. "Suits are a hazard in my line of work. I can't seem to travel without one."

The waiter arrived with a wine selection and they chose half a carafe of Merlot to share. Hearing the appetizers and specials, Leo's stomach rumbled at the mouthwatering suggestions. Once the decisions were made and they were alone, Leo realized he wasn't restless anymore and he'd gone nearly fifteen minutes without obsessing over Lara.

He chose to take it as a good sign. Stressing about her, worrying and willing her to call, hadn't worked. Doing something nice for Aubrey steadied him.

"I know you're employed by an airport in Cincinnati, but what is it you do that requires a suit?"

"I'm an operations manager. There's a uniform of sorts for the day-to-day, but meetings can crop up at the strangest times. It's best to be prepared."

She sat back as the waiter placed a small platter of stuffed mushrooms between them. "You brought a suit in case you needed to attend a meeting while searching for your sister?"

"I packed a suit because it's habit." The worry that had grown out of control didn't help. "And because I was afraid I'd have to deal with police, medical professionals, or even a morgue. A suit gets a smidge more respect in those situations. Assuming the man in said suit isn't a jerk."

"Leo." She murmured his name with such compassion, he thought he'd dissolve. Compassion and zero pity. He'd seen enough pity to know the difference.

He tried and failed to shrug it off. Aubrey made him want to lean in, to take a chance on being accepted. "Do you get this, *ah*, invested in all your cases?"

Her jaw firmed and her shoulders straightened as she pressed back in the chair. "We're trained that some cases or incidents will hit us harder than others." She reached for her wine, held the glass in both hands. "You know, I still haven't heard that apology."

He wished she'd left a hand within his reach so she might feel his sincerity. "I apologize for insisting on going to see Grant. It was rude, not even trying to comprehend your resistance to the idea."

"Thank you," she said, relaxing a fraction.

"I do find it commendable how involved you are with your neighborhood. I meant no offense about the way you invest your time."

Her chin dipped in a silent acknowledgment. "Thanks for that, too. I've taken some heat at the precinct for wearing rose-colored glasses when I look at the city."

"Why shouldn't you? I'd think it would be beneficial to see the best in your community and work toward that outcome."

"Is that what you do?" she asked.

"You could sum it up that way." He noticed the way she kept nudging the conversation away from herself. The last thing he wanted was for her to feel uncomfortable or on the spot. He'd pulled out all the stops tonight with the sole purpose of spoiling her to make up for his gaffes and the trouble he'd brought into her city. "Anything can throw off a normal day at an airport. Local weather trouble, weather in connecting towns, equipment, the list goes on. Although each airline has a policy and system for crises, the airport itself has policies and systems to maintain safety for all."

"It sounds like a normal day for you is hard to define."

"Not unlike police work," he replied. "For your sake, I hope strangers raising hell in soup kitchens isn't a daily occurrence."

"No. Not the way you did it." A lovely blush colored her cheeks. What was she thinking?

"Did you want to talk about Lara at all tonight?" she asked.

He appreciated her thoughtfulness. "Only if you have news you'd like to share."

Her blue eyes widened in earnest. "If I did, I'd have told you already."

"I know." Having this kind of confidence in another person was rare for him, thanks to the tragic loss that had changed his relationship with everyone but Lara. "I'm not implying otherwise. Although I haven't truly put her out of my mind, I've accepted there's little I can do tonight, and I'd like us both to enjoy a nice dinner."

"You believe Grant's people are out there searching?"

"That helps," he confessed. "I know the flyers are getting views, too. I do have faith in you and the PPD."

She watched him over the rim of her wineglass, her expression inscrutable. "If you say so."

He'd been such an ass about this mess from day one, he couldn't fault her for doubting. Leo glanced up when a well-dressed couple stopped beside their table.

"Pardon the interruption," the man began. "Aren't you the man who saved all those people during a robbery today?"

"I escorted a few people to safety," he replied. "Officer Rawlins here did the hard part."

The man turned to the woman at his side. "I knew it was him."

She smiled back at him. "And we're interrupting their meal, honey. Forgive us, please."

"I needed to say thanks." He stuck out his hand to Leo, then to Aubrey, as well. "To both of you. Tina, the cashier at that shop, is our daughter-in-law. Without you two I shudder at what might have happened."

"We weren't exactly thrilled with her decision to work in that area," the wife added quietly. "But she's determined to do something on her own. She swears it's safe over there."

"Tina is great," Aubrey said. "We've made it a priority to improve communication with businesses in the area and dial down the crime rate," she assured them.

"I'm sure it's working," the older woman replied. "Tina's mentioned you often. Officer Aubrey this and that. All good."

"Yes, all good," her husband agreed. "Thank you for your service. We'll leave you to enjoy your dinner."

The gracious couple stepped out of the way as the waiter delivered their meals. For a few minutes Leo and Aubrey ate in appreciative silence. He hadn't realized he was famished until that moment.

"Good?" he queried as Aubrey twirled a length of pasta around her fork.

"Incredible." She angled her chin toward his plate. "Yours?"

"Delicious." In truth, the food was phenomenal, but his attention was all for Aubrey.

Hero-worship or fixation, distraction or outright desire, he couldn't separate one emotion from the other. Wasn't sure he cared. All he could think about was how those lips might feel under his and how on earth he could get her to agree to another date.

"How often do you deal with incidents like the one at the smoothie shop?" he asked when it seemed they'd both had their fill.

"Crime happens." She didn't meet his gaze. "You'd have to access public records for the actual number."

"Is it the restaurant or me in particular?"

She glanced up. "What do you mean?"

"You keep dodging questions about your work. Why?"

Her blue eyes blazed. "Why are you pushing?" she countered.

He was wrecking a pleasant evening by pushing, but he wanted to know, to get to know *her.* "I'm interested. In the job, but mostly in you." Might as well lay his cards on the table. He wasn't good at games and she'd seen too much of his desperation to pretend he had life lined up perfectly. "I admit this dinner wasn't just about an apology or to keep tabs on your search for Lara."

"What if I only agreed to join you to keep tabs on *you*?" she said.

"I deserved that." He grinned. "Care to give me the odds on getting you to agree to another date?"

"You'll just have to take your chances." She propped her folded arms on the edge of the table. "The food is excellent, the company pleasant. To follow your candid example, I enjoy you, too, Leo, when you're not causing trouble in my town."

He pointed at himself. "I'm a hero, didn't you hear?"

"You're a meddling menace." Her lips curled into an indulgent smile.

"Thank you."

"That wasn't a compliment." She shook her head. "Going out again isn't wise. At least not until we find your sister."

Was it really the active case that bothered her? He moved as if he would bolt from the restaurant. "Then I'd better get back out there."

"Stop it. Tonight has been wonderful. Don't wreck it by making a scene and forcing me to take you down."

He cocked his head. "You have your cuffs with you?"

Her golden eyebrows arched. "I'm a PPD officer and I am *always* prepared."

The I-dare-you spark in her eyes set off a firestorm in his blood. He cleared his throat. "Are you interested in dessert?" he managed to ask.

"No, thank you. The sugar rush might dull my reflexes. With you I need to be at the top of my game."

He laughed, hoping it sounded more natural than strained. "Then I guess we're done for tonight."

He asked for the check, only to be told their dinner had been covered by another patron.

"Tina's in-laws," Aubrey said. "That was sweet of them."

And generous, considering the average dinner tab here. "Change your mind about dessert or a coffee?" He wasn't ready for the evening to end.

She waved him off. "No, thank you," she repeated. "I should get home. I'm back on shift first thing in the morning."

He called for the car he'd arranged with the hotel, pleased when she didn't balk at his suggestion that he ride along with her back to her place. He didn't expect an invitation to come inside; he just wanted to see where she lived. It would give him something else to think about, something new to keep his mind off his sister's plight.

He held the door for her when the car arrived and then slid in next to her. The hem of her dress crept above her knees, giving him a tantalizing glimpse of her toned legs.

She'd pressed her hands together between her knees.

"Cold?" He was already shrugging off his suit coat,

draping it over her lap. He hadn't thought to pack his wool overcoat. He'd been too focused on just getting here.

Thanks." Her lips tilted up in a shy smile. "That wind has a bite."

He asked the driver to turn up the heat. A smarter move than drawing Aubrey's body up against his. Wanting the woman and making a move on her were two different things.

The driver had the radio volume on low, but the station played an introduction that had Aubrey sitting forward.

"What—"

She held up a finger to shush him.

He listened as intently as she did to the weather warning about a cold front moving in that would dump heavy snow and ice on the city. People were being asked to prepare for power outages and record low temperatures.

When the report finished, she sat back and tucked his coat tightly around her legs. "We'll be busy tomorrow," she said as they passed the famous Boathouse Row on their way back to her neighborhood.

The lights outlined the rooftop of each building, and the reflections on the river sparkled in the night. The beauty of the scene couldn't compare to the woman beside him. "Meaning?"

"To most people storm prep is stocking up on candles, bread and whatever gets them through an emergency. For the urban precincts we roll out in force and nudge people toward the shelters."

That gave him a better chance of finding Lara. Between the note and her bringing Grant a couple of workers, it seemed like a safe bet that his sister was out here somewhere, helping the homeless community. "Nudge?"

"Well, unless a curfew is issued, we can't arrest anyone who refuses, so we strongly encourage."

It continued to surprise him how committed she was to her city. Sure, it was in the job description, but he'd always thought police departments were so overwhelmed by crime and bad news that they didn't have enough time or manpower for purely humanitarian efforts. Officer Aubrey made him reevaluate at every turn.

"If you nudge the homeless toward open shelters, I should be able to find Lara, right?"

"Only if she *is* on the streets and she chooses to come in."

"She wouldn't risk freezing to death," he said. "Not for any cause." He had to believe that much. The other options were unbearable.

Aubrey opened her mouth, closed it again, as the car pulled to a stop. "Just say it." He braced himself for another brutal truth he wasn't ready to hear.

"We don't know if or why she's out there," Aubrey began, "or where she's staying if she is out there. You have my word that everyone in my precinct will be looking for her as we bring people in."

"Thank you." The warm air in the car suddenly felt stifling with its absolute security and safety. He'd taken so many things for granted. Not Lara, not really, though her inexplicable disconnect made him second-guess that, too.

Maybe she had grown tired of him. Maybe his attempts to stay involved and connected had smothered her, pushed her to a drastic act of independence. As everyone kept pointing out, she was a grown, mentally sound adult, capable of making life-altering decisions on her own.

If he trusted her judgment as much as he claimed, would he be turning over every rock to find her?

Yes.

Because he couldn't accept a world without the unconditional love of his sister. And he couldn't accept that she would willingly put him through this particular brand of hell. She alone knew his darkest secrets and his raw weaknesses. He couldn't believe that she'd deliberately chosen to pour salt into those wounds.

Aubrey touched his arm as she returned his coat. "Leo? Are you all right?"

"Yes." If not right this second, he would be soon. He looked past her to the building. Which window was hers? Who took care of Officer Aubrey's storm prep?

"I assume the hotel knows how to prep for a winter storm," he mused.

"Of course," she replied. "They have generators and—"

"You're probably all stocked up, too?"

Her head tipped to the side as she studied him. "I'll pick up whatever I need after shift tomorrow." She reached for the door handle. "Thanks for—"

He cut her off. "Change of plans," he said to the driver. He draped the coat over her legs again. "Would you please take us to the nearest convenience store?"

"Yes, sir."

Aubrey gawked at him as the door locks clicked automatically when the driver put the car into gear. "I don't understand. What are you doing?"

"If public reactions to storm warnings here go anything like they do in Cincinnati, store shelves will be picked bare by noon. You can stock up tonight and then I don't have to worry about you being hungry or cold after your shift."

She sputtered a protest.

"Please, Aubrey. Let someone do something nice for you. Something helpful."

Aubrey stared at the bags on her kitchen counter. Slowly, she shifted her gaze to the man sucking all the air out of her kitchen. Some trick of Leo's nature that left her breathless. It was the only explanation for why she couldn't utter a simple and polite *thank you.*

He'd not only insisted she stock up on storm supplies; he'd also paid the tab. That annoyed her, she remembered. Opening the app on her phone, she offered to pay him back.

He shook his head. "We can settle up after the storm. You need to get to bed before your shift."

Leo mentioning bed set her nerves humming. Her bed was a short walk away and she had visions of him and her forgetting all about the winter storm rolling in. She'd be in bed right now—alone—if he hadn't dragged her to the grocery store for nonperishable foods and fresh flashlight batteries.

"What is this, Leo? I don't need your charity and really I shouldn't accept it." If anyone found out, she'd likely get another reprimand or, at the very least, another note in her file about inappropriate fraternization. "Just tell me what I owe you."

"Why can't you accept a nice gesture?" He folded his coat over his arms. The coat she'd wrapped around her knees like a blanket during the car ride.

"It just isn't right. You're a civilian and I'm…I'm not."

"You can only accept a nice gesture from a fellow PPD officer?"

"No." Why was he making this such a challenge? "It's just crossing lines." Oh, she didn't want to air all her dirty laundry. Not after a lovely evening. "I appreciate the concern, and this is a thoughtful gesture," she said, trying again. Who would find out, or care, that he'd picked up the tab on a couple bags of groceries?

If she expected IA to move past her mistakes, she should blaze that trail with confidence. "The chauffeur is probably wanting to get home."

Leo had insisted the driver come in with them and stock up for the storm, as well, though he hadn't picked up the man's bill. Leo Butler was a considerate, generous man. A man she wanted to spend more time with, regardless of the status of his missing sister. She wanted to know him. *Intimately.*

"True." He smiled and warmth flowed through her body, pooling in places best forgotten for tonight. "I'll get going. Maybe I'll see you tomorrow while you're out there, nudging people along."

Of course he'd go out and search shelters for Lara. She couldn't fault his devotion. "No chance I can convince you to leave it to the PPD?"

"Afraid not." He pulled on his coat, but he didn't move toward the door. "I promise I won't harass anyone and I won't get in the way."

She almost snorted. Who wouldn't be distracted by his handsome face and compelling reasons for checking around? She moved toward the door, since he didn't seem inclined to make an exit. If he stayed here much longer, she'd be suggesting he send the driver home and call a cab later. As in, *morning-after* later.

Timing was important, she reminded herself, and this wasn't the time to jump Leo and drag him to bed. "Thanks again for a great apology dinner."

"Did it work? You accept my apology?" he asked, his hand covering hers on the doorknob.

Heat sizzled along her skin. "Yes. It was a very effective strategy."

His lips curled upward and she was pretty sure she'd never be cold again. "Good night, Leo."

"Good night." He brushed a kiss to her cheek. The lightest touch, airy. She told herself she was imagining the sparks. So why were her hands suddenly gripping the open panels of his coat? Why was she pulling herself into the heat of his body, closer to the intriguing scent that made her crave more of him?

She didn't want another near-miss. She was past ready for the real thing. "Can I kiss you?" Her lips were a whisper from his. *Please say yes.* The thought pounded through her head loudly enough she was sure he could hear it, too.

He pulled her in tight, up on her toes. Without her grip on his coat, without his hand at her back, she'd fall. Then at last her lips met his and she might as well have been floating. Everything she knew fell away, fell right out of her head and her world, all her focus on that sweet, supple contact.

At last.

Her body melted with a new ease, a new awareness, she couldn't have put into words. Thank goodness he wasn't asking. He explored, the shape of her mouth, teasing and tugging on her lower lip. His arms wrapped her up, firm and secure as she opened to the touch of his tongue. The burst of heat and the velvet slide stole her breath. She didn't care, simply held on, each new wave of sensation dwarfing the last.

He eased back and she discovered she could feel grounded and floaty at the same time. Her feet were rooted to the floor, and she leaned into him, making every breath a sensual adventure. His thumb glided along her jaw, up over the curve of her ear and she nuzzled her cheek into his hand. Dragging her gaze up from his mouth to his eyes, the raw desire in his gaze startled her. Rocked her. Matched the need burning inside her.

"Leo." Her voice cracked.

He kissed her, swallowing whatever else she'd meant to say. He turned her, pressing her back against the door. She appreciated the additional support, used it to let her hands roam over his shoulders, up into his hair.

She caught herself as she started to push away his coat. He couldn't stay. Shouldn't. There were logical, valid reasons he should go. The only one she could recall was the driver waiting downstairs.

His lips feathered down her throat, better than anything she'd imagined. "Leo," she said, trembling.

"Mmm?" His teeth grazed her earlobe.

She let the shiver come and go. "You should go. The driver…"

The tantalizing exploration stopped and he lifted his head just far enough to let her know he'd heard her. "You're right." His gaze roamed her face and his lips found hers for one final, brief kiss. "Can I be honest?" he asked.

"Please."

"I hope we're not done."

She closed her eyes, knowing it wasn't nearly enough to hide her desire for him. Every cell in her body was stating a case for throwing caution, rules and every-thing else out the window. "That makes two of us," she confessed.

He grinned as if she'd handed him a winning lot-tery ticket.

"Good night." He touched his lips to hers one last time and then he was gone.

She lingered in the open doorway like a lovestruck teenager until he reached the first landing. The chilly hallway and the weight of the moment finally doused her glow-y moment with too much reality.

Retreating, she locked the door and dropped her fore-head against the hard surface. What was she doing? All of the reasons *not* to kiss Leo reared up now while she wanted to bask in the aftermath of the hottest make-out session of her life.

He was connected to an active case. She had a soft-hearted reputation to change and a neighborhood to watch over. All of that should matter. Those factors should outweigh the fiery attraction, the desire for more of his kisses, more of *him*.

Turning around she stared at the bags on her kitchen counter. Being on the receiving end of his generous and thoughtful gesture left her gooey inside, like melted car-amel. She took a moment to put away the storm supplies and then went to the bedroom.

Her skin was still sensitive as she got ready for bed. The flannel sheets were a stark disappointment after being in Leo's arms. When she finally gave in to sleep, her dreams were happier, sexy and not at all restful.

Chapter 6

Leo woke refreshed, having slept soundly for the first time in days. His dreams of Aubrey's tantalizing body were a restorative break from nightmares about his sister. He waited for the guilt over that to kick in as he hurried through a cold shower.

He was still waiting for his conscience to scold him while he opened the radio app on his phone, listening to a morning show while he shaved. At the break for local news, a weatherman urged people in the area to take the threat seriously and prepare appropriately.

Done shaving, Leo switched the radio for the television while he dressed in the warmest clothing he had for his search. Just as Aubrey predicted, the storm was the dominant story on every channel. A graphic flashed on the screen with a list of supplies for a storm emergency kit.

The screen split, showing the list on one side and the studio on the other. Seated in front of a fire hearth set, Councilman Keller gave information about where people could pick up ready-made kits if they couldn't afford them.

"Don't be shy," Keller said. "It's times like this when our community shines brightest. There's no reason anyone should go cold or hungry. We're pulling out all the stops to make this a zero-loss storm."

Leo grabbed his phone, taking a picture as a list of emergency shelters was announced. The picture was grainy but readable. He followed the link posted at the bottom of the screen and bookmarked the channel's website in case more shelters were opened.

Lara wouldn't stay out in this nasty weather and she wouldn't let others do so, either. Unless she turned to a friend in town, she would have to be at one of these shelters. He wouldn't hold his breath that a friend would contact him, but he had to keep believing that when his sister had a chance, she'd let him know she was safe.

He would be diligent in his search today. It helped knowing Aubrey would be looking. And Grant. Combining all of their resources, Leo believed they would find her. Find her safe and healthy. And then she could explain what she was trying to prove or accomplish.

While the in-room coffeemaker sputtered through the first cup of the day, Leo tried the visualization technique the family counselor had taught him shortly after his dad died. In that situation, he was to tap into a happy memory and reconstruct it to keep those good feelings top of mind. To maintain the connection to his father and grandfather and reframe the present, knowing he'd been well loved.

The exercise provided an essential reminder when his mother could barely stand the sight of him. Those visualizations helped him feel safe and a bit less battered by the constant sorrow and guilt his mother heaped on his head.

Today Leo brought to mind one of the happy, casual mornings he'd enjoyed with his sister during the recent winter break. They'd shared coffee, jokes and relatively aimless chatter over his kitchen table. The air carried the sweet aroma of cinnamon rolls fresh from the oven. Lara, her hair a mess from sleep, had worn her favorite college hoodie and flannel pants printed with sleepy cats, her feet covered in ridiculous, fluffy purple socks.

When he had that memory fixed in his mind, he simply altered the conversation, imagining what she'd tell him today. About her choices, her safety net and what she hoped to get out of whatever she was doing. It wasn't a perfect exercise and being frustrated with her didn't help, but when he opened his eyes, he felt calmer.

Dressed for the day, confident he and his sister would see each other and talk by nightfall, Leo sipped his coffee while people hustled by on the sidewalk below.

After fueling up at the breakfast buffet, Leo's first stop was the Good Samaritan soup kitchen. The manager, Rosie, wasn't pleased to see him, until he made it clear he was serious about helping. "I can go buy more supplies or stay here and set up cots. Whatever you need, just tell me how to help."

Rosie had the softened look and graying hair of a grandmother, but she could organize people and issue orders with the efficiency and manner of a drill sergeant. She sized him up and put him to work unloading supplies from the delivery truck idling in the alley. Over the next two hours, Leo worked up a good sweat and was starting to understand why Lara had volunteered here. Already he had a fresh appreciation for all the things that had gone right in his life.

Leo enlisted the help of a skinny boy who might be eighteen and learned he had been on the streets since his freshman year of high school. The kid claimed his dad drank too much and no one in the building where he'd lived could remember his mother's name. Shelters and odd jobs had kept him going after they'd been evicted.

Without Lara, it was entirely possible Leo might have run away from a mother who couldn't bear to look at him. The sobering thought made his stomach cramp. He'd been her first charity win; they just didn't know it until now.

When he'd worked through Rosie's task list, he made it clear he was going to search for Lara in other emergency shelters.

"We'll call if she comes in here," Rosie promised. Her gaze dropped to his gloves. "You should raid our stash for something warmer for your hands. The temperature is only going to drop as the storm comes in."

"I'll be fine," he said, touched by her concern. "Keep the good stuff for the people who really need it. If I run across anyone out there, I'll give them a nudge this way," he added, borrowing Aubrey's phrase.

Rosie squinted at him. "You're a good boy," she stated. "A heart as big as your sister's."

He resisted the compliment. "No, but it's something to aspire to."

Leo walked down the street under a bank of clouds already dropping a mix of icy rain and light snow. He saw a patrol car roll by and thought of Aubrey, walking her beat with Calvin, making sure everyone was safe.

He marveled at how well people were heeding the warnings. Fewer cars were on the streets and businesses were already putting up closure signs.

The next nearest emergency shelter was being set up in a school gymnasium. Leo walked in and helped set up cots and a hot beverage station while keeping an eye out for Lara. Other than the volunteers, no one had come in yet. He showed Lara's picture around, but no one recognized her. When he heard a team of volunteers was headed to a known homeless encampment to give folks a ride in, he tagged along with them. It wasn't yet noon and he had plenty of time to visit other shelters in the vicinity before the weather drove him into his hotel room for the night.

When they reached their destination, he didn't bother showing Lara's picture. Instead, he focused on serving coffee from the thermoses the team had brought along, encouraging people to come in from the cold. He hadn't anticipated it would be such a hard sell. Several people didn't believe the weather reports and others feared they'd be trapped or lose a coveted spot.

The van was at capacity and Leo decided he'd walk back if it made room for one more person to have a safe place to ride out the storm. "It's too cold to stay out here," he told an older woman who waved off the coffee, claiming the brew was a curse. "They'll have hot tea," he added. "I set up that station myself." That was apparently all she needed to hear and to his relief, she let him help her into the van.

Leo walked around the camp, giving a wide berth to the people who had refused any assistance. He did a quick head count and sent Aubrey a text message letting her know how many people had gone to the school shelter and how many remained in this particular area. She replied almost immediately, assuring him that officers and more volunteers would come through before the storm hit in full force.

Back in the soup kitchen Leo had felt an affinity with Lara's mile-wide compassionate streak. Out here with the weather worsening, the connection was deeper still. These people had it rough, enduring circumstances that stemmed from bad choices or bad luck. There was no one-size-fits-all solution.

He walked out of the camp, grateful that he had options and means. Of course he hadn't previously given much thought to homelessness or any other societal issues unless it intersected with his work or neighborhood. Typically, he left the relief efforts to those organizations with experience and resources and manpower. Lara was the bighearted person in the family, the one who saw a need and set about meeting it. He'd always found her charitable nature admirable and beautiful. Inspiring, too. But he didn't want her in over her head; couldn't bear the idea that she'd be hurt while trying to help others.

His sister wasn't dumb. Although it hurt him deeply that she'd left him out of the loop about her plans to withdraw for the semester, he had to entertain the idea that she knew what she was doing.

Leo's hands and feet were screaming for better gear by the time he reached the college campus. He trudged along, tucking his chin into the upturned collar of his coat and wishing for a scarf. He noticed news vans parked along the street, framing the corner of the park across from the stately administration building. Cameramen and their reporters were jammed up close to the speaker. Probably for shared warmth as much as to catch a quote.

Walking closer, he saw Councilman Keller was addressing the group. He wore jeans and heavy boots under a down coat. His thick gloves drew the eye when he gestured to the building behind him.

Leo pressed in, listening along with everyone else.

"If you know of anyone in the area in need, send them here. Thanks to Professor Whitten, the school has graciously opened this building to the community and donors have pitched in, so the facility is equipped with plenty of supplies."

Leo's gaze snapped to the professor standing just behind the councilman. Whitten looked cold and uncomfortable and not at all delighted by the praise.

"My aides continue to work with the power companies in an effort to keep the heat on, regardless of account status," Keller continued. "If you have a problem, give us a call or come on down and my team will do whatever we can to help."

Leo studied the closest buildings. Philly architecture had fascinated him from his first visit with Lara. This area boasted an eclectic mix of buildings old and new, restored or razed, with pockets of wealth amid areas where people were clearly struggling to get by. In other parts of the city, neighborhoods might be more uniform, but that wasn't the case here where Lara had spent the better part of the past three years.

Her time at this particular college and neighborhood had changed her in ways no one could've anticipated. If he was going to find her before the storm rolled in, he had to get a handle on why she'd left school to live on the street. Uncomfortable as it was to admit, the professor understood this new side of his sister better than he did.

The clouds overhead opened up and snow fell faster, in wet, heavy flakes, and to everyone's relief, the councilman wrapped things up quickly. In the midst of people rushing out of the weather he lost Whitten, but he overheard a few people who seemed to be part of the councilman's staff discussing a recent foray into another homeless camp.

"Excuse me," Leo said, butting in to their conversation. "A friend of mine is out in this weather. Homeless." He stamped his feet and blew into his gloved hands and then listed the places he'd been so far. "Do you have any other suggestions about where I should look for him?"

"Stick with the shelters," one young man replied, raking Leo with a glance. "You'll be in trouble if you spend much more time out in this weather."

"But—"

"No sense creating drama. We're rounding up everyone who will come with us. If your friend's smart, he'll be at a shelter." He clapped Leo on the shoulder. "Go on in and check around."

Leo didn't need to be asked twice. Inside he found more people than he'd expected to see at a shelter that had just opened. Several people had clearly come in from the street and others seemed to be heeding the councilman's advice to ride out the storm in a place where the power wouldn't go out. There was no sign of Lara. He sent text message updates to Aubrey and Grant, hopeful someone would find her soon.

Needing to thaw out, he joined the volunteers stocking stations with snacks and water while he kept an eye out for Lara. He'd just picked up another case of water when he caught the flash of a familiar bright pattern out of the corner of his eye.

Looking up, he recognized the scarf he'd given Lara for Christmas. He took a deep breath before jumping to conclusions and making another blunder. This could be a coincidence. The cashmere scarf, with a stylized pattern for the Cincinnati Reds baseball team, hadn't been one of a kind. "Great scarf," Leo said.

The man wearing the scarf clutched it to his throat and stepped back from the table.

Leo noted that the accessory lacked the dinge of most items he'd seen in the homeless camp. He reached for the next case of water and tried again. "Cincinnati's my team. Yours, too?" He offered a bottle of water.

"No." The man's weather-beaten hand curled around the bottle and pulled it close, holding both it and the scarf tightly against his chest. "Some girl shared it with me. Said I could keep it. I was coughing."

Some girl. Leo's head reeled. Had to be Lara. Here was the proof his sister was working within the homeless community of Philly. His first instinct was to show the man a picture, but he didn't want to repeat his previous mistakes. "That was really nice of her."

"I know. I said thank you," the man muttered defensively.

"That was really nice of you," Leo said.

The man's chin bobbed up and down once and then he wandered toward a row of long tables. Leo watched him go, hoping his conversation partner would join someone who might be more talkative. No such luck. The man wearing Lara's scarf seemed to be a solo act.

When the cases of water were stacked, Leo retreated to the kitchen where volunteers were warming up after scouring the city for people in jeopardy. "Is anyone heading back out?"

"It's coming down too hard," a young man answered. A concurring murmur rippled through the kitchen. "I think we have everyone willing to come in. Some folks just don't trust anyone no matter what we tell them."

Leo's stomach sank. If Lara had earned the trust of those who refused to come in, she wouldn't abandon them. "This group you just brought in—where did you find them?"

The young driver explained they'd picked up a few people, including the man with the scarf, near a condemned building a few blocks away. Leo shoved his hands into his gloves, grabbed his coat and headed out to find his sister.

Aubrey was cold, despite the foul-weather gear covering her from head to toe. The storm was getting worse by the minute, but there were still some stubborn people out here, refusing to come in.

Councilman Keller's determination to make this a zero-loss event was admirable and the PPD would keep making rounds, urging at-risk people into shelters until the visibility was too low for safety. The police commissioner had quietly pointed out that he didn't want to lose any officers, either.

Although the councilman had excellent intentions, zero-loss was an impossible goal. Aubrey respected his commitment, agreed with it, and she and Calvin continued trudging on, hour after hour, checking alleys and buildings and cars for signs of people trying to survive without assistance. With each round they made, there were fewer people out and about. It was a good sign and normally she would have been delighted that people were taking the bad weather seriously.

But as much as she looked forward to going home to her toasty apartment after shift, she dreaded the call to update Leo if no one spotted Lara at any of the shelters. None of her fellow officers had seen anyone matching Lara's description. Aubrey had even gone against her intuition and pressed Mary-Tea for information, but the older woman hadn't seen Lara since yesterday.

Hearing a call over the radio about activity on the other side of the college campus on their route, Aubrey and Calvin agreed to check on it. They'd been over these blocks time and again. Aubrey had to move quickly to keep up with Calvin's longer stride. She didn't mind since the effort kept her a bit warmer. They reached the address and looked around, circling back to the alley behind the building.

It was marginally warmer, with the structure blocking the worst of the wind. The snow that had blown in around the narrow passage was tamped down from several pairs of feet coming and going.

"See anything?" Calvin asked.

"No." She shook her head.

"Whoever was here must have gotten smart." Calvin turned a slow circle. "Or frozen."

She could all too easily hear the reprimand if they were too late to help or overlooked someone in Keller's district. As she followed Calvin out of the alley, movement caught her eye. A man huddling from the cold was poking at the flimsy cardboard and shelters. The distressed leather jacket was familiar, despite being soaked from the wet weather.

"Leo?" He looked up and the raw grief etched on his

face nearly knocked her back a step. She immediately snapped out orders for Calvin to call for a patrol car as she rushed to his side. "What are you doing back here?"

"Aubrey?" A vapor cloud billowed between them and he squinted at her.

"That's right." His cheeks and nose were red, his lips tinged with blue. She chafed his gloved hands. "Did you walk over here?"

He nodded, his feet shuffling. "She isn't here."

"That's a good thing. No one should be."

"She *was* here, but she's gone."

Aubrey wondered what made him so sure, but that question could wait until he was thawed out. "You are determined to be a problem in my precinct. Come on, let's get you warmed up."

He walked slowly, the cold making him stiff. His shoes were soaked through and his jeans were wet to the knees. It was a wonder he was still standing. "Leo, you're not dressed to be out in this weather."

"She isn't here," he repeated.

The defeat in his voice broke her heart. Her big, mushy, too-soft-for-police-work heart.

"I know," she crooned. Why was the man out here? He wasn't even wearing boots. "We'll find her," she said, adding more nonsense as she chafed his back and arms, trying to get some heat into him. "How long until the car arrives?" she asked Calvin.

"They're on the way."

"Have you seen her?" Leo tripped and Calvin helped her hold him upright.

"Not yet," Calvin replied. "Right now you're my main concern."

Together they shuffled Leo toward the main street,

hoping to intercept the patrol car as soon as possible. Keeping him moving was paramount to prevent any further injury from the cold.

The vehicle met them before they'd walked a full block, and she and Calvin got him into the backseat and cranked up the heat. After a brief discussion, they decided to take him back to his hotel. His teeth chattered through the entire trip and when they pulled up to the front entrance, she looked at Calvin.

Without saying a word, he understood she didn't want to leave Leo to his own devices. Shaking his head, he promised to handle things at the station. "They aren't going to send us back out anyway," he said. "Can you get him upstairs on your own?"

"I'll manage."

Leo was more cooperative, having thawed out a bit on the ride over. He seemed to be thinking more clearly, though his hands fumbled with his key card when they reached his room. She got the door open and helped him inside.

Her radio crackled with the alert that all patrols were being called in and officers would only go out on an emergency basis. Leo shuffled around his room, unable to shrug off his coat, and she realized she was watching an emergency.

"Let me help." She yanked off her gloves and coat and reached for his, peeling them away from his shaking hands.

"I can do it," he protested, landing heavily in the chair by the window.

"You aren't doing it," she pointed out gently. He'd put himself closer to the heater, but that was the only positive thing she could say for his decision making. If she walked out now, he'd likely just fall asleep right there. And he'd be sick by morning. Or worse.

She dropped his gloves to the floor. Reaching around him, she turned up the heat and put the fan on high. Kneeling, she started to work on the laces of his shoes. Her fingers fumbled, stiff with cold as well as a hefty dose of nerves. When she imagined getting Leo out of his clothing, the scene wasn't anything like this.

The man was heartsick and chilled to the bone. When she had him down to a thin white undershirt and his wet jeans, she hauled him to his feet.

"Thank you, Aubrey." His lips collided with hers in an awkward, frosty kiss. With a little hum, he tried again.

She patted his cheek. There were more effective ways to warm him up, though her body was eager to give it the old college try. How could such a meager kiss strike this immediate desire? She really didn't understand herself.

"You need to get warm," she declared. After marching him into the bathroom, she turned on the shower. As the water heated, the small room started to steam up. This was a better way to thaw him out.

Leo might be freezing and shivering, but the little tremors rippling through her were all about an overabundance of heat. After kissing him last night, and even just now, she couldn't keep him locked away in the safe category of "person in need."

He was Leo. Not Mr. Butler. Not report number whatever it was on Lara's missing person case. When he wasn't impersonating an icicle, he was a walking fantasy, a baffled stranger in town, and a brother who'd lost all of his common sense to the worry for his sister.

She wanted every facet of him, and all those facets waiting to be discovered. Ordering her hormones to shut up, she pulled off his damp shirt. He was a victim. A man in need, and her job was to help him in the capacity of a trained, professional first responder. It was a daunting task when she simply wanted to hold him close and promise him things would work out.

She pressed her lips together and reached for the fly of his jeans.

He pushed her hands aside. "I've got it."

"You'll need to turn the temperature down before you get in or you'll hurt your skin."

"Okay."

"Then slowly keep turning it warmer until the chill is gone." She folded her arms over her chest, waiting.

"All right." He fumbled with his fly, but got the button open. His hand went still on his zipper. "I can take it from here."

"You're sure?"

"Go. I'm embarrassed enough already."

She counted that a good sign. She walked out, hearing the splat of denim against the tile floor before she closed the door. He cursed, loudly, and she figured he hadn't dialed down the temperature quite far enough.

His lean torso was as solid as she'd imagined, and the reflection of his back in the mirror would give her plenty of fuel for more sexy dreams of a man who should really be off-limits. Between the blast of hot air in the room and the hotter direction of her thoughts, she had to unbutton her uniform shirt and take off her insulated boots. At least she was dry under the layers of gear.

Distracting herself, she called in a room service order for both of them. If he insisted on pushing too far and putting himself at risk, he gave her no choice but to step up. Yes, it went above and beyond her official duty as a cop. Then again, her shift was over, her partner was handling the report and she couldn't get home without risking her own case of frostbite.

Leo was still in the shower when the delivery arrived. She used her credit card to cover the charge and tip, wishing she could have ordered a change of clothes, as well.

The savory scents of cheesesteak sandwiches and thick-cut, seasoned fries made her stomach growl. It was hard to regret getting stuck here with Leo when the food was such a vast improvement over the can of soup she'd planned to heat up at home.

The bathroom door opened and Leo strolled out, the white hotel towel low on his hips. Aubrey forgot the food, swamped by a completely different kind of hunger.

"You're still here."

She opened her mouth and nothing happened. No words, no sound. What in the world was wrong with her? One fantasy-fueling kiss didn't give her the right to ogle him. She tried again, though her throat was dry as sandpaper. "I wanted to be sure you didn't drown. Ya know, after trying to freeze to death."

"Scalding might have become the bigger risk."

Her gaze slid over him, taking in the deep rosy hue on his cheeks, the expanse of his torso and especially his feet. With heroic effort, she dragged her eyes back to his face. "I told you to turn the water cooler."

"I did. And following your instructions, I kept turning it hotter again until the chills stopped."

Her gaze drifted back to the dusting of golden hair on his chest and she forced her attention to more pertinent matters like his health. "Go on and dress so you can stay warm," she said briskly. "Let's keep you out of the hospital if we can avoid it."

"Yes, Officer."

She snorted. An obedient Leo Butler was a pipe dream. She turned away from him, toward the cart loaded with food. "I ordered cheesesteaks and fries. And coffee."

"Hot chocolate, too, I hope."

She heard the dresser drawer glide open and close again, the rustle of denim and softer fabrics. Her mind gleefully filled in the blanks, taunting her with the view she was missing. What she'd already seen wasn't torture enough? She couldn't seem to drag her thoughts back into a professional lineup.

"I did." She turned a mug upright. "Would you like some?"

"I'd like to know you ordered it for yourself."

Oh. "I did," she repeated.

"Good. You deserve more than a hot chocolate for saving me."

"I plan to have one of these sandwiches," she said.

A low chuckle sounded behind her as he moved around. "You can look. I'm decent again."

The amusement in his voice made her smile, relaxed her. They were new acquaintances, sure, and she'd enjoyed the sensual chemistry. More than that, despite Leo's pushing every limit, she recognized a trust and respect that ran both ways.

She poured a cup of coffee for him and nearly bobbled it as he crossed the room. He was obviously feeling more like himself, evidenced by the masculine confidence that shredded what was left of her composure.

He wrapped his hands around hers, holding her gaze

as he took the coffee cup. His lips pursed as he blew across the hot surface before he took a sip. "Strong and hot," he said. "Perfect."

Need coiled into a tight spring in her belly. Was he trying to get her to jump him? Because it was working. She didn't know what to do with her hands or where to look or how to handle whatever was going on here.

She motioned to the covered plates of food. "You should eat something."

"You don't expect me to eat alone, do you?"

She had no idea what to expect with Leo. Pulling the chair away from the table, she plopped down. "What were you thinking out there?" Appalled by the outburst, she held up a hand. "Sorry. Eat first. Please. My questions can wait."

"You deserve an explanation," he began.

She cut him off. "Later." She nibbled at a steak fry to appease her growling stomach while he loaded a plate with a chunk of the sandwich and a pile of fries.

"You're not eating?" he asked.

"I'm getting there." He'd scared her, nearly becoming a statistic out there in the alley. Now that he looked and acted like himself it all hit her. Hard. Left her hollowed out and weak. She didn't have the luxury of weakness. Not on the job or off.

Her stomach rumbled and she loaded up a plate for herself.

"Wouldn't it be more comfortable without the gun?" Leo asked. "Or are you planning to draw on me?"

"Ha," she said. "Although…if that's the only way to keep you out of the storm, I won't rule it out."

"Ha," he echoed. "I'm sorry I created more trouble."

"Play to your strengths," she quipped. Immediately contrite, she added, "I know you're worried about Lara."

He took a big bite and chewed, leaving her to wonder how many more blunders she might make before the weather let up. She should check on the availability of another room here at the hotel. It would bust her budget, but it was better than mooching off Leo. He was clearly out of danger, and a little space was better than sticking here and giving in to temptation.

She rose, moving toward the phone on the desk.

"What are you doing?" Leo followed her. "You can't go out in this."

He was absolutely right. Through the window she could see the storm had reached whiteout proportions. A person could get lost crossing the street. "Calling to see if they have another room available for tonight."

Clouds gathered in his eyes. "Why not stay here with me?"

She arched her brows. "Did you want the reasons in alphabetical order?" She hoped not, since any desire to resist was fizzling fast.

"Chronological," he challenged.

She actually tried to accommodate his request before she gave up and picked up the phone. He took it from her grasp before she even realized his intent. "Leo," she warned. "I can't stay overnight."

"Who's around to even know?"

Calvin, the patrol team who'd helped rescue Leo, Sergeant Hulbert, who had to notice she didn't come back with her partner, plus the hotel security team. "Plenty of people saw me come in with you." They'd definitely passed two or three surveillance cameras on the way to his room.

"Why would anyone bother to track when you leave?"

She wasn't about to share that cautionary tale. He was so close she could touch the burnished gold scruff shading his jaw. "Are you growing a beard?" Not quite twenty-four hours ago, at dinner, his jaw had been smooth as silk.

"Not your best segue," he said, dragging his knuckles across the whiskers. "It was an attempt to insulate my face from the cold front."

"Needs more time."

"Agreed." He stared at her with such concern an observer might think she'd been the one in need of rescue. His gaze slid down her body, and her nerves tingled in anticipation. "Stay. Here."

"Leo." She was suddenly all too aware of the utter disarray of her uniform. Boots and coat and hat by the door, her uniform shirt unbuttoned.

"We haven't even talked about Lara," he said.

She rolled her eyes at the obvious ploy. "You know I would've said something if I had news. Go eat and stay warm."

He caught her hand, laced his fingers with hers and gently tugged her back toward the table. Her pulse raced and her skin tingled all over. "I'm the one with news," he said.

"What?" That revelation cooled her right down again. "You followed a lead to that alley?"

"I'm not talking until you've eaten half a sandwich and had a cup of hot chocolate."

"Is that a threat or a bribe? It's not smart to aim either one at a police officer."

He pulled out her chair, waited for her to sit. Then

he leaned down, putting them cheek to cheek. "You can take care of yourself," he said, his lips brushing her ear.

The brief contact set off a chain reaction, and an insuppressible tremor flowed down her spine. *More*, she thought, her mind on the man rather than the case or the food. Somehow, she managed to keep her hand steady as they ate in silence jam-packed with anticipation. Not awkward, just aware.

As much as she wanted to stuff her face and hurry this along, she couldn't bring herself to rush the meal. No one cared where she was, as long as she was safe, and believing otherwise was starting to feel paranoid. Her goal was to be healthy, mind and body, as a cop and as a woman, and in all of her relationships.

So she enjoyed the food and relished a hot chocolate dessert. Leo told her a story of sledding with his younger sister after a big winter storm and she could almost see their rosy cheeks and hear the wild laughter. She'd had similar fun and escapades with neighbor kids growing up, but it wasn't the same as having someone there with you all the time, sharing the good and the bad.

"I always wanted a big brother," she said without thinking.

He smiled. "I hope your mother explained that families rarely work that way."

She rolled her eyes. "Lara's lucky to have you. That's all I meant."

"Did you need a big brother in your corner?"

"No." She didn't care for the protectiveness in his tone. Leo didn't need more worries. "These days I have Calvin. And Sergeant Hulbert. That's plenty of oversight already." And still she'd been duped by her lousy, drug-dealing ex. She tried to laugh, but it sounded croaky to her. "You've held back long enough," she said, stacking their dirty dishes on the cart. "Spill whatever led you into that alley."

"One condition," he began.

She shook her head. "No. No changing the rules now. Talk."

Leo refilled his coffee and took a cautious sip. "The councilman we saw at the club." He snapped his fingers. "What's his name?"

"Keller?"

"Yeah, that's right. He was doing some press near the college when they opened the shelter. Promised a safe place for anyone with concerns about heat or whatever."

"Sounds about right." The man had done the full circuit of local radio and television this morning, promising assistance. "It will be interesting who pays the bills when they come due."

"You don't seem to like him," Leo said. "Why?"

She rubbed at her face, wishing for her fleece sweats and fuzzy socks. "I don't *dislike* him. He talks a great game, but he's a politician and it always falls to those of us on the front lines to fulfill his promises." She waved off the political tangent. "How does that tie to Lara?"

"I went inside to help them finish setting up. As people trickled in, I saw a man wearing a scarf like the one I gave Lara for Christmas."

"Leo." The lecture was right on the tip of her tongue.

"The scarf was clean, Aubrey. Cashmere, too, and it was a distinct Cincinnati Reds pattern. Lara loves the team. I talked to him about baseball, but I didn't push him or anything."

"You've given up on the aggressive inquisition approach?" she asked.

He chuckled. "Will you ever let that go?"

Not a chance. "As a first impression, it's a lasting one," she teased. Sobering, she propped her elbows on the table. "You were warm, in a shelter, doing good work. People were arriving, so why leave?"

"The man with the scarf said he got it from a nice girl."

"You showed him a picture of Lara?"

"No. Didn't want to make him uncomfortable." His lips tilted in a sheepish grin. "See, I can learn."

"Good to know. That doesn't mean he got the scarf from Lara."

He stared at her. "Do you really think there are two girls out there sharing their cashmere scarves?" Without waiting for an answer, he continued. "He was the first person who'd seen Lara. I hadn't heard anything out of you or Rosie or Grant all day."

She sat on her hands before she got up and hugged him or did something equally foolish. "Leo, no one is giving up."

He rolled his shoulders, restless. "I asked the volunteers about where they'd picked up the man with the scarf. Hearing there were others who didn't come in…" His voice trailed off.

"You went looking."

"She doesn't leave people behind. I had to go."

"Leo." Her heart swelled with love. It was too soon, too silly, too impossible. Calling it compassion or infatuation was a copout. She was falling for Leo. There wasn't any other explanation for the hard squeeze behind her sternum or the sweet, fizzy tenderness that didn't fade. Unless she took a leave from work and simply kept herself glued to Leo's side, there was no way to protect him from himself.

As tempting as that idea was, considering her feelings for him, taking leave meant one less person available to help in crises like this storm.

"Maybe it wasn't smart." Leo picked up a steak fry and broke it in two. "But what if she was stuck? What if she wasn't helping someone, but in serious trouble? What if she needed me?"

All questions without answers. "You're worried, with good reason," she said. "If I could wave a magic wand and make her appear, I would." When they did find Lara, and she had to keep believing in a positive outcome for Leo's sake, she would be hard-pressed not to shake the girl senseless for putting her brother through this heart-wrenching ordeal. "The shelters aren't the only places to ride out the weather," she said. "If your sister is half as determined as you, she's found a safe place."

"None of Grant's people have seen her, either. I checked with him before I went down that alley."

She did her best to suppress her reaction to Grant's involvement in an active PPD case. Leo needed that additional ray of hope.

"What's really your beef with him? It felt more personal than the vigilante rant you gave at the meeting."

"Sorry about that."

"Come on, Aubrey. Is it so hard to open up?"

"I don't usually," she said. Here, away from the precinct and the man in question, she could speak freely. She bit her lip and decided if he could learn and change tactics she should give him the same courtesy. "The campus security chief sent you to Grant because he's known to pick up cases that fall through the cracks of normal police work. Your sister isn't that kind of case."

"But you warned me that the PPD wouldn't put much into the search."

"Leo." She pressed her fingers to her eyes for a moment before meeting his gaze again. "Everyone, Grant included, has reminded you that your sister is an adult."

He scowled, but didn't comment.

"Grant has connections, from his years on the PPD and through his business as a club owner. He's good for the community overall. I just think he runs the risk of undermining the system when he takes on his own projects. Lara is an active case."

"All right. I can see your point."

She appreciated the olive branch. "My opinion isn't the popular one. And to be fair, I know his reputation of helping starts with how he gives first responders a way to stay busy while rehabbing an injury or whatever. He was also one of the first business owners to create a house policy that gives potential victims a way out if a date is going badly."

"A cop can only respond to a crime that's been committed." Leo's scowl had softened into contemplation. "Does Grant intervene too early?"

"In my opinion," she said. "More than once Grant has called in PPD just in time to hear a confession, handing detectives open and shut cases."

"That bugs you."

"It does," she admitted easily.

His finger circled the edge of his coffee cup. "I respect your point of view, but I can't be sorry more people are searching for Lara."

"I wouldn't want you to be. Your sister isn't mentally

unstable or physically ill, so I doubt she'll risk frostbite or worse when there are other options. That means someone will spot her eventually."

"Do we know that?" Leo stretched his arms wide, then folded his hands behind his head and stared up at the ceiling.

She scolded herself for ogling again. Why did they have to meet at the precinct over an official report? "Pardon me?" She'd lost the thread of the conversation.

"Do we know she's stable?" He dropped his arms back and sat up straight. "Seriously. Who pulls this kind of stunt? Shutting me out has never been an option."

Someone committed to her agenda. Aubrey kept the thought to herself. "I'm pretty sure we do know," Aubrey replied. "There would've been other signs of emotional or mental issues long before now."

"I don't know." Leo pushed back from the table and paced the width of the room. "She loves *me*." He tapped his temple. "That's a pretty big indicator she's got a faulty wire or two."

Why did he think he was unlovable? The guilt and misery on his face stirred up those all-too-willing urges to comfort and soothe. Along with a new temptation to offer him a distraction they could both enjoy. She admired his tenacity and his conviction that Lara was in trouble, even when it made her job more difficult. "You're nine years older than your sister?" she asked.

"Yes," he replied.

"What did she do when you went to college? Did you call every week?"

His gaze drifted to some point in the past and his lips shifted into a half smile. "She cried. Until she finally believed that I wasn't going away to school. I stayed local, lived at home. I couldn't leave her alone with our mom."

Clearly, those hadn't been easy years. Whatever had happened to their family, the siblings had formed a deep bond to survive. It sure would be nice to know if pushing would help her understand Lara's actions or just cause Leo more pain. She was still debating when he stopped in front of the window. She immediately worried about him standing in the draft but managed to keep quiet.

"It's beautiful," he said, watching the storm outside. He held out a hand. "Come watch with me."

She joined him at the window, done resisting this closeness that felt so right. Big, fat snowflakes had turned her city into a sparkling wonderland. At least from this vantage point several stories up. Down on the street, the conditions were creating dreadful hazards. She hoped people stayed in so everyone could be safe.

A plow and salt truck rumbled by and Leo slid his arm around her waist, drawing her close. She couldn't help checking the windows across the street for any faces aimed their way. And what could she do about it if she saw anyone?

Turning into his arms, she relaxed against him. "I'm glad you're safe."

"I'm glad you and Calvin found me. I might still have to file a complaint."

"Do tell." She liked the glint in his eyes when he teased her.

"Isn't shared body heat the best tactic for preventing or resolving hypothermia? I feel like you didn't do *everything* possible." He touched his forehead to hers. "Seriously, thank you, Aubrey."

"You're welcome." She wanted a kiss, needed the tangible, incontrovertible evidence that he was better. Stronger than he'd been when she found him.

His lips brushed across hers, a mere whisper of what she craved. "Thank you for saving me from myself. Again."

"Serve and protect," she said. "That's me."

"Hmm." His hands linked at her back and he leaned away to study her face. "So you'd do all of this for anyone you found on the street?"

She nodded, inexplicably delighted by the way his mouth kicked up at one corner.

"So I'm nothing special?"

"I wouldn't say that." Her fingers trailed up and down the placket of his thermal Henley shirt. The fabric hugged his shoulders, emphasized his sculpted form. "Why weren't you wearing this earlier?"

In lieu of an answer, he kissed her. A kiss full of glorious intention loaded with an invitation to so much more. She unbuckled her belt, setting it and her gun aside. Then she gave herself over to the moment, to this man, doing her best to send her excess body heat into him.

His fingers worked under her uniform shirt and silk undershirt. She shivered at the first contact, sighing into the sweet, welcome feeling. His hands weren't icy anymore. His hot palms cruised up over her ribs to cup her breasts. She arched into the touch, her nipples straining through her bra. Under her hands, the muscles of his back rippled with his movements until she was ready to claw off his clothes and strip him bare. Again.

"It's too hot in here," he said, trailing kisses along her throat.

Leo had such a talented tongue and lips. And teeth,

she added as he nipped and soothed her skin in turns. "No such thing for you tonight."

He hummed, low in his throat. "So this." He kissed her hard, slid his hands up and down her back. "This is only therapeutic activity."

"I hope not," she admitted breathlessly.

He laughed, holding her so close the sound vibrated from his body right through hers. She'd never known laughter could be so erotic.

"I can't think of a better way to chase off any hidden cold spots." He eased away from the window, drawing her closer to the bed. "Stay."

Slowly, she drew his mouth down to hers. Any argument she might have posed was beyond her now. She took her time with the kisses, lingering over every point of contact, learning what made his breath hitch, what made him sigh.

Had anything ever been this perfect? Her heart fluttered in her chest, merrily reminding her she'd never experienced anything quite like this before. He tempted her in new, amazing ways and thanks to his job, he'd be gone before her past mistakes could dim the glow of a hot, fast and oh-so-enticing connection.

She eased back, just out of his reach, and unbuttoned her shirt. His gaze locked on to the movements, and a thrill jolted her pulse to a new high.

"Aubrey—"

The lights went out. The sudden silence of a power outage always took her by surprise. She found the absolute lack of ambient noise as refreshing as it was intimidating. With no distractions, she could hear the snow and ice pelting the window as the wind gusted.

"Aubrey?"

Her entire body homed in on Leo's voice, yearning for him, as if they'd been separated by a continent rather than a few feet. "I didn't do it."

His laughter might as well be a beacon in the dark. "Just making sure you didn't disappear."

Here, with him, was the only place she wanted to be.

She could just make out the shape of him, one more substantive shadow in the layers of darkness. "Give me a second." She moved toward the door, dutifully double-checking that the emergency lights were on in the hallway.

The minimal glow was creepy. Up and down the hallway, other doors were opening, heads peering out.

"Trouble?" Leo's hand curled around her shoulder.

She squeaked and jumped, instantly ashamed of herself. "Looks good."

His low, brief laugh was so much better than the pain in his voice when he worried for his sister. "Afraid of the dark?"

"No."

"What if I told you I was?" His lips grazed the back of her neck.

She scooted back into the room. "Are you?"

"Just a little." He pressed the words into the sensitive skin at her nape.

She had the strangest feeling he wasn't joking. "The lights will be on soon." She hoped so anyway.

"Probably true." He turned her, claimed her mouth in a kiss hot enough to divert a wicked winter storm. "You're thinking of leaving."

"I don't want to." Desire rampaged through her system. Her head fell back and she moaned as the scruff on his jaw rasped against her throat.

His hands gripped her hips and he pulled her flush against his body. He was hard, heat radiating from his demanding lips to his erection nudging her hip to his thighs flexing against hers. She melted against that heat, everything going soft, inside and out. Her whole being, from her heart to her skin, yearned for him.

Leaving was the responsible choice. Leo was safe; she could go home with the confidence that he wouldn't venture out again tonight. But then she'd be alone and when he kissed her like she mattered, as if he wouldn't be safe without her, specifically, that filled her with an unbearable longing. She arched into him, captured her mouth with his and gave in to the temptation at last.

Chapter 7

Leo felt the shift, the subtle give when Aubrey's internal debate over duty versus desire ended and she gave herself up to him. To them. To this moment. She was his, here in the dark where he could pretend they'd met under more typical circumstances.

Cradling her face, he kissed her soundly, his tongue stroking hers. He'd never have enough of her sweet flavor. A chill was already creeping into the room without the heater. Maybe he was more prone to it after nearly freezing in the alley.

If the hotel had a generator, he wasn't sure he wanted it to kick on. Aubrey—supple, giving, glorious Aubrey—was all the heat he needed tonight. Possibly forever. In the near-total darkness, he had to trust his hands and hers, her sighs and murmurs to guide him. When he ran out of buttons, he pushed her shirt off her shoulders and slid his hands over the silky layer underneath. The long-sleeved shirt might ward off the nasty weather, but it slithered over her sweet, rounded breasts, tantalizing him with what he couldn't quite touch.

As if sensing his frustration or fascination, she yanked the garment away and flowed back into him. Her skin was softer than the silk. He tasted her. Lips, throat, lower still until her heart pounded under his kisses. She arched and he obliged, nipping at the tight peaks of her nipples through her bra.

He let her shove him back toward the bed, pulling off his shirt on the way as he heard her dealing with the boxy uniform pants. He wanted to see her, wanted to enjoy the reveal of her lush body. Without any light, relying only on hearing and touch, taste and scent, he found every discovery a mesmerizing new experience.

She was a lithe shadow, a dip in the mattress as she joined him on the bed. And she was naked, shivering as his hands glided over her skin.

"I'll keep you warm," he vowed. Here tonight, anywhere. He cut off the wayward thought. No sense wrecking this magic by overthinking tomorrow.

"Counting on it," she said between kisses and nips along his shoulder, up to his ear. How did she already know the touches he craved most?

He was desperate to give her more. Enjoying the discovery, his hands and mouth roamed over the swells and dips of her sweet body. She was muttering threats about being teased and getting even right up to the point that her first climax ripped through her. She bucked and clung and dragged him up until their mouths meshed once more.

"Leo." She whispered his name in the dark, breathless and satisfied.

Feeling as if he'd set the moon and stars in the sky only for her, he caressed and coaxed until she was hovering at the edge of another orgasm. He left her long enough to find a condom from the travel kit in the bathroom. Returning to the bed, she reached for him, drawing him down to cover her again. On a sigh that was the most erotic sound he'd ever heard, he sank deep into her tight, hot body.

She arched, moving with him and matching his pace until they were both spent and breathless, tangled in a lover's knot of satisfaction. With four of his five senses full of her, he promised himself they'd do this again, with enough light to watch pleasure play over her face and skin.

He got up and dealt with the condom and turned the switches on the light fixtures he remembered being on. At the bed, he pulled back the blankets and tucked her in, sliding in beside her. Body heat was a thousand times better than a solo shower for chasing away any chill.

Leo woke less than an hour later when the power came on. The desk lamp was shining right into Aubrey's face. He started to roll out of bed again, only to have her body follow.

She was still asleep and he decided the light could wait. He enjoyed studying her when she couldn't protest or divert his attention. Relaxed as she was right now, she seemed almost fragile. Her hands were tucked under her chin and her pert nose and bowed lips begged for his kisses. His heart pitched to his toes as he faced this softer, vulnerable view of her. She'd always displayed such stoic and reasonable professionalism. It was impossible to overstate her commitment to her city, her neighborhood and her role in it.

So what was he doing here? Why was he letting himself grow attached to a woman he couldn't share a life with? Even if he ignored the crushing weight of guilt that destroyed his relationships with everyone but his sister, he could see that he and Aubrey had vital, essential careers in separate cities.

Maybe the lack of any future was an integral part of his attraction. He forced himself to examine that uncomfortable potential truth. Had he used her to dull the pain of Lara's disappearance?

Adjusting the pillow and tucking his hand behind his head, he stared up at the ceiling. Beside him, Aubrey snuggled closer, one hand resting over his heart. He covered that hand with his and realized she meant more to him than a convenient release. In the morning they should probably talk about it. Or ignore it. Talking changed things, put a significance and a burden on what might be better if kept simple.

He had another week at most, before the airport needed him to decide about taking a formal leave of absence. Somewhere in the days ahead he and Aubrey could figure out what this was, what they wanted it to be.

He might very well be trying to strategize over something she didn't want at all.

The alarm on Aubrey's phone went off right on time. Blinking sleep from her eyes, she sat up to turn it off and discovered everything else was wrong. Wrong bed, wrong room and definitely the wrong man.

Though it was hard to remember *why* he was the wrong man when he rolled over and drew her in, kissing her as if they had all day for only each other. Tempting as it was, thorough as he was, they both had an agenda. He would want to speak with Grant and get back to searching for his sister. She had to report in at the precinct and hope no one realized she was wearing the same uniform.

After a hot shower for two, breakfast had been a quick affair with another room service delivery. As she downed the last of her toast and juice, she debated whether or not it was smart to kiss him goodbye. Did sex make them that kind of couple?

She shoved her feet into her boots, scolding herself for not bolting from the room first thing. He'd looked so despondent over the lack of activity on Lara's bank account, she couldn't do it. He didn't look that much better now, but she couldn't be late.

"I'll keep you posted," she said, buckling her belt and shrugging into her coat. Hat in her hands, she watched him refill his coffee mug. This wasn't the time to lecture him on healthier choices. Besides, it was hard to argue health when he'd demonstrated his stamina and virility so effectively last night.

"Same," he said. He crossed the room as she reached for the door. "Hang on." He kissed her soundly. "Be safe."

"You, too," she replied, her heart pounding in her ears.

Leaving the hotel, she wasn't surprised to see several people out and about. The traffic lights were working, a good sign considering the power outage, and sunlight sparkled on fresh snow.

As she returned to the precinct, the previously piping hot eggs and bacon became a slippery lump of angst in her belly. It didn't matter that no one else knew where she'd spent the night, the walk of shame put heat in her cold, wind-chapped cheeks.

Calvin raised an eyebrow as she joined the morning briefing at the last possible second. As expected, those teams on foot were to search for any victims of the storm and assist when possible. When Hulbert opened up the meeting, Aubrey asked if anyone had seen Lara yesterday or overnight. No one had. She hoped with every fiber of her satisfied body that they wouldn't find her out there today, a casualty of the storm.

Thankfully, Calvin waited until their second circuit before he brought up anything related to Leo. "You're not giving up on the Lara Butler case."

"Can't."

"Because of the brother?"

She blew into her hands. Lying to Calvin wouldn't do any good. "In part. Mary-Tea asked me not to search for Lara."

Her partner reared back. "And you're just now telling me?"

"Yes. It happened while I was posting the flyers." When the signal changed, she started across the street. Calvin, in shock, apparently, had to jog to catch up with her.

"Does the brother know?"

She shook her head. "I didn't trust him to stay cool about it. Then the note and…"

"He went to Grant."

"Yes." They were approaching the Good Samaritan. "I'm stuck," she admitted. "Mary-Tea might have written that note to Leo or had nothing to do with it. Either way, it seemed to me like she wants Lara to keep doing whatever she's doing."

"What are you going to do?"

"My job," she snapped. "Just like I told Mary-Tea and Leo and Grant, too."

Calvin held up his hands. "Take it easy. I'm not judging."

"Others will and you know it." She caught the twitch as Calvin winced. Her stomach dropped to her toes. She knew that face. "What now?"

"Nothing serious," he promised. "I overheard Hulbert take a call yesterday afternoon. He mentioned that you weren't in."

She groaned. "And the caller didn't ask for you." Calvin shook his head, though the question had been rhetorical. "Let's go," she said, resigned. "If IA is hovering over me again, we should get some good done before the hammer drops."

The work was her best distraction as they checked in with the volunteers at the emergency shelter that had been opened at the gymnasium. As they walked by a table where people could pick up hats, gloves and coats, she hoped Leo was being smarter about the weather today. No one had seen Lara. Although the worst of the storm had passed, a foot of snow layered with ice still meant dreadfully low temperatures compounded by the wind chill.

She sent him a text message as they left the temporary shelter but still didn't have a reply by the time they reached the precinct. It was tempting to make a pass by his hotel, but she couldn't ask Calvin to cover for her again.

Hulbert caught her gaze as Aubrey and her partner walked by his desk. "Back already?"

"Short and effective beats frostbite," Calvin said.

Aubrey stomped snow off her boots. "So far it's an all-clear on our beat."

"Count your blessings," Hulbert said. "I've heard of two confirmed fatalities so far."

Her throat dried up. Please don't let it be Lara. "Here?"

"Nah. Across town." He shook his head. "Sure would be nice to get through one winter without finding a human icicle."

"I'm with you," Aubrey said, "Let's hope that's all." Across town meant Keller wouldn't call out their precinct directly, although she expected him to be vocal about the deaths.

"Any luck on your missing coed?"

"No news is good news." She checked her phone, but there were no messages from Leo.

"Any reason to believe she's still in town?"

Aubrey nodded once and took an elbow from Calvin. "Mary-Tea knows something about her."

"That's as real as a heart attack."

"Exactly," Aubrey agreed. "But you know I can't push her."

"Be patient," Hulbert said.

"That's the plan," she said, turning with Calvin to go find something hot to drink before heading back out.

On a gust of cold air Tina and Ray walked in. They were both wearing smiles bright enough to rival the sun reflecting off the snow. "Officer Aubrey!" Tina exclaimed, rushing forward. "We brought your favorite."

Calvin stepped forward, taking a crate of hot drinks out of Tina's hands. "This smells incredible," he said.

"There's hot chocolate with whip and without, mochas and more." Tina beamed. "Plus, your smoothie," she said to Aubrey. "We came to you today. As a thank-you."

"Wow!" Aubrey exclaimed.

"This is awesome," Hulbert chimed in. "Come on back, guys."

Aubrey wasn't exactly hungry and it was hours yet before her usual break, but the thoughtful gesture warmed her up, inside and out. "How are you feeling?" she asked, sipping the frozen blend of fruit and yogurt.

"I'm over it," Tina said. "Mostly." She clutched her wool mittens in her hands. "My cousin's a grade-A jerk, to be sure, but you responded so quickly." She grinned. "I keep reliving that takedown. In a good way."

Aubrey laughed a little. "Good to know."

"Between you and me?" Tina leaned close. "Ray is hoping to sweet-talk the sergeant for the contact information for the man who led our customers out of harm's way."

"Oh, um…" Aubrey glanced over to see Hulbert chatting with Tina's boss. "Policy is we don't share that kind of thing."

Tina frowned. "I get it. You shouldn't under normal circumstances."

"Sergeant Hulbert will make sure the man gets the message."

The other woman brightened. "That'll work. We want to give him a reward."

Aubrey couldn't see Leo accepting a reward.

"I'd give him a kiss," she continued, fanning her face. "He was a hottie. Don't tell my hubby I said so."

Aubrey felt a prickle of jealousy slither over the back of her neck. It was the worst reaction. Tina was happily married. Even if she hadn't been, Leo wasn't hers. Was he? She sucked down more of the smoothie to cool the sudden blast of emotions.

"Aubrey?"

"Ignore me." She tapped the center of her forehead. "Smoothie-induced headache."

"Uh-huh." Tina folded her arms and leaned back. "You're into him. The hero guy."

As if she needed the clarification from Tina. "I'm certainly not against people who do heroic things," she evaded.

Tina shoved her shoulder, none too gently. "Stop. It's me." Her expression fell. "We're friends."

Aubrey did stop. "You're right. About being friends," she hurried to add when Tina did a quick happy dance. "The hero guy," better to use Tina's phrase than Leo's name, "is from out of town. That's really all I can say."

"Oh, tell me you'll have a fling," Tina whispered. "You looked good together. After." Tina smiled. "My mother-in-law sent me a picture of you two at the restaurant."

She rolled her eyes, hiding her discomfort over being caught unawares by a stranger's camera.

"You deserve all the good stuff, Officer Aubrey." She waved, trotting after her boss as they left the precinct.

Calvin sipped from a tall cup. Hot chocolate rather than coffee, Aubrey noticed, when the whipped cream lingered on his upper lip. "Good, right?"

"The best," he said. "You should dump that frozen fruit nonsense and indulge."

"You don't need to twist my arm." After stashing her smoothie in the freezer, she took a cup of hot chocolate as they went back out for another circuit of the neighborhood. The warm, rich aroma was as effective as an extra layer of silk underwear.

It was impossible not to think of Leo, of room service,

power outages and all the rest of it. She never should've stayed or let herself obliterate that professional boundary. Letting her heart trump common sense was an idiotic move that would end badly if she wasn't careful.

Leo was nothing like her drug-dealing ex, but if her fellow officers caught wind of where she'd spent the night, there could be serious ramifications. Her secret was safe; it had to be. Calvin wanted her to get her personal life back. Maybe not specifically with Leo, but with some decent guy.

Her lips tingled, more from the memory of his kisses than from the hot chocolate. She should reestablish a professional distance with Leo. *Mr. Butler.* One mistake during a storm could be forgiven. The thought alone was enough to put a pinch behind her sternum.

She wasn't the one-night-stand type, but that was what this had to be. Anything more would raise too many red flags. Turning a corner, a blast of wind pushed her back. She leaned into it and ducked her chin deeper into her scarf. She wouldn't allow last night to become a problem.

No one could fault her for how she conducted herself on the missing person case. She'd take a step back, regroup and reassess. Last night—off duty—had been fun once the danger of hypothermia passed. Once they found Lara, Leo would probably take her back to Cincinnati.

Assuming they found her at all.

Aubrey was a cop to her soul. Whatever her peers said about her rosy outlook on life, she understood there were crimes, big and small, along with some seriously ugly dark spots in the day-to-day of life in Philly. The same held true for any major city. Crime typically corresponded with population density.

She also understood that when people did inexplicable things—like leaving school and cutting off communication—they always thought they had a good reason.

What was Lara's reason for leaving a relatively safe campus for the street? Why withdraw from school and cut off contact with a brother who clearly loved her?

Not that Leo was hard to love...

"Officer Aubrey!" She and Calvin turned toward the voice and spotted Mary-Tea huddled in the shadows of the alley.

"What are you doing out here?" Calvin asked. "Let's get you back to the shelter."

She shook her head and scuttled out of his reach. "They cleaned out the folks near Thirty-third Street. Posted a guard."

Calvin's eyebrows shot up. "We can take a look and sort it out," he said.

"No one is driving anyone away," Aubrey added. This was the battle they fought every time the cops tried to relocate people for their own safety. The worry was always that they wouldn't be allowed to return. Volunteers would be working overtime until the weather cleared, trying to get as many as possible into better situations. "We just didn't want anyone getting sick."

Mary-Tea's chin came up. "There's a guard chasing 'em off," she insisted. "That sweet Lara girl has pictures but she's no match for the guards. You have to help her."

"Have you spoken with Lara?" Aubrey asked, her voice remarkably calm, while inside hope exploded with a fireworks display better suited to the Fourth of July.

"This morning."

"She's well?"

"I just said so." Mary-Tea pointed a finger at Aubrey. Instead of the dingy wool gloves she normally wore, she had a nice clean pair made of leather. "She's no match for that guard. Go on now."

"We will." Calvin reached for his radio.

"I need to speak with Rosie first," Aubrey said. That was why they were here.

Mary-Tea huffed impatiently. "If we lose that girl…" She flapped her hands and shuffled away. "You're wasting time!"

As mad as Mary-Tea was at the moment, Leo would be worse if they lost Lara. She had to get down there, but she also had an obligation to Rosie and the people she took an oath to support and protect. She could always text Grant. Though the thought rankled, it was the option with the best chance of successfully supporting Lara.

She used her teeth to pull off her glove and sent the message before she could come to her senses. Shoving her phone back in her coat, she stalked into the soup kitchen to get a report from Rosie.

The manager was all smiles, reporting they'd been full to capacity—which meant she'd gone over the legal capacity limit—but the power had held and they still had plenty of food for today's meals.

"Your deliveries should be able to get through by the end of the day," Calvin said.

"Even if they can't make it, we have canned goods to work with," Rosie replied.

"Great," Aubrey said. "Any sign of Lara or her brother?"

"No." Rosie shook her head. "I'd tell you, I swear."

"I believe you," Aubrey said. "Mary-Tea says she's out there right now, trying to help the folks who camp near Thirty-third." Rosie's lips flattened into a thin line. "You know anything about it?"

"No, I heard people grumbling about being shoved out, but no one mentioned Lara. Not to me." Rosie shoved her hands into her apron pockets.

"Can you shed any light on why she's out there advocating and keeping everyone who loves her in the dark?"

Rosie bit her lip. "As I said, she's trying to help by living it firsthand."

"Help how? Who's backing her? I'm told her bank accounts haven't been touched."

"She can't carry money or use a card," Rosie said with a snort. "You know she'd be robbed or worse if she did that."

Aubrey glanced into the main dining room where Calvin was talking with a few folks distressed by the trouble. "This is the place she knows," Aubrey said, thinking aloud. "Why wouldn't she come here? As far as we can tell she didn't come in out of the weather last night."

Rosie cringed. "Her brother knows this place, too. She's avoiding me and this spot for that reason alone. You know the grapevine. She knows by now that he's looking for her."

"Then she should find a way to let him know she's all right."

"If she comes in, I'll make sure she does," Rosie promised. "From what I hear, she is making friends, winning people over."

Aubrey glared at her. "What kind of friends?"

"You must believe me, Officer Aubrey. Everyone she meets is happy to have her help. She is working on behalf of those who need her most."

That wouldn't be enough consolation for Leo. What was the catalyst that made Lara take on a complex, city-wide challenge right now?

"She's getting folks in here to eat that don't normally bother. Are you sure putting a stop to her efforts is the right thing?" Rosie asked under her breath.

Aubrey swallowed the string of curses. "You know I don't have any problem accepting good help for the community, but she owes her loved ones an explanation."

Rosie dropped her gaze to her hands. "I heard some chatter last night," she said. "Lara might be staying in a car near the tracks."

If it was true, it put Lara right between her former campus and the camp on Thirty-third. "That's a big help, Rosie."

"I swear I didn't know until last night. Mary-Tea is worried about her."

"Several people are worried about Lara," Aubrey said none too gently. "Calvin and I will do what we can. I expect you to call if you see her."

Rosie nodded. "Check that diner the men's church club runs," she said under her breath.

Aubrey hadn't thought to check the diner. They didn't specifically call themselves a shelter or soup kitchen, but it was known that they fed anyone who walked in. "More chatter?"

The manager only pursed her lips and turned away, calling out orders to her kitchen volunteers.

Aubrey and Calvin compared notes as they walked down toward the tracks to check on the status of the known homeless camp as well as look for signs of the car Lara might be living in. Calvin notified the precinct of their intention. This might actually be the only day that Lara would be officially at the top of her priority list, and she intended to make the most of it. For the case, not just for Leo.

"I was told time and again," Calvin said, "that Lara's brother is a nuisance."

"First impressions leave a mark," she muttered. "That has to be as much gossip grist as truth. If Leo was raising hell, we'd be answering those calls."

"True."

She checked her phone, just in case Leo or Grant had something helpful to report, but nothing had come through. With any luck, Leo had listened to her and was safely in his hotel room, avoiding frostbite. She understood his determination but he needed to understand his limits. She'd been scared to find him so cold last night. It had taken everything she had to stay calm, keep her head.

And that was before she'd spent the night in his bed. His arms. It seemed knowing he was temporary didn't change that she wanted to enjoy every available minute.

They walked the street along the tracks first, just a pair of cops on a beat. Although they didn't find Lara, several cars were good candidates for further investigation, and she and Calvin had a list of license plates to look up when they got back to the precinct.

Their next stop, the Thirty-third Street camp, was exactly how Mary-Tea described it. Snowed over like everything else in the city, but definitely under guard. Two men in hip-length black coats and snow pants and boots were standing around. Not obviously patrolling, but periodically hauling away the inadequate housing items left behind in the lot. A black sedan was at the curb and a panel truck was backed up into the lot, the cab not quite out of the flow of traffic. Thanks to the weather, no one was driving on this street to get irritated.

"What the hell?" Aubrey whispered.

"They could be shooting a mafia movie," Calvin said as they passed the corner.

"Mary-Tea was right. They're definitely cleaning out the camp," she said.

"On whose authority? They don't look like sanitation to me."

They kept their distance as they walked the area. Aubrey used her cell phone to take several pictures of the men and the vehicles before they approached.

The two men saw them coming and strode forward. "Officers. Tough day for walking a beat."

Calvin looked from one man to the other. "I'd say it's a tough day to stand outside doing…"

He gestured, encouraging one of the men to finish his sentence. They didn't. "What is going on here?"

"We're just taking an opportunity to clean up while everyone's elsewhere." The man with a bit of gray at his temples stuck out a hand. "I'm Jim. This is Max."

Aubrey took in the whole scene while Calvin asked for identification and kept the men talking. She snapped a picture of the plates on the panel truck but she wasn't fast enough to get a glimpse inside before the men called her over.

"They have a permit to clear the lot," Calvin said.

"And a tough new boss down in Florida," Max said. "Doesn't understand snow days."

"I see." Aubrey smiled, following Calvin's affable example. "Well, be sure to take breaks and stay warm."

"You betcha." Jim leaned in to read her badge. "Officer Rawlins."

She and Calvin walked a couple of blocks before Aubrey felt calm enough to speak. "They made my skin crawl."

"It wasn't just you, but the paperwork looks legit."

"Let's get back and see what pops," she said, picking up her pace.

Calvin matched her stride and whatever he might've said was swallowed by the call over the radio. The dispatcher reported a public disturbance in an alley practically around the corner. Aubrey and Calvin paused, listening to the dispatcher. She was surprised she couldn't hear raised voices bouncing off the snow and buildings. Calvin jogged ahead and she called that they were on the way to the scene.

The sounds of the fight escalated as they approached. She stopped at the mouth of the alley, looking around Calvin to take stock. Two men were facing off, circling. One bigger and clean, his dark jacket looked new. The second man was stout and grimy, clearly less fortunate. Neither man was Leo, she thought, grateful for life's small favors. The men were shouting at each other and the larger man held something in his hands. A plastic grocery bag, she saw as he turned again. The stout man was focused on the item as he shouted.

"Mine, fair and square."

Aubrey wanted to roll her eyes.

"Nicky," Calvin said in a put-upon tone.

Nicky, the stout man, was a regular on the street and often a troublemaker. He liked his space, his freedom. She was sure that so many people trying to save him from the weather yesterday had put him on edge. "Gentlemen!" she called out, pitching her voice over their loud argument.

The bigger guy turned and a sly grin flashed across his face. His dark hair was slicked back and he shot her a cunning glare. The face clicked. This was the guy who'd been asking about Lara at the pub. Was he still armed?

With her hands open, she marched forward around Calvin with measured, deliberate steps. They'd learned the hard way she could often defuse a fight faster. "What's the trouble, guys?"

"He has my food!" Nicky shouted, lunging for the bag.

The other man pivoted, keeping the bag and himself out of reach. "You had your chance. I found it."

"You stole it!"

Nicky shoved a hand in and out of his pocket. The sunlight glinted off the blade of a knife. "It's mine!" Nicky threw himself at his opponent, missing by a mile as the man sidestepped out of the way.

Aubrey shouted for him to drop the weapon. Behind her, Calvin did the same. She didn't want to fire on Nicky, or anyone else, but she couldn't let him stab anyone. Not even a man going out of his way to cause a scene.

Nicky attacked again. This time the first man tossed the bag in Nicky's face. A moment later he and his slick hair and perfect coat were gone, up and over the fence, while Nicky shuffled after him, screaming obscenities and impossible threats.

"On it." Calvin raced after the other man.

"Nicky?"

He spun around, his eyes glassy, lips tinged blue. In his shaking grip, the bag rattled in one hand, the knife in the other. His hands were bare.

"Where are your gloves?" She'd seen him with a decent pair of wool gloves on his hands the last time he'd been in the soup kitchen.

"Go away!" The screech, ricocheting between the frozen brick and iced-over steel garbage bins, hurt her ears.

"Take it easy, Nicky," she said. "Tell me what happened."

"It is my food," Nicky insisted.

"That's fine." It was too soon to ask for the knife. "Come on now." Aubrey spoke quietly. This wasn't her first time talking Nicky down after a dustup.

"Gone!" He shook the knife at the fence, started back that way. "No take backs."

"No take backs," Aubrey agreed, guiding him toward the exit of the alley again. As far as Aubrey could tell, Nicky's emotional development had stalled out around the level of a first grader. Whether he'd always been that way or he'd regressed due to a drug habit or mental illness wasn't clear. Didn't matter.

"I bet you're hungry," she said. "Let's get you some soup."

"I got food." He clutched the bag to his chest. "Got food here."

"Okay." He must have pulled something from the Dumpster. Except the bag looked clean. "Can you put the knife away?" She'd prefer to seize it, but it was too soon for that.

He frowned at his hand as if he didn't recognize the weapon.

"What kind of food?" she asked.

"Roast beef sandwich. Fresh."

"Good." She looked back toward the fence. "Did that other man give you the food?"

"No! No. No. New Girl did."

He said it like a name. Talking with Nicky was never

easy, but this was weird even for him. He didn't like new people. "When did you see her?"

"New Girl?" He gestured with the knife. "She was over by the deli." He shook the bag again. "It's closed for the storm."

If only *that* narrowed things down. The bag didn't have any logos on it. And it raised the question, how did New Girl get food from a closed deli? Aubrey desperately wanted control of that knife, but Nicky wasn't in the mood to share weapons any more than he was willing to share his food. "One second." She put herself between Nicky and the street and showed him the picture of Lara on her phone. "Is this New Girl?"

He squinted, leaned in. "Uh-huh. New Girl." He rattled the deli sack. "She's nice. She gives things without taking them back."

"That is nice." Aubrey glanced around, wishing Calvin would get back here. Who was giving things to Nicky and then taking them back? Though it was completely possible that any slights were in Nicky's imagination, her instincts were humming.

"Have you seen New Girl anywhere other than the deli lately?" Delis were prevalent around the campus and any clues would narrow the search.

Nicky scowled, his head tipped back to the sky. "Dunno." His knife arm relaxed a bit. "We had soup once."

Again, that could have happened almost anywhere. Frustration built in her throat, but screaming wouldn't help anyone. Screaming in Nicky's vicinity was particularly unwise, especially while he was armed. "Where'd you find the knife?"

His baffled gaze locked on her face and he blinked owlishly. "Officer Aubrey?"

She gave him a small smile. "That's right." A noise behind her on the sidewalk drew her attention. And Nicky's. Nicky leaned around her for a better view, the bag in his hand rustling as he tried to hide it from the newcomer.

It was Leo, relief stamped on his face when he recognized her and walked closer. "Hi. Rosie told me you and Calvin were out this way. I thought I'd..." His gaze narrowed when he spotted the knife in Nicky's hand. "You okay here?"

"I'm great." He was bundled up today. She didn't need to ask what he was doing. He was searching for his sister. "Was about to call."

"Really? I—"

Whatever Leo meant to say was cut short. It happened so fast, in a blur of motion and raised voices as Nicky rushed by her, knife outstretched. She shouted for him to stop, but he'd clearly had enough of strangers today. She grabbed his coat and held on for dear life, leaning away with all her weight to keep him off Leo.

"Drop the knife!" She yanked on Nicky's coat but made little progress. "I can handle him," she said to Leo. "Get out of here!" she yelled.

"Not a chance." Leo stepped closer, placing himself in Nicky's path so the man couldn't make it to the street. "I'm not leaving you alone."

Nicky's outrage apparently overwhelmed him and she stumbled back as he spun around, aiming all that rage at her.

Could a shift get any worse? This couldn't be happening. "Drop the knife, Nicky."

"No take backs!" he screamed.

He raised the weapon overhead and brought it down in a swinging blow. She blocked the move, ducked under his arm and spun away. She would not shoot a confused, unwell man because someone else had riled him up.

Aubrey had every intention of disarming Nicky as gently as possible. Nicky's only intention seemed to be drawing blood.

"Nicky, it's me." She spoke quietly, raising empty hands. "It's Officer Aubrey." She needed to get him warm, get some food in him, let him rest. Only then did she stand a chance of learning about the man who had upset him.

"No, no, no." Nicky advanced again. "Leave me alone!"

"Let's go."

"No!" He screamed and advanced. Sunlight bounced off the blade and she shied away from the bright reflection. From the corner of her eye she caught a flash of movement and she braced for two attackers. Her reaction, her shift, must have been obvious to Nicky, who glanced over his shoulder.

Leo. Of course it was Leo. He took Nicky to the ground, but thanks to her, he'd lost the element of surprise.

She swore, no more than a bystander now as the men wrestled for control of the knife. It was her job to keep the peace, not let innocent people get hurt. Her shouted orders for them to stop went unheard. The urge to fire her weapon bubbled through her system, made her fingers twitch. They rolled around, kicking up the fresh snow to reveal the less than pristine condition of the alley. Slashes of muck and trash marred the blanket of white.

At last, Nicky lost his grip on the knife and she leaped into the fray, hauling him off Leo. She planted him hard on his butt in the snow. "Stop and settle down."

She crouched in front of him. Sad eyes full of remorse darted side to side, avoiding her gaze. Blood dripped from his nose and a scrape over his eyebrow. More blood seeped from a shallow wound on his hand. "Stop this right now. Nicky, it's me."

"Officer Aubrey?"

"Yes. I'm taking you in." She held up a hand when he started to protest.

"I'm sorry." Tears rolled down his cheeks. "I'm sorry. You can take the knife."

"That won't cut it this time, Nicky. You came at me with a weapon and attacked two other men. We need to get you warm and cleaned up so we can sort this out."

"I just want my sandwich." He reached for his nose, but she caught his hand before he poked at the bloody mess.

"I know." Behind her she heard Leo moving, his breaths caught somewhere between a pant and a hiss. When would he stop interfering? She was mentally writing him tickets for everything from jaywalking to obstruction.

"Jail? No, Officer Aubrey." Nicky cried harder. "I don't like jail."

"I know." She helped him to his feet. "Only until we can get you warm and fed." She had no intention of pressing serious charges against him, but she needed him steady enough to tell her about his interactions with Lara.

"I had to be in the shelter last night," Nicky pouted. "I don't like the indoors, Officer Aubrey."

"I know." The whining would increase, alternating

with apologies and demands. At least Calvin had radioed for backup. A patrol car was waiting on the street and she handed over Nicky and his knife. She checked inside the bag for any logo on the sandwich wrapper, but it was plain. "Make sure he gets to eat this." It wasn't standard practice, but it would help everyone involved if Nicky had some real food.

She toggled her radio to check on Calvin's current location and learned he'd caught the other man, had him at the precinct already. It should be a good thing, but Aubrey couldn't muster much enthusiasm in the moment.

Walking back into the alley, she was all set to deal harshly with Leo. Regardless of her unflagging belief in the goodness of people, she knew how to handle herself when things went sideways. It was her *job*. Civilian assistance wasn't required, despite the local press naming him a hero the other day.

"What were you thinking?" she said, staring down at him.

He tilted his head, peering up at her from where he sat in the snow, propped up against the wall. "I was thinking he had a knife and you weren't pulling your gun fast enough."

"When I use my service weapon is my decision. This wasn't finding a way to get civilians out of a building."

"No, it wasn't," he admitted.

"So why didn't you let me do my job?"

"Aubrey."

"You call me Officer Rawlins while I'm in uniform."

His gaze narrowed. "Fine. I was scared. I was thinking, Officer Rawlins, that I couldn't lose you." He dropped his head back to the brick and stared up at the sliver of sky overhead.

The bold declaration set her back and softened all the hard words she had lined up. "I can handle myself. Training, awareness, procedure. You know the value of those words."

"Uh-huh."

She extended her hand to help him up, but he didn't take it. "All you did was overcomplicate an edgy situation." His bomber jacket was smeared here and there with Nicky's blood and there was a long scratch on his face that needed cleaning.

"I think I did more than that." He looked down toward his midsection, where his hand was tucked under his coat.

She lifted the battered leather and saw the red stain blooming on his shirt. She swore all over again.

Chapter 8

Leo, having run out of defenses or excuses and more blood than he would part with voluntarily, was grateful when Aubrey stopped demanding an explanation. The pain in his side had increased with every breath, a sharp pinch that made him think the knife must still be inside him.

It wasn't. Of course it wasn't. He'd seen her hand that off.

Still, he didn't regret taking the blow. Better him than Aubrey and that man had been intent on hurting someone. Yes, as she repeatedly reminded him, she had the training and skill and the familiarity with the maniac. He'd been wrong to jump in, but he couldn't sit back and watch one more person he loved get hurt or die. If that made him some kind of throwback chauvinist, he'd work on fixing that character flaw later. When he could breathe again.

Her face had been a mix of temper and concern in the ambulance. The emergency room team had made her stay on the other side of the curtain while they cleaned the wound, stitched it up. The resulting fog was nice, but he couldn't figure out why it was taking so long to burn off.

The fight hadn't been intense or drawn out. Less than a minute, if he had to guess. Flashes of that knife coming down over her head played behind his eyelids. A grotesque nightmare he couldn't shake. He wasn't sure if Aubrey's mention of the knife-wielder seeing Lara was reality or painkiller-induced fantasy.

He shifted, his side protesting, but bearable. Handling scared and unhappy people, managing and defusing risky situations was Aubrey's job. She might be right that he'd had no right to intervene. He'd seen her in action, knew she could handle herself. Still…love.

Love.

That wasn't just the pain meds. That was real. Of course he'd fallen for Aubrey. Lara would tell him it was *because* the relationship couldn't go the distance. Different cities and demanding careers. He swiped away a wayward tear, hoping like hell he'd get to hear Lara deliver that lecture in person.

He was a fool on so many levels. A fool for thinking he could find Lara on his own or that she needed to be found at all? A fool for falling for Aubrey, although that went deeper than the knife. She was smart and brave in her work and beautiful and lovely off duty. The compassion ran through both facets of her life equally. Compassion for her neighborhood and the stubborn stranger who'd lumbered in and upset the flow.

Definitely a fool.

He should go back home, back to work and wait for Aubrey to call with an update. The insecurities from his childhood flooded through him. He'd been through enough counseling to know that feeling unlovable didn't make it true. But he kept making mistakes, this knife wound being the latest example. The ones that were too big to forgive crashed through his mind. Lara had been the only glimmer of acceptance he'd had from the time he was ten.

What did that make him if he couldn't live without his sister's presence? Not a whole person, clearly, since he'd hopped into bed with the first woman who demonstrated that heady combination of personal concern and sexual interest.

Maybe the fog was burning off after all, since the pity party was starting to annoy him. So he'd had a rough childhood. He was attracted to a cop who would probably never forgive him for taking a knife to the belly. And he was still the kind of fool who rushed in without thinking.

"Overcompensating to the end," he muttered, shying away from the light overhead.

"What was that?"

The voice belonged to Aubrey, and for a moment he thought he was hallucinating. She was sitting beside the bed, her fingers curled around his hand. He stared at their joined hands for a long time, expecting the vision to fade.

He turned his palm up, laced his fingers through hers. A warmth and comfort filled him when he finally accepted she was real. She was here. And she wasn't glaring at him. "You stayed?"

"Well, I went home to change clothes while they stitched you up."

"When can I get out of here?"

"I'd say you're on the right track. They knocked you out to clean the wound properly, considering where you were injured. Plus, they wanted to get in a round of antibiotics."

He followed her gaze to the IV taped to the back of his opposite hand. "I'm sorry for interfering."

"So you've said." Her lips curved into a reluctant smile. "In the ambulance and again about an hour ago. Twilight, they called it."

Great. "What else have I said?"

"Nothing juicy or helpful," she replied.

He wasn't sure if that should be a relief. "Why did you stay?"

Her smile turned weary. The affection in her eyes was shadowed by something he couldn't put a finger on. "You're a meddling-prone tourist in Philly. Someone has to keep tabs on you."

His bubble burst with her logic. He had no right to expect some declaration of love. They barely knew each other. "Thanks." He pulled his hand away to swipe at an itchy spot on his forehead. She caught him, stopped the motion.

"There's a cut at your hairline. Leave it be."

"Great."

She kissed his knuckles before resuming her seat and hope bloomed in his chest. The affectionate touch lifting away a layer of dread and frustration. "You should see the other guy," she quipped.

Leo hoped never to see the other guy again. "Is he all right?"

"He will be. Nicky gets riled easily when things aren't going according to his schedule." She caught her lip between her teeth and all Leo could think was how much he wanted to kiss her. He wasn't sure he'd ever get his fill of her.

That probably came with being emotionally broken. He should probably tell her the truth. In the interest of transparency. She should know enough to nudge him aside if he did something stupid and admit he loved her.

"Did I ever tell you why Lara and I are so close?"

"No," she replied.

"We shouldn't be. By rights she should hate me as much as my mom does."

Aubrey frowned, her brows pinched. "Your mom can't possibly hate you. Do you need another painkiller?"

If only there was something to take the sting out of what he had to say. "The drugs can't change the past. I need to tell you."

Her grip tightened on his hand. "It isn't necessary."

"You've gone above and beyond to find Lara. Even doing things you don't agree with."

"Leo."

"Just let me get this out." *Don't think, just talk.* If she heard the truth and stayed, then he could figure out what to do next. "I should have told you this earlier." Before they wound up in bed. "When I was ten years old my dad and grandpa took me camping. We did weekends like that all the time. This time, on the way home, there was a car accident. I was the only survivor."

There were the bare facts. Out in the open. He looked down to see Aubrey still held his hand.

Now for the rest of the story.

The sympathy in her eyes burned off the last of the fog blurring his senses. He didn't want pity. But what *did* he want?

Understanding. Acceptance. She couldn't give him either until she had a full picture and an explanation—not an excuse—for why he'd been such an idiot and generally upset the delicate balance in her neighborhood.

"We were a normal family until that day. My sister's first birthday party had been the weekend before. Presents, balloons, cake. The four of us were on the same team. Hugs. Jokes. Bedtime stories. Seven days later my mom was a widow." *Because of me.* "She never quite came out of it."

"Grief is tricky," she said. "We can talk about it later. I should let you rest."

"My sister grew up without a father because of me. Dad was driving, my grandpa next to him up front. I was bouncing around in the back. Chattering."

"Kids do that."

He hated the platitudes that cleared him and put the blame on his dad. "I distracted him and he went off the road. They died. I didn't."

Everything about Aubrey locked up, frozen in a horrible, dread-filled moment. She didn't blink. Her hand on his was still. He wasn't sure she was breathing.

"You were ten," she said at last.

And a part of him was stuck back there, trapped in that wreckage, unable to move on. "But I haven't learned a damn thing. Haven't changed. I nearly got you killed, too." Just like the car accident. He'd distracted his father and then they were careening off the road. Tumbling, rolling. Glass shattered, metal screeched against trees, crumpling more with every impact.

"You're wrong about that, about today. Nicky causes his own trouble. I was ready for him to act out." She released his hand, spreading her arms wide. "Look at me, Leo. I'm fine."

When her hands wrapped around his again, the tension in his chest eased. "I'm sorry, Aubrey."

"You've apologized enough. We can talk about it more when you're feeling better. Hospitals make everything look worse. Whatever happened when you were a kid wasn't your fault, either."

"I survived." Just in case she hadn't noticed. "That was the real crime in my mom's eyes. I've never understood why Lara doesn't hate me, too, but she never has."

"She doesn't hate you because you're a good brother."

"She's never once shown an ounce of resentment," he continued. "We had a great dad and when he was alive we had a better mom. Maybe dropping out of college, refusing to talk to me, is just her way of finally writing me off, too."

"Hush. I don't believe that and you can't think that way." Aubrey hugged his hand with both of hers. "You're hurting, Leo. Emotions run high at times like this."

He'd been hurting for almost two decades and his emotions were usually low to absent. Except for Lara. He should've told Aubrey about this earlier. Before they'd slept together. She had a right to know the kind of man he was. "Lara's the only person who's ever stuck by me. I just thought you needed to know the whole story."

She stared at him, an unfathomable expression in those big blue eyes. Only waiting for her to say something did he understand why he'd bared his soul. He expected her to walk away. If it was inevitable, he needed her to do it now. Before he tumbled completely into love as deep and terrifying as that ravine had been.

He didn't trust love to last, to ever be enough, unless it was Lara. Loving his father and grandpa hadn't been enough to keep them alive until help arrived. Loving his mother had backfired time and again. He dated and fell into deep like, never trusting himself to go further.

Aubrey was the first woman who made him wish he could give more. Only his sister accepted him despite his history of errors. Whatever he offered to Aubrey would be a shadow of what she deserved.

"Family is important," she said. "Whatever the story." She leaned down and kissed his forehead. "Thanks for telling me."

The curtain swept open and a nurse walked in with his discharge orders. Behind her was Aubrey's partner, Calvin.

The cop did a double take and his gaze went unerringly to their linked hands. She let go in a hurry. One second he and Aubrey were connected and the next she might as well have been on the opposite side of the country. The sudden distance rattled him, annoyed him more than a little, even if it was practical. Clearly, she didn't want to advertise that there was something between them.

The observation slapped another layer of shame and irritation on the whole mess. Aubrey had gone above and beyond, despite his screwing up right and left, getting in her way.

"I thought you went home," Calvin said.

She plucked at her casual sweatshirt. "I did."

"Okay. The sergeant sent me over to see if our victim's pressing charges."

"I'm not," Leo said. "It was as much my fault as his. Officer Rawlins told me the man was struggling after all the extra precautions with the storm. Seems I added to it."

Calvin made a humming sound while the nurse removed the IV. "That's a compassionate outlook." He tilted his head toward Aubrey. "Isn't it?"

She shocked Leo by taking his hand once more. "I think so."

"Is this your decision, Mr. Butler?" he asked, his eyebrows arching.

Aubrey sucked in a breath. "How dare you?"

"You know I have to ask," he said, pointing to their joined hands.

She closed her eyes. "Yeah. I get it."

"So do I," Calvin murmured. With a jerk of his head, he demanded Aubrey join him away from Leo's bed.

With the nurse rattling off discharge instructions, he couldn't hear any part of the conversation. The way Leo kept screwing up, Aubrey's partner probably didn't want him to hear any bad news or catch wind of a lead.

Aubrey hated leaving Leo alone even for a few minutes after he'd shared such a heartbreaking history, but she had to catch up with Calvin. "Hang on a second. What did Nicky say?"

"He ate his sandwich and talked nonsense."

"Then what about the guy you chased down?"

Calvin shook his head and kept walking. "Dead end."

She didn't believe him. Aubrey hustled to get in front

of him and cut him off. "Calvin," she said. "You're stone-walling me."

He nodded.

"Why?" Habitual rosy outlook or not, she knew her job.

"Why won't you or your new friend press charges?" he countered. "At the very least, it'd do Nicky some good to be off the street."

Food, warmth and shelter aside, Nicky would be miserable behind bars. "He identified Lara Butler as the person he calls New Girl."

Calvin swore. "And you think Nicky can lead you to Lara."

"It crossed my mind." She glanced around, made sure no one was watching too closely. "I don't have a better idea, and anything that will reunite the Butlers is a good thing."

"You sure about that?"

"I am." Leo wanted to see his sister safe with his own two eyes. Only then would he be able to understand what Lara was doing and that she was, hopefully, being safe about it.

Leo's admission about the past put every reckless thing he'd done in a new light. Her heart ached for him as a child, bearing an impossible guilt, and for him as a man, uncertain of his worthiness. Yes, she cared for him, more than was wise considering she didn't know if he would ever move on and be open to being loved by someone else. By her.

"Maybe the sister has good reason to ditch the brother," Calvin said.

Outrage blasted through her, leaving her hands hot, her teeth clenched. "What are you implying?"

Calvin hadn't missed any facet of her reaction. "That right there, Aubrey." He did everything but drill a finger into her chest. "You're too involved," he accused. "After Neil, you know better than anyone people aren't always what they seem."

The hot blast iced over. Never before had Calvin slapped her in the face with that lapse in judgment. It hurt, badly, but she'd have to deal with it later. "There's no reason to suspect Mr. Butler is anything but a worried brother. Nicky gave me the impression Miss Butler is close. Tell me why you would ignore our best lead on a missing person case."

"You stayed with Butler at the hotel last night. In his room?"

He was fishing. Had to be. Still, she couldn't muster a reply. This entire conversation was out of character for the partner she relied on. She hadn't done anything wrong. Tiptoeing along that line, maybe, but it was hard to regret her night with Leo.

"What is going on?" she asked when she trusted her voice again.

He stepped back from her and closed his eyes, one hand pressed to his mouth. When he met her gaze again, she saw frustration and sympathy on his face, in his eyes. "Check your phone."

She pulled her cell from her pocket and frowned at the icons indicating a missed call and a voice message from their captain.

"You're suspended," he whispered. "I'm sorry, Aubrey. I tried to head it off."

The floor seemed to tilt under her feet. She slumped against the wall. "Why?"

"Conduct unbecoming," Calvin answered.

Who would've reported that? Why? "I—I don't understand."

He reached out and gave her shoulders a gentle shake. "It's bull, Aubrey. Listen to the message, talk to the captain. Hulbert and I are doing what we can to find out where the report came from."

"And Lara?"

"Did you hear me?"

"Yes." She pressed a hand to her throat, swallowing back the wave of tears that wanted to fall. There was no room for crying here. Not over this. "Who will work Lara's case?"

"Guess that's me."

Her thoughts were jumbled, her mind spinning. None of this made any sense. Temper simmering, she straightened her spine. Her past mistake could not blow back on Leo and Lara. She couldn't allow this to wreck their first solid lead.

"I need to get Leo back to the hotel," she said.

Calvin muttered a quick count to ten. "You have to stay away from him if you value your career," he said. "Let Sullivan help him."

She stepped in close. "I haven't done a damn thing wrong," she said. "And I won't allow some rumor or witch hunt or whatever to stop me from continuing to do good work."

Calvin walked out and Aubrey sent Grant a series of text messages about everything since she'd run across Nicky and the other man in the alley. It was the only way to ensure the search for Lara continued in earnest while Leo recuperated and she was shut out of the precinct.

Once Leo was settled in his hotel room and she'd ordered a light dinner of soup for him, Aubrey stepped out to listen to the captain's message. It was an order to come in immediately to turn in her badge and gun.

After quickly promising Leo that she'd be back, she walked over to the precinct. Even without the heads-up from Calvin, Sergeant Hulbert's grim expression when she walked in was plenty of warning.

"Any advice?" she asked as he called the captain's office.

Her burly friend only shrugged a shoulder. "I just work here."

She snorted. They both knew he was the heart and soul around here. The brains, too, more often than not. "If you call this work, I'll take it," she said, following the pattern of their old joke.

"Careful," he teased. "I only make it look easy. Go on."

Directed to enter Captain Yancey's office, Aubrey was surprised to find she wasn't the only guest. Another man, wearing a dark suit, held his camel-colored wool coat folded perfectly over his arm. He struck her as a well-dressed shark. It took her a moment to recognize the predatory gleam in his eyes. The leather coat was gone and his hair was styled back from his face, without the assistance of any product. This was the man from Pomeroy's. The man who'd set off Nicky.

Was he an attorney, an investigator, or a new addition to IA? She didn't trust him on sight. Had he been following her? Is this why Calvin called him a dead end? She was left wondering as Captain Yancey began without making any introductions. "Officer Rawlins, as I said in my phone message, it's come to my attention that you've exhibited conduct unbecoming of a Philadelphia police officer."

She had to stand here and endure this while a stranger looked on? "I beg your pardon?"

"You are hereby suspended for one week," Captain Yancey said with quiet authority. "Please hand over your badge and service weapon."

Aubrey hesitated, eyes locked with her captain's. Yancey had been held up as a shining example of women in law enforcement when Aubrey had been in the police academy. She was known to be stern, but fair and she'd assumed the role of captain for this precinct a year after the debacle with Aubrey's drug-dealing ex.

The captain tapped her desktop. "Now, Officer Rawlins, or I'll make it two weeks."

"I'll comply," Aubrey assured her. "May I ask for clarification about the source of this complaint? I'm sure there's been a misunderstanding."

"It's no misunderstanding, Ms. Rawlins," the stranger said. "A complaint was filed and corroborated with video evidence from surveillance cameras in the city."

"And you are?" she demanded.

"My name isn't your concern," the man sneered. "I represent the person who is unhappy with your inappropriate behavior."

"Aubrey," the captain interjected. "I've read the complaint and I've reviewed the evidence." The expression on her face could only be described as pained. "I advise you to discuss this situation *only* with your union rep. We don't want any negative publicity to undermine your future with the PPD."

"Captain?"

"This isn't a decision I came to lightly," she said.

"Who are you?" Aubrey asked the stranger again. She was tempted to rattle off where she'd seen the man and his differing appearance at that time, but her survival instinct kicked in. A little. "Why are you allowed to be part of this meeting?"

"I'm the person sent to see this suspension is carried out properly and without delay," he replied.

The captain's eyes narrowed at his statement. What kind of pull did he have? "I have rights," she protested. And she knew them well after her past fiasco. "I'd like to know precisely what behavior has been red-flagged and corroborated." After Neil and before she'd met Leo, she led the most boring personal life imaginable.

"Again, your union rep can be of assistance," Yancey said. "Because of the unfortunate precedent in your record, your suspension is effective immediately."

"With pay?" Aubrey queried, just to prolong the farce.

"Another question your rep can assist you with."

"Who do you work for?" she asked the stranger.

"That's not your concern," he repeated.

"Ma'am, I formally object to this suspension."

"Duly noted and I understand," she added unexpectedly. "Your badge and service weapon, please."

Again, she considered admitting she recognized the man from previous encounters in the neighborhood, but she would tell the union rep. Her captain seemed as uneasy as Aubrey felt. Stifling her protests, she handed over her badge and gun.

"We'll see you in seven days, Officer Rawlins."

"Yes, Captain." She'd be back sooner if she could get to the bottom of this. The shock of the moment combined with the overwhelming despair made her reckless. "Ma'am, I have a right to know who filed this complaint and submitted the video evidence."

The stranger opened his mouth, but the captain stood

up, cutting him off. "Your suspension originated at the top of the food chain." Her precise enunciation was razor sharp and the look she leveled at Aubrey was a warning to stop arguing. "You're dismissed."

Aubrey left the precinct feeling numb and disconnected. It was as if she'd been trapped in an impenetrable bubble, unable to interact or engage with anyone. If this had come from *the top of the food chain* she didn't want anyone else to get in trouble by associating with her or showing support.

If only she knew who wanted her out of here.

She walked, or more accurately, stomped, through the snow to her apartment. Once behind closed doors, she dropped into the nearest chair and let the tears fall for a few minutes. A week off sounded nice when a vacation was in the offing. A suspension wasn't the same thing at all.

She looked up her union rep and made the call, left a message.

Next, she sent a text to Leo to check in. His reply came almost instantly, assuring her he was doing fine. Would he feel the same way when the pain meds wore off in another hour? She should follow Calvin's advice and stay away from Leo. Stay away from Lara's case.

Looking around her apartment, she'd be stir-crazy by noon tomorrow. Home was a haven, after her shifts. She loved the action of being a cop, keeping an eye on the people who lived and worked within her precinct.

Being seen with Leo must have been the catalyst for the captain's hasty—*forced*—move. She couldn't think of any other instance that could be considered inappropriate. The idea took root, wouldn't let go. They'd been seen together at Pomeroy's by the same man who'd crashed her suspension meeting. Though she hadn't done anything wrong while talking Nicky down earlier today, the annoying stranger had been involved in that incident. The coincidences made her skin prickle. It would be interesting what the union rep shared with her when they connected.

Seven days. She could search for Lara, carefully. She could monitor Leo's recovery and make sure he didn't do too much too soon. She sure couldn't sit around here and mope. In her bedroom, she pulled out a suitcase and started tossing clothing and necessities inside. Staying here was predictable and safe and she was done with that.

Odds were good Leo would let her stay over again tonight, if only because the painkillers muddled his thinking. Tomorrow, if necessary, she'd find a different place to crash. In the meantime, she planned to pick this apart until she understood who wanted her out of the precinct.

Who could wield the authority to take her off the job? And why? She wasn't working on anything significant. Maybe that was the problem. Getting absorbed by Leo's search for Lara must have interfered with some case that needed to be solved for one of Philly's wealthy or influential citizens.

The closest she'd come to a victim in that demographic was Tina, whose in-laws had commended her and Leo sincerely. Bought them dinner. Had someone found out and deemed *that* inappropriate behavior? That had been completely out of her control.

For the life of her she couldn't put another case into that category. Following Yancey's example as a cop, Aubrey made a habit of knowing what was going on in her precinct at all times. Down to where the homeless camped and which bars had slacked off on the ID checks.

They hadn't had big trouble in her precinct for months. So why would anyone high up the ladder care where she spent her personal time?

Visiting Leo's hotel and having dinner with him across town were the only places she'd been that intersected with the type of people who had the clout to get her suspended so quickly.

Of course, that still left her wondering why anyone other than Leo cared where she spent the night. Police officers were allowed to have lives, even messy ones. So why come at her this hard?

Chapter 9

Though the limits of recovery frustrated him, Leo behaved himself for the first forty-eight hours, staying in the hotel room while Aubrey went out and searched for Lara. At first, he'd thought she was only being kind and using her time off, but when she told him about the suspension, it was a no-brainer to have her stay with him.

He owed her for everything she'd done with Lara's case. And the list kept growing. More important, he enjoyed her company. Somehow, she kept him from feeling useless while he recovered. She gave him hope. For Lara and for himself.

To help, he continued reaching out to the people Lara had been close to, keeping an eye on her bank records and doing whatever he could remotely. That included daily conversations with Grant. Though she might not admit it, Aubrey needed someone other than her union rep working on the cause of her suspension.

Leo honored Aubrey's request not to discuss her situation, but he didn't like the timing of Aubrey's dismissal. Grant had agreed with him. Just when she'd found breadcrumbs that might lead to Lara, she'd been slapped with claims of unbecoming conduct. Though he didn't have the answers yet, he was determined to find a way to help Aubrey beat the suspension.

As he regained his strength, he ventured farther from the room. The day he walked around the block, with Aubrey's supervision, he might as well have won a gold medal. Back in the room, before she headed out to check the area around the tracks again, he promised to take her to the hotel restaurant to celebrate.

There was no need to dress up the way they had the night after the robbery, but she looked gorgeous in a ruby-red sweater that hugged her curves, black slacks and heels that put a kick in his pulse.

"I'm almost out of vacation time," Leo said over a pasta dinner loaded with roasted chicken and vegetables. "Unless I take a leave of absence."

"You can do that?"

"It's possible." He felt trapped, staying in Philly, and he felt like a quitter when he wanted to return to Cincinnati.

"When we find Lara, what will you do?" she asked.

"Take her home." He sipped his water. "With luck, and time, I'll get some answers."

"Have you heard anything from Grant?" she asked.

Her casual tone set off a warning in his head. They avoided the topic of Grant's assistance, even though she wasn't officially bound to the PPD this week. He planned to better respect that boundary.

"Nothing more than I shared earlier." He set down his fork. "I don't understand how Lara continues to evade everyone except the people she wants to see."

"Your sister is smart. We're looking for an idealistic, fresh-faced college girl," Aubrey said thoughtfully. "But if she looked like one, the homeless community would write her off."

Leo bit back the curse. "Am I the only person who hasn't thought of that?"

"It's the only explanation that makes sense to me." She lowered her voice. "We know she's here. We have a handle on the area where she's working. I'm trying to convince people we don't want to interfere, just chat."

He studied her face. "What good deeds did you hear about this afternoon?"

Aubrey grinned. "A food truck delivered leftovers that would normally be trashed to a camp down by the river yesterday."

He was proud of his sister. "Maybe I should just leave her to it." For days now he'd been trying to connect Lara's extreme decisions and helpful acts with Aubrey's trouble. Who could be threatened by either or both women? "The paper had an article today on housing solutions. Councilman Keller is proposing temporary tiny homes, supervised by social workers and police, of course."

"Of course." Aubrey swirled her pasta through sauce. "Since he first suggested it, everyone at the precinct argues about whether or not that makes anything better in the long-term."

"What do you think?" he asked.

"Keller is a developer by trade. A good one," she added quickly.

"But it still feels sticky to you?"

"That's a great word. And yes, a little," she admitted, setting down her fork. "The plan probably comes from the right place. There will always be stragglers, but the idea could be effective."

Leo craved another bite, but he was stuffed already. He'd ask for a to-go box and take it back up to the room. "Life isn't perfect. Some people will always struggle, either by their choices or decisions made by others."

"The key will be getting everyone onto the right page," she said.

"Meaning?"

"Programs like Keller's proposition need a clear goal and a timeline. Otherwise, the rest of us are out here chasing our tails or cleaning up unintended consequences. Keller campaigned on big promises about safety and cleanup. Resolving the homeless situation should be about the people, not just the curb appeal."

She made an excellent point. "Lara volunteered for a couple street cleanups. Not people, but trash and graffiti. She sent me pictures."

"You never mentioned that. Can I see them?"

"It was her freshman year," he said. "I didn't think it was relevant."

"Do you have the pictures?" she asked. "It might spark another place for me to look. She's staying somewhere nearby, but I have yet to find her."

"Sure. They are all backed up on the cloud on my laptop."

She looked at his plate, then raked those eyes over him. "Are you full?"

"I was going to take the leftovers upstairs."

"That works," she said.

By the time they reached the room, there was a sizzle in his veins that had nothing to do with new ideas of where to look for his sister. He was eager to be close to Aubrey. Since the stabbing, she treated him with kid gloves, giving him space to heal and time to think. There had been kisses, but far more rest, even though they were sharing a bed. His body was starting to demand more.

When they were shoulder to shoulder at his computer, he breathed her in, steadied as always by her presence. He was going to miss her when he returned to Cincinnati. Would she come with him if he asked? The idea of inviting her to move surged to the front of his mind. This city was in her blood, he knew that, could see it in her eyes whenever she spoke of her career or her personal interests.

He couldn't help believing she shared the depth of feeling he had for her. She'd stuck around after he shared the worst skeleton in his closet. That had to mean something. He hadn't said the *L*-word—it was way too soon for that declaration—but he was trying to show her in every moment.

His sister smiled at them from pictures with friends at events around campus and elsewhere. The floodgates opened as he shared what he remembered with Aubrey. It was startling to see the transformation through her two and a half years of college in Philly. "She really has changed," he said, scrolling back to the most recent pictures.

"Can you go back to that first cleanup day?" Aubrey asked. She clicked on the picture and zoomed in, studying the background.

Leo was consumed with how happy and carefree his sister appeared, surrounded by friends in her old jeans and new college sweatshirt. Behind the group the trees blazed with autumn color.

"You're lucky," Aubrey said. "Who she is doesn't seem to have changed a bit."

He should probably take comfort in that and trust his sister to reach out when she was ready. It just wasn't that easy, not the way things had unraveled. There was something at play he couldn't see, something that kept Lara from giving him the reassurance she had to know he needed.

"Big heart," he said. Leo reached for Aubrey's free hand. "I am lucky to be her brother." Catching her chin, he turned her face and rubbed his nose against hers. "Luckier still to have found you."

"Leo."

He wanted her, without his missing sister monopolizing their thoughts. He stood and tugged her along with him. "The first impression wasn't my best, but the rest of it…" His voice trailed off as he pushed a hand into her hair and brought her mouth to his.

She slid her hands over the nape of his neck, her fingers sifting through his hair.

"Be with me tonight." He skimmed his lips along the warm, silky column of her throat. "No research, no worries. Just you and me." His hand trailed over her waist, over her hip, under the hem of that bold sweater.

"You're sure we won't do more damage?" She traced the line of his shoulders, his biceps.

"Not a chance," he promised.

"You swear you'll stop if it's too much."

"Not a chance," he repeated, pulling her hips into his.

She laughed, the sultry sound music to his ears as they moved toward the bed.

This woman was one of a kind. He'd trusted her with everything, past and present. Being that open with her scared him as much as it thrilled him. He gave her all the tenderness she stirred in him, and with her body wrapped tightly around his, he knew she was where he was meant to be.

Aubrey drifted on a cloud of satisfaction. He was definitely feeling better and he made her feel incredible right down to her soul. She should be delighted, giddy even, but she knew it couldn't last. With Leo she felt beautiful and strong, able to find a balance between her sunny view of the world and the reality. Just being near him, she experienced a joyful sense of belonging. It was like coming home.

Curled beside him, she rested her palm over his heart as hers slowly returned to a normal rhythm. He kissed her hair and she'd never felt so cherished.

"I love you," he whispered, his fingertips caressing her shoulder.

For a moment everything inside her froze. He couldn't mean it. Then her heart erupted into an ecstatic flutter. She loved him, too, but the words were locked behind some kind of haze in her mind. She could see them, but couldn't get them out into the open.

Better if she didn't reply. What sort of future could they have, even if Lara was found? Long-distance relationships were filled with pitfalls. She wanted to believe he meant it. Desperately wanted to cling to the gift he'd given her.

Love is enough.

Where had she heard that? Not on the job. Love definitely had not been enough to keep her ex from doing something stupid. Had that really been love?

Snuggling closer, she realized that old relationship had been nothing more than a bad impersonation of the real thing. Love could be enough. For now. Did it matter if they had days or years ahead of them? This time, just the two of them together, was priceless. If they never had more than this, she knew she'd never settle for anything less than real again.

She pressed a kiss to the warm skin of his chest, wrapped a leg around his and hoped he could feel the words she couldn't speak.

Leo didn't press her for a response, though he had to know she was awake. He continued to hold her, trailing his fingers over her bare skin as if he couldn't get enough. Maybe she was as hard as Neil had claimed. Too much cop, not enough compassion. Only hours before she'd dragged his drug-dealing butt into the precinct in cuffs, he'd told her he loved her.

She hadn't responded to the false declaration then; why couldn't she be honest with herself and Leo now? He'd shared his worst personal moments and he deserved equal openness from her. "I really should explain."

"Shh." He tipped up her chin and kissed her. Sweet, soft. "No need."

Oh, there was every need. She wriggled to sit up, tucking the sheet under her arms. "There's one more factor that contributed to the suspension."

He rolled to his side, eyes intent on her.

She swallowed. "A few years ago my boyfriend was dealing drugs. Practically right under my nose. I knew he smoked weed with his pals on the weekend, but I overlooked it. When I caught him dealing harder stuff, I hauled him straight to the precinct."

He arched an eyebrow, didn't say a word.

"Internal Affairs went through my life with a flea comb, looking for dirt. They still do periodically."

He frowned, immediately leaping to her defense. "That's not fair."

"Maybe not, but it still happens, due to my overly trusting nature. I have a rep around the precinct for seeing the best of people, rather than the cold, hard truth."

"Then they need glasses. You're the best cop, the most dedicated, I've ever seen in action."

She started to giggle and couldn't stop.

"What's so funny?"

"A few of the cops I work with gave me rose-colored sunglasses as a gag gift," she said when she'd caught her breath. She leaned over and kissed him. "And you might be a little biased."

"Maybe," he allowed, holding his thumb and finger about a half inch apart.

The quiet was gentle, easy, and she rested there, thinking about how to help Leo and his sister. The light glinted on the golden hair dusting his torso. Her hands tingled, recalling the heat and texture of him. She watched, fascinated as the honed muscles in his arm bunched when he pushed a hand through his hair. He really couldn't be still unless he was asleep.

"You're smiling," he said, his knuckles grazing her cheekbone. "Why?"

She thought the top reasons were pretty obvious, considering where they were. "Your sister has good intentions, I'm sure of it."

Leo grunted. "You don't even know her, but you're right."

Aubrey felt like she did know her, though, after everything she'd learned from him and her interviews with people Lara interacted with as a volunteer. She wondered if Leo's plans to take Lara home would work. "What does she plan to do with her poli-sci degree?"

"Assuming she finishes that degree, her plan was to 'make a difference.'" He used air quotes. "Politics might have been in her long-term plans. She'd done an internship with one of the political analysis firms last summer and she enjoyed it. As you've learned, she really likes being in the thick of things. If Lara had her way, she would split her time between teaching at the high school or college level and charity work."

She'd come to a similar conclusion after her last conversation with Professor Whitten. "Tough road," Aubrey murmured. "But you said Lara has a knack for looking at the good in people."

"Yes, she does. Maybe I'll get her a pair of rose-colored glasses."

Aubrey rolled her eyes. "She'll take it as a compliment."

"Like you did?"

He was massaging the tension from her palm, tension she didn't even know she carried. Better to keep things light, to remember this was supposed to be about the two of them. "Exactly."

"You're in a similar, draining job situation with the PPD. Is there any sage advice I should try to impart when I do see Lara again?"

Aubrey took her time, wanting to give him the right words. "Dealing with the public can be stressful," she

said. "Balance is my advice. Charity work can be draining. Teaching can be draining," she replied. "If your sister's goal is to do both, I hope she finds enough reward
in one endeavor to recharge and keep her energized for
the other."

"How do you find balance, Aubrey?"

He was completely focused on her again. For a moment she simply enjoyed the heady sensation. "Well, not
every day is a good one, but I like to focus on the good
people I meet every day."

"Like me," he teased.

She took his face in her hands. "Just like you."

He smiled. "What happened to your ex?"

"He went to jail." She anticipated the next question.
"I handled everything up front and by the book, but the
PPD doesn't want another scandal. By getting personally involved with you, a man tied to an open case, I
make them twitchy."

"What do you want?" He stroked her arm, elbow to
wrist and back again.

"I want to find your sister so you can get some peace.
Then I want to get back on the job. I don't know what I'd
do without the PPD and my normal beat. It's who I am."

"Why?"

"Why did I become a cop?" She chewed on her lip
when he nodded. His touch lit fires, soothed them, lit
more. The story just flowed right out of her. "My friends
and I were mugged outside a movie theater back in high
school. The cops who intervened were an inspiration to
me." It sounded corny, but it was the simple truth.

"Did they catch the mugger?" He scooted closer and
kissed the back of her hand, her fingertips.

"Yes," she murmured. "I testified," she added, her

voice quaking more from his touch than the memories. "One of my friends is agoraphobic now. We do movies at her place."

He kissed her with so much tenderness she thought she'd fly apart.

"Then that's what we'll do." His embrace kept her grounded.

"What do you mean?" She was breathless from the magic of his mouth.

"We'll find Lara *and* get you back on the job." He kissed her again, sparking fresh need through her body. "And we'll start first thing tomorrow."

Chapter 10

The next morning Leo poured himself another cup of coffee and turned off the television. The morning news wasn't giving him anything helpful. He checked in at the airport in Cincinnati, assuring them he would be back on the job soon. They all sent their concerns and hopes that Lara would be found.

Last night, in Aubrey's embrace, was the first time he'd felt remotely like himself since the stabbing. He'd meant what he'd said about finding Lara and clearing Aubrey's name within the PPD. There was a way to do both.

Analysis was his strong suit, though he usually applied himself to business interests. Operations and logistics at the airport were far easier to figure out than emotions and personal motivations. But Aubrey was special, to him as well as countless other people. Seeing her in action around the neighborhood proved that.

He loved her and he acknowledged that factor played into his decisions. That didn't mean it hampered his ability or limited his choices. Yes, it would've been cleaner if he'd met her in Cincinnati or under better circumstances here in Philly. He would've preferred it if discovering all the good stuff about her and about being *with* her wasn't also tied up in the mess with Lara's disappearance.

Still, he didn't regret telling her how he felt. He didn't even mind that she hadn't given him the words back. One of his therapists had told him love was always better shared than hidden away. He hadn't expected her to reply in kind; hadn't expected much of anything really. What he'd received instead was the gift of her trust as she shared the story of her ex. Although things were somewhat unsettled emotionally, her affection for him was clear and knowing she trusted him, experiencing her sincere care and concern, eased his mind and his heart.

If she wanted back on the PPD, despite the way they doubted and treated her, he'd help make that happen, even if it meant he couldn't be with her in the long run. It would be worth it to know she was happy.

At last, his cell phone rang. Seeing Grant's name on the screen, he answered immediately.

"I have a lead on Lara," Grant said, wasting no time on the pleasantries.

Leo did a double take. He'd expected news about Aubrey's situation. "Good. Good," he repeated, mentally shifting gears. "Where is she?"

"It's more about where we expect her to show up," Grant said cryptically. "I just left Professor Whitten's office."

"I *knew* that jerk was involved," Leo snarled. "What did he say?"

"He wasn't eager to cooperate, but he did admit he's storing her belongings. Free of charge. Also, he meets with her every week in a park near the campus."

Leo swore. He imagined breaking up the weekly meeting by teaching Lara's professor a lesson or two in common sense, but this wasn't the time for that daydream. "Tell me where and when."

"It might not be that easy," Grant continued. "He promised Lara hefty research credit for doing this. Her job is to gather in-depth, firsthand experience with the homeless population and hand over real-time statistics to verify the city's claims about assistance."

"In winter," Leo grumbled and pinched the bridge of his nose. That was his sister all the way. How many times had she declared that accountability was the only way to make real change?

"I had the same thought. He claims he'll put her name first on the paper," Grant said, his voice loaded with sarcasm.

"What a stand-up guy." Leo tapped his foot, eager to get out there and save his sister from her warped mentor. "My sister's out there risking her life for his glory. Rosie at the soup kitchen told us from the start Lara was a good girl trying to help."

"That's the picture everyone is painting," Grant confirmed.

Leo walked to the window. "Are you suggesting we leave her to it?"

"No," Grant said quickly. "The professor came clean because Lara missed her last meeting. In light of Aubrey's suspension, I think the sooner we bring Lara in, the better. My gut tells me something bigger is in play."

"Mine, too." The new information worried him that

someone didn't want Lara's firsthand reports going public. Odds were good it was the same someone who didn't want Aubrey to find Lara.

"Do you have someone watching the park?" Leo asked.

"I do. I've sent this information to Aubrey, as well. I think it's best if you stay out of it. The professor is convinced she's committed to seeing this project through."

"And if she sees me, she'll bolt?"

"That's my fear," Grant said.

"With good reason," Leo admitted, trying to be objective. "I'm all kinds of overprotective. She knows that and she damn well should've told me or sent me a convincing message."

Grant chuckled. "So she brought this search on herself?"

"Let's go with that, sure. It makes me sound less like a helicopter parent."

"Family is important," Grant said. "If my sister did something like this, I'd be pulling my hair out, too."

"I'm not good at waiting," he said. "Let me know the minute you have something, please." He wasn't happy about sitting back, but if it increased their chances of getting Lara back safe, he'd do it.

"Hang in there," Grant said. "I have a couple people headed that way," Grant said. "Aubrey will be in place, too. When Lara shows up, they'll bring her in so we can hash this out."

"Is there a scenario that gives me ten minutes alone with Whitten?"

Grant chuckled. "One more reason for you to sit tight. You've had enough run-ins with the law since you rolled into town."

Leo could only be grateful Aubrey had answered that initial call at the Good Samaritan. With nothing better to do, Leo searched for more information on Professor Whitten. His classes, his publications and everything else he could find. When he crossed paths with that man again, he wasn't going to leave anything unsaid. Or undone.

Thanks to the information Grant had gained from Whitten, Aubrey was in position, monitoring the park near the college campus. Fifteen minutes ago, she'd watched the professor cut through the park on his way to and from a coffee shop on the corner.

Aubrey had been sorely tempted to dump his coffee over his head. If anything happened to Lara, Leo would blame the professor, and rightly so.

Aubrey wasn't sure which of the other people in the park were connected to Grant, only that the three mothers with toddlers building a snow fort weren't Lara. It helped to know there were more eyes than hers watching for Lara. She'd specifically asked not to be told which people were from the Escape Club and she appreciated that Grant respected her wishes. If he'd found the request petty, he didn't say so. She just couldn't risk another smudge on her PPD service record.

She raised her camera, aiming at the building across the street. Framing a particularly lovely roofline outlined by icicles gleaming in the sunlight, she took the shots, then checked the display. Not bad, though she didn't entertain any illusion that this could be a fall-back job. Photography was the simplest excuse for being here alone and she did her best to look like an artist rather than a cop without a beat.

Lara entered the park and Aubrey caught herself staring. She wasn't sure how she recognized Leo's sister in the stained coat and battered hat. It was the confident stride, she decided, as Lara marched forward and dusted snow off a bench and sat down.

It was all Aubrey could do to hang back and watch. Where was Whitten now that Lara was here to report in? Warm in his office, no doubt, Aubrey thought darkly.

Walking away from Lara's position, she sent a text message to Grant, in case it made any difference to his team. Along the way, she snapped a few pictures of Leo's sister, just to give others an idea of how Lara was dressed now. She circled the perimeter, focused on the ice-covered ironwork around a sculpture, and then knelt down to get a curious angle of trees and sky.

Standing, she realized Whitten's office overlooked the park. He had a good view of Lara, should he choose to look.

"Ms. Rawlins. How nice to see you enjoying your time off."

The voice raised the hair on the back of her neck. She swiveled around to see the man who'd crashed her meeting with the captain. "Again, I'm at a disadvantage. What's your name?"

"None of your business." He'd shed the suit and classy overcoat for the black leather coat he'd worn the first times she'd seen him.

"You're making it my business," Aubrey said. "In fact, I'm thinking of filing a complaint."

"You go right ahead, sweetheart."

She couldn't see his eyes behind the mirrored sunglasses. Still, she noticed when his attention shifted to a point behind her. He'd spotted Lara. He tried to shove by her, but Aubrey blocked his path, pretending to slip on a patch of ice and dragging the big man down with her.

His knee hit the walkway with a loud crack and he let out a string of curses that had the mothers covering tiny ears and reeling kids in close.

Smart. This man's an animal.

He scrambled to his feet and Aubrey managed to trip him again. With a violent shout, he gained his feet and caught her by the collar. He shook her, hard. She fought back, but she couldn't get the right angle. She might as well have been a gnat.

One of the mothers ran toward them, shouting about 911, her phone raised. Aubrey tried to wave her off. If Mr. Nameless hurt a bystander, Aubrey would never forgive herself. The man tossed her back on her butt and ran off. When she looked over, Lara was gone. That had been their best chance to reunite the Butler siblings and she'd blown it.

Picking herself up, Aubrey gave her assurances to the woman who'd rushed in, a pretty redhead named Kenzie, who was doing a favor for Grant between shifts with the fire department. They'd lost Lara, thanks to her. She sent a text message to Grant and started back to the hotel to confess her blunder to Leo.

He met her in the lobby and pulled her into a hug. "It's okay."

"It isn't. She was there, and then she was gone."

"And where would she be if you hadn't dealt with the creep eyeing her?"

She started to ask, but she knew the answer. "Grant filled you in."

"Better, he sent me pictures." Leo kept his arm around her as they walked to the elevator. "Lara looks like a mess, which she should under the circumstances, but she isn't hurt."

And she might well have been. "This guy in the black jacket keeps showing up," Aubrey said. He had been intent on reaching Lara. "We need to figure out his connection to your sister."

"We will," Leo promised. "We're closer, thanks to you."

The praise didn't sit right. Lara was clearly in trouble and who knew what she would do now that the meeting place was compromised. "Leo, I'm so sorry," she said again when they were back inside the room.

"It's fine," he replied, though she didn't see how it could be. "You didn't let that jerk anywhere near her. That means more than you know."

She appreciated his vote of confidence, but nothing would ease the strain around his eyes and mouth until they found his sister. She rolled her shoulder and flexed her arm. The winter gear absorbed most of the damage but there would be some bruises in the morning.

"I should report the incident at the precinct," she said, bridging the next unpleasant topic. "When I do, they'll pull the missing person report on Lara."

"Then why would you do that?" he asked, stepping back and shoving his hands into his pockets.

"It's practical." She fiddled with the zipper on her coat. "Lara is of age and it seems she is determined to stay out on the streets."

"You know there's more to it."

"Technically, I *suspect* there's more to it." She hated how snobby that sounded.

"That's it?" He stalked over to the window and glared

out at the street. "You're just going to dismiss my worry as overreacting?"

"Of course not." She wasn't about to dismiss anything. Not Lara's actions, Mr. Nameless's interference, or Leo's feelings.

Given a choice, she'd focus solely on finding his sister. That was what really scared her. She'd let emotion become a blind spot and had paid dearly for the error. Even though Leo was completely different—and temporary—she couldn't afford to make another wrong move because her heart wanted one thing while her job demanded a different course of action.

"I'm not giving up on any of this," she said. "I still have oodles of free time to try and find her."

He crossed the room. "Crap. I'm a jerk."

"You're not," she assured him. "I understand how stressful this is for you."

"Let me apologize," Leo said. "I'm not mad at you. I'm angry *she* ran." He pushed a hand through his hair. She resisted the urge to smooth it back again. "What next?"

"Let's try and pin a name on that creep. He's up to his eyeballs in this."

"In a minute." He unzipped her coat and helped her out of it. "You can notify the precinct by phone, right?"

"Might be better that way." The captain wouldn't appreciate her coming by. She could call Calvin or Hulbert and let them update the official report.

"Good." He kissed her.

She was sinking into the sensual heat when his cell phone went off with a nerve-jolting ringtone. He jumped to answer the alert and his face paled.

"Leo?"

"It-it's Lara."

She peered at the screen with him.

"The number's blocked, but this message. It's her."

She read it over his shoulder.

LEO WE NEED TO TALK

"Are you sure it's her?" Too short for any subtext, Aubrey hesitated to assume Lara sent the message.

"I have to go. I have to meet her." He sent back a text that he would meet her anywhere, anytime.

She laid a hand on his arm. "Wait for the reply, Leo." She didn't need both Butler siblings drifting around her city, targets of whatever was going on.

He gave his phone a shake as if that would make a reply appear faster. "I'll go to the park. If I'm alone, maybe she'll talk."

"Just hang on a second." She would not let him go until she knew the details of the meet. "Let's do this the right way."

He bounced on his toes. "Come on," he growled at the phone.

Aubrey was antsy herself. If Leo thought he was going to meet Lara anytime, anywhere alone, he was in for a rude awakening. He would need someone to cover his back. No matter what she said, when he saw his sister again, he'd be too consumed with her to be cautious.

She didn't think Lara was doing anything illegal, but she was increasingly convinced that someone, someone who kept Mr. Nameless in spiffy leather coats, was out to stop her.

Leo continued to prowl the room.

I love you.

He'd really said it. And she really hadn't. And now what she'd left unsaid was mocking her.

If another chance presented itself, she'd confess her feelings. She wouldn't hesitate again or second-guess because a future looked unlikely. *Love is enough.* She would keep that front of mind.

"Tomorrow!" Leo shouted. "Tomorrow morning at the Good Samaritan." He looked up. "Should we call Rosie?"

"No." As much as it pained her to say it, they needed Grant's help to make sure things went smoothly. She held out her hand for his cell phone. "Show me the message. I'll give Grant a call."

"Should we go over there, maybe stake it out overnight?"

She glared at him. "Sit down," she said, pointing to the desk chair. "You have one job, Mr. Butler."

His eyebrows shot up. "I like it when you're bossy."

"Stop." She leaned over and kissed him anyway.

"Is that my job?"

"It will be later," she teased. "Right now see what you can find about this guy." She showed him the pictures from her camera.

"What's your job?"

"I'm going to speak with Grant."

Leo jumped to his feet. "Don't do that, Aubrey. Let me. I know how you feel about him."

"Relax. I'm okay with it." She realized the words were completely true as they passed her lips. "Who else can we rely on for extra eyes tomorrow?"

"You're sure?"

She kissed him, smiled and then walked out of the room before she changed her mind. They needed help and they weren't going to get it from the precinct. On paper, Lara was an adult who'd chosen not to tell her family what she was up to. Sad but true.

Taking the elevator down to the lobby, she knew it had been more than fabulous sex or three small words that changed everything, especially her. It was one specific man. *Leo* had challenged her all or nothing faith in the system.

She sat down in a chair away from the front doors and dialed Grant's number.

"Officer Rawlins," he answered. "How are you feeling? Kenzie told me about that scuffle in the park."

Miserable. Grumpy. Resigned. "I'm good. Lara just made contact with Leo."

"That's great. Did she give him anything helpful?"

"No specifics, and the messages were coming from a blocked number."

"You're worried it's not Lara."

"I am," she admitted. "After the way things went today, I want a better plan in place for tomorrow. Please?"

"You do realize I'm not a security service. I'm just a cop who retired too early and still cares about his community."

"Mr. Sullivan—"

"Grant," he corrected.

Fine. "Grant, I apologize for what I said and my negative attitude about what you do. You've helped people that would have possibly slipped through the cracks of normal police work."

"Probably," he corrected her again.

"That's fair." She swallowed the sigh. "I did my best to be sure Lara and her brother weren't overlooked. But…" She'd practiced this in her head. Shifting her beliefs wasn't easy. She was glad she was sitting down.

"Leo needs your help. Lara agreed to meet with him tomorrow at the Good Samaritan, but I can't back him up on my own."

"Because IA keeps you under a microscope?"

Did the man know everything? He certainly had the connections from his years on the police force. "Yes." She laid it all out. "The man I tangled with at the park was also at the meeting when Captain Yancey suspended me. I think Leo was right all along and Lara is in serious trouble."

"Go on."

Of course he would know what she hadn't specifically told Leo. "I've used my own network in the neighborhood for the past few days." Mary-Tea and others had kept watch for her. "The camp on Thirty-third was cleaned out the day after the storm. Officer Rice might have more detail on the men we spoke with at the time. I was suspended before I could learn anything."

"And you don't want to drag Rice down with you?"

"No. My priority is Lara. According to my sources, she's helped those displaced find other shelter, kept them fed. In turn, several of them are keeping her protected, but I've been told men are following her."

Aubrey hadn't told Leo because she didn't want him freaking out when there wasn't anything he could do about it.

"The people I have keeping an eye out for her have reported seeing familiar faces, as well. Give me the particulars of the meet." She did. "All right. I'll make some calls and be in touch. We'll get Lara in safely."

Her instincts were humming. Grant had more information he wasn't sharing. "Did you speak with Leo?"

"Not about this, Officer Rawlins."

"Aubrey."

She heard a rumble on the other end of the call that might have been a chuckle. "You want to know why I'm so willing to help you in particular?"

"I do, yes." She'd been rude to him, in his own place. Her cheeks flamed with embarrassment at the memory. "Please."

"Because I used to be you," Grant said. "I understand the overload and overwhelm. I understand doing everything right and having it turn out all wrong. I understand how it feels when you know that the people in your community should all have equal priority, yet one of them strikes a new chord you can't ignore."

Technically, Leo wasn't part of her community. His sister was. It was the same with certain shelter and charity workers and even the people they served. Some of them just clicked with her, motivating her to go above and beyond. Leo had tripped that new chord, long before she was personally invested. "We're not supposed to play favorites."

Grant scoffed. "You're human. We all are. I'll be in touch."

"Thank you," she said. Relief coursed through her. Leo needed his sister safe and whole. Life had stolen so much from him, far too early. She'd taken an oath to protect and serve her community and as much as she'd resisted it, working with Grant was part of fulfilling that vow, for Leo.

"You should come by the club," he said. "We're just a few weeks away from a grand reopening."

"Oh. I…" Would going out to the Escape Club make things better or worse for her with IA and the PPD? She was human, entitled to a personal life. "Thanks," she managed. "I'll look forward to it."

"Great."

The call ended. Aubrey remained in the lobby, replaying it all in her head. They'd have support; that was what she would focus on. Leo and Lara would soon be reunited.

And then what?

They'd all go their separate ways. She'd be back on the job, where she belonged. Leo and Lara would work out their differences. At home.

No sense crying over the facts she couldn't change. So why were tears sliding down her cheeks? She dried her eyes, wondering how, in a city as big and busy as Philly, she'd fallen in love with a man whose presence was only temporary.

Chapter 11

Leo needed to focus on Lara. His sister needed his help, needed his full attention. Unfortunately, he couldn't keep his thoughts away from the quiet woman in the passenger seat beside him. The anticipation of what they were about to do didn't mute all of the new feelings for Aubrey rolling around in his chest.

Under normal circumstances he might have talked through it with Lara, let her set him straight on the whole being in love thing. Was that irony?

"What are you thinking about?" Aubrey asked.

"Irony," he answered without thinking. He reached over and gave her hand a squeeze while they waited for the traffic light to change. His heart skipped when she laced her fingers with his.

He'd fallen in love with her and, like a man with a fever, he'd spoken up, laid it all out there and she…had yet to respond in kind. What had he expected? They'd met under fraught circumstances barely two weeks ago.

As an adult, he understood, did his best to give her space. But the broken little boy he'd been was scared. Scared of more disappointment and crushing rejection.

Which was stupid.

He'd worked through all of this, learned to reframe and appreciate the good, normal life he'd started out with. Yes, the accident had changed everything, especially his mother and the family dynamics. He'd sorted out those twisty layers with a counselor during his college years.

Grief changed people and some people, like his mom, broke under that pressure. He drifted, lost and lonely, using Lara as a touchstone. Lara had simply adapted, growing from a happy baby to a happy toddler to a happy kid who had no illusions about her mother's weaknesses. Still, she'd become a fairly well-adjusted adult, even if she had taken an unorthodox approach to uncovering the plight of inner-city homelessness.

His sister had always had a big heart and now it was his job to get her, and her heart, home in one piece. Parking the delivery van in the designated loading zone behind the soup kitchen, he cut the engine. Rosie had arranged for them to make the delivery today.

He should say something. Maybe she would. The silence stretched between them. He was sure she could hear his pounding heart. "Thank you." He gave her hand another squeeze.

She raised their joined hands and pressed her lips to his knuckles. "You'll have her back soon."

With a determined nod, they climbed out of the cab and went around to the back of the truck. After unloading crates of produce, they walked into the soup kitchen. They were a few minutes early and he hoped Lara was already here.

"You holding up?" Aubrey asked when they went back out for the next load.

"I didn't see her."

"We will." Her smile eased the worst of the doubts.

Leo slid a crate of onions onto the steel worktable in the kitchen. Aubrey would probably be shocked if she knew how his attention was split. Yes, he wanted his sister back, but he was equally concerned about Aubrey's feelings for him, beyond the undeniable sexual chemistry.

"If she runs again…" He couldn't finish the thought.

"She ran out of that park because she had to," Aubrey reminded him. "Meeting here was her idea." She patted his arm. "Take a breath."

He obliged, then kissed her lightly on the lips. "Thank you for being here," he said. "For helping a worry-crazed brother."

She smiled up at him. "You're welcome. Let's keep moving."

That was advice he could get behind. He believed in Aubrey. She'd shocked him by so willingly involving Grant, but she didn't show any regret over that choice.

"When we get her back, can I wring her professor's neck?" he asked in a whisper on the way back to the truck.

"No," she said, smothering a laugh. "Warranted or not, I'd still have to arrest you for assault. Besides, we don't know the whole story."

Leo knew Lara, and he was almost certain Whitten had manipulated her big heart for his own glory.

When the truck was unloaded, he and Aubrey stuck around to help Rosie and her team while they waited for Lara to show up. He lost count of how many people they served before Aubrey nudged him. "She's here," she whispered, carrying a refill of stew to the serving line.

It was all he could do not to bolt out of the kitchen to make sure it wasn't a mistake.

Aubrey popped his ribs with her elbow. "Stick to the plan."

He nodded and served stew to those in line for lunch. When Aubrey moved to the bathroom per the plan, Leo checked his watch. He'd wait five minutes and then move to the delivery van. Aubrey and Lara would meet him there and they would all drive away.

Simple and secure.

He couldn't call it easy. Nothing would feel easy until all three of them were back in the hotel suite. Maybe not until they were back in Cincinnati. Of course, Aubrey wouldn't join them there. But that was a problem to solve after Lara was out of danger.

He heard a crash in the dining room followed by raised voices. He exchanged a look with Rosie, but held his ground, speaking kindly to the bearded man in front of him. He would follow the plan. A woman's shriek punctuated more shouting, and the original plan evaporated from Leo's mind.

"Call the police," he snapped, dashing out of the kitchen and scooting around and between people as quickly as possible. In the dining room a man in a long, battered trench coat was shouting at a group of women about the "new girl." He hadn't come through the food line. His dark hair was a mess and his beard scraggly, but Leo's attention locked on to his shoes. The guy's shoes were too nice. Cross-trainers, wet from the weather, but the uppers were mostly clean and the laces looked new.

"Hey!" Leo raised his voice just to get the other man's attention. It took all his willpower not to search the room for his sister. She'd specified meeting in the bathroom, but what if this altercation changed her mind or scared her off? He held his palms out wide. "Can I help you with something?"

The bearded man's eyes weren't glassy from substance abuse or shadowed by hard circumstance. No, his gaze was too sharp and far too calculating for Leo's comfort.

"Come on over and talk to me." Leo waved him closer. "Let the ladies eat."

"Ladies?" The other guy snorted.

"The next words out of your mouth will be respectful," Leo warned.

"Or what?" The man shrugged off the worn coat and stood tall. The wild hair and beard were a ridiculous contrast with the clean sweater, jeans and shoes. He stalked toward Leo.

Leo shifted, drawing his attention away from the hallway where he hoped Lara and Aubrey were making their exit. Both he and Aubrey had keys to the truck, as a contingency.

The jerk charged at him. Bent at the waist, Leo angled his hip and threw his weight into the move. The man went up and over, landing on the floor with a splat.

Leo ran for the hallway just as Aubrey and Lara stepped out of the bathroom. Per the plan, Aubrey had given Lara a change of clothes and a Phillies ball cap. His sister looked almost like the college student he remembered. Almost. The sorrow in her eyes was new and hit him harder than the attacker in the dining room.

"Go, go!" He urged them out the back door.

He fished the van key out of his pocket as Aubrey threw open the back door. They only had a few yards to cross from the building to the van. The plan was to be cool, walk out, get in and drive away.

The shouts following him convinced Leo the plan was blown. He gave Aubrey a look and she nodded once. Stepping outside, she rushed forward, Lara on her heels and Leo bringing up the rear. They hadn't taken more than two steps when the sharp report of a gunshot confirmed Leo's worst fears.

His first instinct was to drag Lara and Aubrey back into the building, but that gave the man behind him too many options, including potential hostages. He pressed closer to Lara, protecting her with his body, and shoved both women ahead of him. "Go!"

Lara cried out and stumbled to her knees. Leo swore, apologizing as he tried to help her up.

A pop and hiss had him turning toward the street. Smoke was filling the delivery lane, blocking them from the shooter's view.

Aubrey had the side door open and turned to help Lara into the shelter of the vehicle. He assisted Lara from his side, his hand coming back red. He couldn't process what he saw. Wiping the sticky blood on his jeans, he slid into the driver's seat and started the engine.

The rear and side mirrors showed a bank of thick fog, so Leo drove straight ahead and away from the chaos. At the side street, he turned away from the flashing lights of the PPD, who'd responded to Rosie's emergency call.

He caught Aubrey's gaze in the rearview mirror. "How bad is it?"

She winced, her mouth pulled to the side. "Take us straight to the ER," she said. "Lara's hit."

Leo glanced at the dried streaks on his palm. "How bad?"

"Not so bad," Lara said, her voice tight with pain. "Aubrey's hit, too."

"What?" He'd thought things couldn't get worse. For a moment the past and present merged. He wasn't a safe bet. Couldn't do a damn thing right to keep the people he loved safe.

"Leo," Aubrey snapped. "It's not serious." She met his gaze in the rearview mirror. "But hurry."

She didn't have to ask him twice.

Aubrey ignored the sting in her side. "I'll tell Grant to meet us at the ER." It took her two tries to get the text message sent. She'd been grazed by a bullet meant for the woman sitting beside her. "You must have stirred up some hornet's nest."

"Apparently so," Lara said through clenched teeth. "When the professor missed our last scheduled meeting, I found another way to upload the information I've been gathering."

Aubrey smoothed her hand over Lara's face. According to Grant, the professor claimed Lara was the one who'd gone AWOL. She stared into the girl's eyes, which were the same color as her brother's. "We'll get it all figured out."

"Thanks, Officer Aubrey." Lara's eyelids fluttered. "That's what Mary-Tea calls you."

"How bad is it?" Leo called back over his shoulder.

"I'm fine," Lara answered. "It's a flesh wound." Her voice was steady, but pain was etched around her mouth and eyes.

Aubrey gave a start when Leo laughed. "If this has been a theatrical farce from the beginning, I'll kill you, sis."

Aubrey's cell phone rang and seeing Grant's number on the display, she answered. "Lara's been shot."

"We saw it," Grant said. "We're holding the shooter and I expect him to cooperate."

"Good news," Aubrey allowed. "We're on our way to the ER. Lara needs a hospital more than a conference in the back room of your club."

Grant snorted. "You make it sound so unethical, Aubrey. I'm on your side. Put me on speaker?"

"Sure." She shifted closer to the cab so all three of them could hear. "Go."

"Leo?" Grant's voice filled the vehicle.

"Present."

"We can debrief at the hospital unless they release Lara right away."

Aubrey didn't expect it to go that way. Lara was bleeding pretty heavily and she didn't see an exit wound.

"No one is following you," Grant continued. "Whoever hired the shooter won't make another move right away."

"You sound confident," Aubrey said. How could he be so sure? She gasped, bracing too late as Leo turned for the hospital.

"I am. I'll explain more in person," Grant replied. "Are you okay?"

"We're here," Leo said, pulling to a stop in front of the emergency room doors.

Aubrey disconnected the call, sliding her phone into her pocket. Whatever Grant had uncovered would have to wait until they were done here. These days there was no way to keep any gunfire out of the news or the police blotter. The red tape of bullet wounds and reports would be plentiful as soon as they walked inside.

She'd stick with the facts. It was the only way she knew. Though she hadn't wanted Grant involved, she was grateful for the backup. She'd never expected anyone to try and kill Lara.

Unanswered questions plagued her as she and Leo waited for Lara to be treated. Aubrey's effort to preempt what might be a career ending incident involved calling Hulbert and giving him a brief report. Then it was a matter of waiting for the officers who'd caught the case to find them at the hospital.

Officers Small and Woodson had spoken with Leo and Lara first, catching up with her while a nurse treated the wound from the bullet's track across her ribs. Woodson took notes as she explained she'd been volunteering at the soup kitchen with Leo when the shooting started.

"Butler. He's been a pain in the ass around here, searching for his sister." Small said.

"He's also the man who helped customers exit a store during a robbery last week," she replied, inexplicably annoyed with her fellow officers.

Woodson frowned. "He said he found his sister by volunteering at soup kitchens around town."

"More effective than posting flyers," she said with all the sarcasm she could muster.

"And you were there volunteering, too," Small stated.

"Yes." Her jaw clenched hard enough to make her

teeth ache. "Helping Rosie while I'm suspended beats twiddling my thumbs at home."

"Aubrey." Small patted her shoulder. "We're on your side."

Once the nurse finished and gave her discharge instructions, Aubrey hopped off the gurney. She wanted to walk out of here and just go home. If she did, she wouldn't know what Lara had found out, or what Grant planned to do about it. This was her city after all, the place she called home and where she intended to stay.

"Thanks," she said. "I don't mean to be defensive. Never thought I'd have to cope with gunfire without my service weapon."

Her fellow officers murmured sympathetic responses. The emotional layers were hers and had no bearing on the report they filed. So she kept her feelings locked down. From this point forward, whatever Lara had to say was probably best handled by Grant and his PPD connections.

Leo and Lara would go home, she would return to duty when her suspension expired and the world would keep on turning. The happy glow in that picture of her future had dimmed considerably in recent days because of Leo. She wanted a life and love and a partnership beyond her career.

Spotting Leo down the hall, she looked away, listening to Small. "The shooter was delivered to the precinct," he was saying. "Rice is taking his confession. The guy is in the mood to talk."

"Good." That would make all of this easier for the Butlers and for her.

"Any chance you could make an ID?" Woodson queried. She shook her head. "My attention was on Lara. When the gunshots started, I was focused on getting her out of harm's way."

Woodson patted her shoulder. "Let us know if you think of anything else, all right?"

"I will."

Small followed his partner to the exit.

"Are you all right?" Leo wrapped her in a gentle hug. "Did they grill you?"

The tenderness was temporary and that made it sting worse than the antiseptic solution the nurse had applied. "I'm fine." Nothing inside Aubrey was any match for the warmth of his touch or the sincerity in his gaze.

Whatever came next, she couldn't deny that what they'd shared was real. Her every instinct about Leo had been on target. Maybe her intuition wasn't as far off-kilter as she'd thought. If only the revelation brought solely happiness, rather than trailing a shadow of impeding loneliness she knew would come when he was gone.

"I'm fine," she repeated. "How's Lara?"

"On the mend. The bullet wasn't embedded too deep, so they took it out with a local anesthetic."

"Wow. That's wonderful news." Leo looked different, more handsome than ever without the stress and worry lining his features. "Has she spoken to Grant?"

"Grant was hoping you'd join us for that." Leo walked backward, tugging her along for a few paces. "They moved her upstairs already."

"Good." She let him keep hold of her hand all the way to Lara's room, locking away the sensation for later. The gesture swelled in her heart, becoming bigger than it should be. When they reached the room, Lara was sitting up in bed and Grant was in the chair beside her. They were both smiling.

"Aubrey." Lara extended her hand. "It's nice to officially meet you."

"You, too." The girl's grip was strong, steady. Aubrey had expected her to be out of it with painkillers. The younger woman had backbone in spades. "Leo's told me so much about you."

"He exaggerates."

Aubrey didn't think that was an accurate assessment, but she let it slide. "How are you feeling?"

"Like an idiot that took a stroll through a shooting range." Her gaze fell to her hands and she smoothed the wrinkles from the cotton blanket that covered her from the chest down. "I'm not just talking about today. The intention was to spend three months on the street and three months working on the paper afterward. I was going to get research credit."

"We heard," Leo muttered.

"I'm sorry I worried you," she said, her eyes filled when she looked at Leo. "This wouldn't have been your ideal plan for me, but I didn't just dive in unprepared. It just turned out I wasn't prepared enough." She glanced at Aubrey. "You know how it is out there."

"I have a better idea than most," she said. "What you did took remarkable courage."

"Not really. I had backup and a time limit."

"Your professor is a jerk who used you," Leo barked.

"Maybe." She sat up straighter. "To make the most of it, I cut all ties and tried to blend in, but a few people recognized me from the start."

"Why take such drastic measures to help?" Grant queried. "You were already volunteering with great organizations and on your way to graduating with honors on schedule."

Lara turned to him and cocked an eyebrow in challenge. "You're the last person I'd expect to ask me that."

"My reputation precedes me?"

"Yes," Aubrey and Lara replied in unison. Then they exchanged a smile.

"I don't do much to help the homeless directly," Grant said.

"You helped the guys I brought over," Lara said. "It's your reputation for employing people who give a damn that gets around."

Grant arched his eyebrows, his fingertips tapping together.

"This is about you," Leo said. "You didn't do it for the research credit."

Lara's gaze met Aubrey's. "Mary-Tea was the catalyst," she admitted. "Not Whitten. She came into the soup kitchen with a black eye and she wouldn't tell me how she got it."

It wasn't unusual for a victim to be vague on details. People were hurt or attacked and, much like Leo, weren't convinced the police would budge enough to help. "I know where Mary-Tea spends most of her time," Aubrey explained. "She's well liked. Unless she'd been drawn away from her usual haunts, someone should have seen something."

"Exactly." Lara shifted, a spark in her eyes. "And when she's mad, she doesn't pull punches or spare names and feelings."

Now things were making sense. Why Mary-Tea helped Lara hide from all of them and why she'd delivered messages and warnings on Lara's behalf.

"She convinced you to help her?" Grant asked.

"No. She convinced me there was something questionable going on in her community. If Mary-Tea had been attacked by someone she knew or someone she could deal with, she would've said so. She wouldn't talk to me. Others were being attacked, too. No one would talk to me."

"Until you were one of them," Leo said.

Lara nodded.

Grant rounded on Aubrey. "You didn't know about these attacks?"

"This is the first I've heard of it," she replied. "People come and go, especially around the holidays." She was surprised and pleased when Leo stepped closer in tacit support. "There are frequent altercations or accidents. I can't help when I don't know."

"So did you find anything that made it worth it to take this semester off?" Leo asked.

Aubrey listened closely as Lara explained how she finally got Mary-Tea to admit she'd been roughed up by strangers. Not anyone new to the street, but thugs who'd come in strong with threats and orders to move away from the Thirty-Third Street camp. When she didn't budge, she took a beating that convinced her.

"Hired muscle," Grant mused.

"Had to be," Aubrey agreed quietly.

Leo sighed. "And my heroic little sister thought she could singlehandedly find the money behind the muscle."

"Pretty much," Lara said with a cheeky grin. "I fed the information to Professor Whitten, who dug into it through normal channels. The camp on Thirty-Third and two other places were sold to new owners just weeks before the attacks began."

"They're being pushed out by a developer?" Leo queried.

"That was my guess," Lara said. "I'm not sure of everything Whitten found out while I was on the street. The beatings and trouble subsided, but I stayed to gather real numbers and a full account of the problem so we can come up with more effective ways to help people."

"Not a bad plan," Grant said. "You needed better backup."

"Professor Whitten doesn't count," Leo said. "He's a coward. He's not even here."

"Stop it," Lara snapped. "He's not as bad as you think. He just didn't help you."

"And you nearly got killed," Leo pointed out.

"Take it easy." Aubrey pressed her shoulder to his, her turn to give support. "She's safe, Leo."

"I hope so," Grant said to Lara. "You'll need to take some precautions while the dust settles."

"That won't be a problem," Leo declared. "You're coming back to Cincinnati with me. You can write up your paper and recommendations from home."

"No." Lara's chin rose, defiant. "I'm staying. I'm not even in much pain."

"That's the painkillers talking," Leo countered.

They bickered, though Aubrey didn't hear any of the specifics. Just the mention of Cincinnati made her heart ache in her chest. "I—I need to go," Aubrey stammered, speaking to no one in particular. She slid a look toward Grant. "Thanks for the assist."

Then she bolted from the room like a scared rabbit. Lara had done something huge and courageous and now Aubrey had to find a way to step up and make sure things changed in Philly. Her breath backed up in her lungs. She would get the details from the professor and then figure out the next step. Alone.

A sob caught in her throat. Why was she upset? Leo hadn't ever given her anything but the truth about his plans to take Lara home again.

"Officer Rawlins? Aubrey?"

She turned to find Grant right behind her. Apparently, she'd made it all of about ten yards from Lara's room. "Are you all right?"

"Sure," she lied bravely. "Just too many sleepless nights."

Grant nodded, his bushy salt-and-pepper eyebrows lifting a bit in doubt. "Understood. Before you talk to anyone else about this, I'd like to ask you to give me a few days."

"Why?"

"Well, you're still suspended, and I might be able to pull strings you can't."

He wasn't wrong, though it stung enough that she wouldn't admit it. "All right. The man who tried to catch Lara at the park is a key player. He must have ties to the new property owner," she said. "I'll use the rest of my forced free time to learn what I can from Mary-Tea and anyone else who will talk to me. I'm not the only cop in the precinct who wants to see those people safe."

"I know," Grant soothed. "If there's anything we can do, any support we can give, say the word, okay? You're welcome at the club anytime, before or after we open."

She nodded, misery overwhelming her. There was an ache in the pit of her stomach, knowing Leo would be leaving, even as her heart soared with joy that he had his sister back. She had to get out of here before she broke apart.

Chapter 12

Leo couldn't believe his sister wanted to stay and follow this through, even going back undercover, but she wouldn't let it rest. "You could work up your report from Cincinnati. At least think about coming home while you recuperate. Here, you'd be dealing with a hotel room, since you gave up your dorm."

Lara held out her hands. "Truce. I give. Just stop badgering me."

"What?" He'd just been getting warmed up. "You're giving in?"

"I'm not even close to giving in, but your girlfriend is giving up on you."

He spun around and belatedly realized they were alone. For how long? "Where'd she go?"

"Not behind curtain number three, you dork." Lara rolled her eyes. "She left while you were pestering me to do things your way. Go find her."

He was through the door before she finished. Standing so close to Aubrey, he'd felt her reactions to Lara's story as if they were his own. This woman cared so deeply, even beyond her role as a PPD officer. She'd cared for him; she'd shown him tremendous grace and compassion as he'd been frantic, trying to find his sister.

Now he hurried down the hall toward the elevators, just as desperate to find Aubrey. He paused, hearing a conversation, and followed the sound of her voice around the corner where she was speaking with Grant.

"Everything okay here?" he asked. Aubrey had been through enough with him, her suspension and then rescuing Lara. He didn't want Grant to be further aggravation. The other man was only involved because of Leo's insistence.

"Sure," Grant replied. "You two stay in touch," he added, striding away without waiting for an answer.

"He was just letting me know I had options for the rest of my suspension." She pressed her hands to her eyes for a moment.

"Of course you have options," Leo said. "Why do you need them, though?"

She shrugged. "Grant helps first responders as much as he helps strangers. Rosie might get sick of me hanging around."

"What if I gave you an option to trump both of those?"

When she looked up at him something inside his chest loosened. That clear blue gaze was so precious to him now, he couldn't imagine not seeing it every day for the rest of his life. That was a big leap, bigger even than when he'd blurted out that "I love you."

What they needed was time. Time away from the chaos and pressure. Time without his worry for Lara and her concerns about the PPD painting a black cloud over their every thought and action.

"You walked out," he said.

"You and your sister needed the privacy." Her smile wobbled. "It's a sibling thing that I'll never understand."

He chuckled, but there wasn't any humor in her eyes. He was supposed to be making her a better option. "Come to Cincinnati. Lara will probably be released tomorrow and ready to travel. It's not a long flight. I have plenty of comp tickets available."

She frowned at him. "Why?"

He struggled as all of the answers jumbled up in his head. *Because I love you. Because you're my only source of peace. Because I need you the way I need air.* He couldn't give her any of those answers. They were words, declarations she would write off as overblown feelings induced by the crisis.

"Because you need the change of scenery as much as Lara does. Think of what the two of you can accomplish for Philly if you get away for a few days."

"You think I'm too close to the trouble here?"

"No, I think a break can be energizing, restorative. Come visit, get the whole story out of Lara and the two of you can brainstorm workable solutions."

She folded her arms over her chest. "And let Grant do *all* of the heavy lifting with the shooter and Whitten."

Yes! Surely, she saw the value in that. "At least temporarily." Like Lara, Aubrey showed no sign of relenting. Shouldn't she be excited about spending more time together? At the moment she looked as if she couldn't wait to be rid of him.

"I can't," she said. "Leaving now sends the wrong message. Only good people, working inside the system with the people who need help, will make this situation better."

She wasn't the only good person in Philly, even if he did manage to get Lara to go back with him. "What's the real issue, Aubrey?" he demanded, hurt by her lack of enthusiasm.

"No issue." She dropped her hands, rolled her shoulders back. Didn't she know he recognized the signs of her bracing for the worst? "You need to see to Lara's recovery. I need to do the same for Mary-Tea and the others."

"What about *us*?" Had he just said that?

"I don't know what you want to hear, Leo."

Yes, she did. He could see it in her eyes. Why did he have to lay his soul bare again? She wasn't even trying to meet him halfway.

"I want to hear…" *I want to hear you say you love me.* He cleared his throat, breaking up the ball of need and fear choking him. "I want to hear you'd enjoy spending a few days with me away from threats and demands."

"There's an entire segment of my community rattled and worried. I can help them."

"You're *off duty*." Desperation raked sharp claws through his gut. He reached for her, more than half-afraid this would be the last time he saw her face. "I'm not asking for that much."

"I wish I could give you the time. I do." Tears shimmered in her eyes. "We both have our responsibilities. Your sister needs your attention."

He wanted to argue, but she wasn't wrong.

She took a step backward and his heart lurched after her, though his feet remained rooted to the floor.

"Aubrey—"

She shook her head, taking another step away from

him. "I've enjoyed getting to know you, Leo, and I'm happy we found your sister. Take care."

Her words clanged through his head as she walked away, cycling over and over on a loop as uneven and unsteady as a rusty merry-go-round.

She'd refused his offer. Refused him. He'd hated Philly on arrival, but seeing it through her eyes had changed his mind. He'd wanted to show her his town, his home. His heart. Except his heart was hers now. He rubbed at the hollow space in his chest.

Why did one more rejection hurt so badly? He should be an expert by now. The place where his heart had been didn't give a damn about logic, only Aubrey. He'd given her the space, all but rolled out the red carpet for her to trust him with her feelings.

She'd made her choice.

Now he had to live with it.

He trudged back toward Lara's room. His sister would go home with him. He needed to see her healthy again, needed the reminder that he wasn't as alone as he felt right now.

The nurse was checking her vitals, giving them both a reprieve. As soon as she walked out, Lara stated her case for staying.

"No," Leo said. "I'm not losing you to a cause. Let things cool down."

"Leo, I'm an adult," she pointed out.

"I've heard." He was tired of hearing it.

"I'm not going back to Cincinnati," she said, coughing a little. "I want to finish my degree here."

"They should just hand you the diploma today," he muttered. At her glare, he raised his hands. "Sorry. Your professor is a jerk for going along with this."

"He can be a jerk, but those people need a voice and reliable assistance. Good cops like Aubrey need support from people like me."

Leo studied her face, recognized the signs. He would never convince her to leave this town. Was that so bad? Yes. Absolutely without a doubt, that was the worst. The last thing he wanted to cope with now.

"You want to finish what you started with this research experiment, that's fine. We'll do that." He stalked over to the window. Sunlight danced on the snow, making what was still white on the trees and window corners sparkle like diamonds. He could call Philly home until Lara was out of school and ready to be on her own. It was what he should have done from the start.

"I'll call the airport and put things in motion," he said. He could cash out his leave and tap into his emergency fund if he couldn't find work right away. "A moving company can pack up the house for us. We'll find a place here," he added.

"You've been thinking of relocating?" Lara asked. "Here?"

"Sure." From the moment Aubrey refused to even visit Cincinnati. "It's a great city."

"Leo," Lara said, her tone skeptical.

"Without you, what the hell do I have in Cincinnati?" Leo was adaptable, his career easier to transfer. With or without Aubrey, he wouldn't have any peace if he left Lara here to recover on her own. "It's what I should have done your freshman year."

"Please. I adjusted flawlessly to college life."

"You did." He sighed, his breath fogging the window glass. Adulthood and real life were the current threats.

"We're stronger together and if you need to be here to reach your goals, I'll be here, too, to support you."

"In it together, huh?"

"Always," he muttered. Moving allowed him to stay closer to the most important person in his life, the person who'd never given up on him. And if, by some miracle, relocating gave him a second chance with Aubrey, he'd take it.

"What do you want, Leo?"

He turned his back on the window and forced himself to answer her honestly. "Family. A partner for this thing called life." He scrubbed a hand through his hair. "That would take some pressure off you," he admitted. "I thought that kind of messy, emotional stuff was for other people. Turns out I was wrong."

Her gaze dropped to her hands, one bandaged, one free. "But you want all that messy stuff for yourself now? Not because you think it's what I need?"

"More than I've ever wanted anything else." Aubrey had shown him a better way, if he was man enough to change and take a risk with no guarantee of the reward.

"You were never Mom's problem."

Leave it to Lara to cut to the chase. Until Aubrey, he'd never allowed himself to be that vulnerable. She hadn't given him the words—she'd even walked away—but not before she'd shown him nothing was stronger than love.

"Did you hear me?" Lara winced as she shifted the bed to sit up a bit more.

He rushed forward, but she waved off his concern. "Relax. I'm tougher than I look." She paused to sip from the water glass on the bedside table and then tried to smile. "You were Mom's whipping boy, sure," Lara continued. "It was cruel and horrible and unfair. But that's her loss, her failing, not yours."

He knew what she was doing. He even tried to appreciate it. "No one has a perfect life." The words were dry as sand. "My mom didn't like me. You grew up without a dad."

"Because of a freak accident, Leo. An accident you survived. Do you ever think about how proud he'd be of you?"

Not often. There were other things to think about.

"And Mom's depression and rejection hurt both of us. Maybe more than we think." She pleated the hospital blanket between her fingers. A nervous habit she'd had since she was a toddler.

What else had she kept inside, hidden behind her sweet smile?

"Lara."

She closed her eyes and rested her head against the pillow. "I mean it, Leo. Move to Philly, but only if it's what *you* want to do."

"It is." Sticking close to the place he'd grown up had worked while Lara had needed him to help her navigate their mother's moods. As much as he'd like to pin this urge to relocate solely on her shoulders, that wasn't his primary reasoning.

"Great. We'll negotiate boundaries later. Right now, if you love Aubrey, go tell her," Lara said. "You're the best man I know, Leo. You've always deserved love and kindness and affection."

"But can I give those things in return?" he asked, voicing his greatest fear.

"You've been doing it all your life," Lara replied confidently.

"When did you get so wise?"

She laughed, cringed. "About the time you and Aubrey rescued me from myself. I like her, Leo."

"She's amazing." Leo took her hand in his, stilling the nervous movements. "You'll stay and do what you do best. Just don't shut me out again."

"Deal. Will you go tell Aubrey you love her?"

"Already did," he said. Lara sputtered, indignant. "You focus on getting better and I'll figure out how to win her trust."

He waited until she dozed off before he stepped into the hallway to start making arrangements. His course decided, the pieces seemed to fall into place. On the phone with his boss, they quickly came to terms about splitting his time with his department and training up his replacement. Now all he had to do was find work here in Philly. To his surprise, his boss had ideas about that, too.

He might have called it fate but the most essential piece of the puzzle was Aubrey. There was no guarantee she'd come around even once he completed the relocation.

He hoped, when he reached out to her as a new resident of the city she loved so much, she'd willingly make room in her life for him, too.

Aubrey didn't expect to miss Leo so much, especially not when it had been her choice to walk away. Somehow, she'd let another man slip through her practical and smart defenses and get close enough to hurt her.

Yes, Leo was different. The pain was her fault. That was the problem.

She'd spent the first forty-eight hours since leaving him reminding herself that he wasn't her type. Too polished, too handsome, and too willing to bend the rules to save someone he loved. His sister. Her.

He loved her and she'd kept quiet, even after promising herself she'd speak up. He must hate her now. She sure hated herself. She'd used the internet to get a street view of his house in Cincinnati. She'd even looked at job openings within the local police department. And then she'd pulled a pint of ice cream out of her freezer to ease the burn of turning down the best man she'd had the pleasure of meeting.

When she finally did get back on the roll, she'd been surprised by the support of her fellow officers. No one had bought in to the conduct unbecoming nonsense, especially not when the "evidence" of her supposed indiscretions amounted to her helping a clearly incapacitated man to his hotel and later sharing a meal with him. Hulbert, she was sure, was behind that information leak. Every day she wanted to hug him for it.

During her first shift back, Calvin filled her in on what she'd missed. The shooter had given up the real names of the men they'd found clearing the camp on Thirty-Third Street. Those arrests led the police to the thug who'd followed Lara and been present when Aubrey had been suspended. Mr. Nameless had been hired by Councilman Keller to get rid of Lara because her research threatened to expose him as the actual owner behind the development company.

Aubrey had been as shocked by Keller's abuse of power and criminal actions as everyone else in the city.

The media had picked up the story and uncovered Professor Whitten's arrangement to send a student undercover to expose the plight of the city's homeless population. He was now facing a peer review, among other problems. Aubrey suspected Grant was behind that, though she couldn't bring herself to ask him to confirm those rumors. The professor had made egregious errors in how he'd handled the entire situation and deserved all the embarrassment and unpleasant consequences the school and police could throw at him.

Beyond her immense gratitude, she still hadn't figured out how she felt about needing Grant's connections and assistance to wrap up the whole mess.

Walking the neighborhood with Calvin only reminded her of Leo. She thought she saw him everywhere. It was pathetic and frustrating and why didn't she call him already?

Pride. Pride and cowardice. She'd seen the flare of pain in his eyes when she refused his invitation to visit Cincinnati. So she worked her shifts at the precinct and with Rosie at the soup kitchen. She'd even coordinated with Grant, following Lara's example, and they were developing a better jobs network for people in need. She worked until she could drop into bed and not dream about Leo. Maybe, with time, losing him would stop hurting.

Before Leo, she never would have asked Grant for any kind of help. The former cop was far more than an outlier with an ego and even after days of rehashing the scene and reviewing the reports, she couldn't see how they would've rescued Lara without his help.

Leo's fault, she thought, grasping for some anger. Anything to mute the aching loss wedged deep in her chest. Love sucked. Loving *him* sucked. He had the power to wound her more deeply than any criminal. And she'd handed over that power willingly.

At the end of her shift, she opened her locker and

the rose-colored glasses inside the door mocked her. It was high time to get real. Maybe crushing those glasses would give her some perspective. Some spine. Some peace.

A week of nights in an empty bed and an emptier apartment sure hadn't done it.

She left the glasses where they were and slammed the door closed. Locked it. Battling back another surge of tears, she waved to Hulbert on her way out of the building.

"Hold up," Hulbert said. "Got a message for you." He handed her the small square of paper.

She frowned at the number as she entered it into her phone. The call rang and rang until at last a woman answered.

"Officer Rawlins, of the Philadelphia Police Department, returning your call."

"Hey, Aubrey, this is Lara."

Aubrey sagged against the wall. "How are you?"

"I'm better than new," she said. "I'm here in town and Grant and I were hoping you might have time to talk after your shift."

"Talk?" Aubrey echoed, butterflies racing to the flight line, ready for takeoff. Leo had once vowed not to let Lara out of his sight. If she was in town, was Leo with her? Could she have a second chance with him?

"I was hoping we could work together," Lara began, "to document some of the measures that are working and…"

Aubrey tried to listen, but her focus was shot as she kept hoping for a mention of Leo. Should she ask? Of course she'd work with Lara to help the homeless community. Teaming up with Leo's sister would be painful as hell, though. At first. The pain of missing him, of missing her chance, would dull with time, right?

"Aubrey? You there?"

"*Hmm?* Yes, I'd love to hear more. Whatever I can do to help." She hoped that was a reasonable response, seeing how she hadn't registered anything Lara might have said about a plan.

"See you at seven at the Escape Club, okay?"

"Sure." Grateful for the time cue, Aubrey replaced the receiver, fairly sure Lara knew how much she hadn't heard. Embarrassing, but what was forlorn distraction between two people who'd been shot together?

What could be better than another meeting with Grant at his club? It hadn't officially reopened, but they must be close to ready. She walked home, her thoughts and stomach churning in opposing patterns. She changed out of her uniform, choosing dark jeans and a sapphire turtleneck. Tugging on ankle boots in deference to the inch of snow that fell last night, she grabbed her polar fleece PPD jacket and went outside to meet the car service she'd called.

She confirmed the address with the driver and spent the ride sorting out the best way to ask about Leo without looking like she was asking about Leo.

When she arrived, she stood and just stared at the club. The construction equipment and debris were gone and the new sign was up and lit, though the inside remained dark. Walking to the door, she saw the posters announcing the grand reopening next week. Good for Grant and his team, and the community, she thought.

She opened the door and a light came on over the dance floor. In the center of the glow, she saw a familiar figure.

Leo.

Her heart leaped, banging against her rib cage. "Leo?" Was he really here?

"Aubrey."

He sounded real. He looked real as he walked over. And his hand, wrapping around hers, felt as real and right as ever. Oh, she'd missed him. She didn't know what to do, so she followed like a lost lamb as he led her toward the table. "What's going on?"

"We're having a date."

"I was supposed to meet Lara." He tensed up and she wished she could reel the words back in. "She was in on it," she said as the pieces clicked.

"She was," he confirmed, though her remark hadn't been a question. "She's a good sister."

The inside of the club looked better than new. The famous bar had been restored with care, the tables and booths arranged around an expansive dance floor and wide stage.

In the center of the space, under that soft light, one table was set for two people, complete with a white tablecloth, a pair of lit candles flanking a small arrangement of deep red tea roses.

"It seems bigger."

"It might be," Leo said.

He pulled out her chair and soft instrumental music floated through the air. "Who else is here?"

"No one. This is just for us."

Time alone, just the two of them. Guilt prickled the back of her neck over her refusal, her fear of telling him how she'd felt. How she still felt. "Leo, I…" The words he deserved to hear failed her again. "I don't know if I can do this." Not if he was going to leave again.

"I haven't asked you to do anything," he said. "Let's enjoy ourselves." He lifted the cover from a platter to reveal a selection of crackers, cheese and stuffed mushrooms. "Your favorite, right?"

She nodded, her throat too dry to speak.

"I've missed you."

"I've missed you, too." What an understatement. She pulled herself together. This was Leo, a man she admired and trusted. Brother of the woman she hoped to work with to create a real change in the city. "How is Cincinnati? You must have been relieved to be home."

"It isn't Philly," he said with a twinkle in his eyes. "And it isn't home anymore."

She set down her water glass as his statement registered. "What are you saying?"

"Lara is determined to stay here for her degree and to finish what she started. I don't expect she'll call Cincinnati home again. So here I am."

"Here you are," she repeated, stunned. "What does that mean?"

"I moved. Here to Philly. We bought a house."

"You didn't." But of course he had—for Lara.

"I'm working an inside line on a potential new job, too."

She was happy for him. Truly. "Much to celebrate."

"It pales."

"Pardon me?"

"The new city, new house and eventually a new job, all pales in comparison. That's just a way to stay close to my sister. It's not a life."

"Then what is?" She hoped he knew, because good work, friends and great ice cream weren't making the grade for her anymore.

"Love. Companionship, affection, laughter. Those things make the rest of the necessities shine. Those things make a life full, Aubrey."

This was her chance to tell him she loved him, too, to ask him to look at her with the love and all the rest he'd said.

"Leo—"

He cut her off, shifting his focus and lifting the chafing dish at the serving cart next to the table. The savory aroma lifted on a billow of steam. Cincinnati chili, she realized. The laughter bubbled up and out of her, a sweet release for all the pressure she'd carried this past week.

"I conned the secret recipe out of a friend and one of Grant's guys made it for us." He loaded her plate, and his, and resumed his seat.

It smelled delicious, but she was too afraid to eat, with those butterflies back at the flight line, wings humming and ready.

"Leo, you once said you loved me."

"I did." He met her gaze and she saw the love in his eyes.

"It scared me," she admitted. "What I thought it would mean. Being loved."

"Could you elaborate?"

She had to, didn't she? If she got the words out, he might be able to help her put them in the right order. "I didn't want to lose myself, my goals in a relationship. I didn't want long distance hassles or resentments. And I was a coward not to say I loved you, no matter how much time we did or didn't have together."

He stirred his chili while the silence grew heavier. "I'm here," he said at last. "I want you to stay *you*. That's why I moved here. To give us the best possible chance."

"Now you've changed everything for me and I'm only…"

"Do you love me?" he asked with such gentle vulnerability she felt her heart tremble.

She nodded. "I do. I love you, Leo." The words slipped out effortlessly, bringing all the rest along with them. "I probably started falling somewhere around the second time you rapped your head against the wall in the soup kitchen that first day. I love who you are, how committed you are to Lara and helping her."

"I'm here for you," he said.

She wished he'd reach out and touch her again, but it was long past time for her to make the first move. He'd uprooted a life he'd built to be here. For his sister, sure, but for himself. For her. For all of them. "You want a family."

"I do."

Her heart soared to the rafters. "I want that, too. With you." She pushed back from the table and came around to his side. Cupping his face in her hands, she bent and kissed him softly. "I love you. And it's so much more than I thought it could be. You give me courage."

He pulled her into his lap and kissed her long and deep, the promise of forever in every breath they shared.

"I looked at jobs in Cincinnati," she confessed. "I was working up the courage to apply."

"Now you don't have to. I'm good at strategy and adapting," he murmured against her throat.

"We haven't been apart long enough for me to forget that," she said, arching into his kisses. "You strategized this date perfectly. How did I get so lucky?"

"I'm the lucky one. You listened when you could have arrested me."

"And you listened when I didn't even know how much I was sharing." Tears threatened, but she was too happy to let them fall. "We're going to have an amazing life."

"We are. And it starts right now." He drew her out to the dance floor and held her close, swaying to the sweet music. It was the perfect beginning to the lifetime of love ahead of them.

* * * * *

Read the previous volumes in Regan Black's
Escape Club Heroes series, available now
from Harlequin Romantic Suspense:

Braving the Heat
Protecting Her Secret Son
A Stranger She Can Trust
Safe in His Sight

#2139 COLTON 911: GUARDIAN IN THE STORM
Colton 911: Chicago • by Carla Cassidy

FBI agent Brad Howard is trying to solve a double homicide—possibly involving a serial killer. He never expected Simone Colton, daughter of one of the victims, to get involved and put herself in jeopardy to solve the case.

#2140 COLTON'S COVERT WITNESS
The Coltons of Grave Gulch • by Addison Fox

Troy Colton is a by-the-book detective protecting a gaslighted attorney beginning to fear for her life. Can he keep Evangeline Whittaker—and his heart—safe before her fears become reality?

#2141 CLOSE QUARTERS WITH THE BODYGUARD
Bachelor Bodyguards • by Lisa Childs

Bodyguard Landon Myers doesn't trust Jocelyn Gerber, the prosecutor he's been assigned to protect, but he's attracted to the black-haired beauty. Jocelyn finds herself drawn to the bodyguard who keeps saving her life, but who will save her heart if she falls for him?

#2142 FALLING FOR HIS SUSPECT
Where Secrets are Safe • by Tara Taylor Quinn

Detective Greg Johnson expects to interview Jasmine Taylor for five minutes. But he's quickly drawn to the enigmatic woman, and the case surrounding her brother becomes even murkier. With multiple lives—including that of Jasmine's niece—in the balance, can they navigate the complicated truths ahead of them?

SPECIAL EXCERPT FROM

⬥HARLEQUIN
ROMANTIC SUSPENSE

*Detective Greg Johnson expects to interview
Jasmine Taylor for five minutes. But he's quickly drawn
to the enigmatic woman, and the case surrounding her
brother becomes even murkier. With multiple lives—
including that of Jasmine's niece—in the balance, can
they navigate the complicated truths ahead of them?*

Read on for a sneak preview of
Falling for His Suspect,
USA TODAY *bestselling author Tara Taylor Quinn's
next thrilling romantic suspense in the*
Where Secrets are Safe miniseries!

Greg had been heading to his home gym when his phone
rang. Seeing his newly entered speed dial contact come up,
he picked it up. She'd seen his missed call.

Was calling back.

A good sign.

"Can you come over?" The words, alarming in
themselves, didn't grab him as much as the weak thread in
her voice.

"Of course," he said, heading from the bedroom turned
gym toward the master suite, where he'd traded his jeans for
basketball shorts. "What's up?"

"I…need you to come. I don't know if I should call the
police or not, but…can you hurry?"

Fumbling to get into a flannel shirt over his workout T-shirt, Greg was on full alert. "Are you hurt? Is Bella?" Had Josh been there?

"No, Bella's fine. Still asleep. And I'm...fine. Just..."

He'd button up in the car. Was working his way one-handed into his jeans.

"Is someone there?"

"Not anymore."

Her brother had shown her his true colors. And she'd called him. "You need to call the police, Jasmine." They couldn't quibble on that one. "He could come back."

"He?" For the first time since he'd picked up, he heard the fire of her strength in her voice. "Who?"

"Who was there?" She'd said *not anymore* when he'd asked if someone was there.

"Heidi."

Not at all the answer he'd been expecting.

Grabbing his keys and the gun he didn't always carry, he headed for the garage door and listened as she gave him a two-sentence brief of the meeting.

"Hang up and call the police and call me right back," he told her, pushing the button to open the garage door and starting his SUV at the same time.

He was almost half an hour away. The Santa Raquel police were five minutes away. Max.

Heidi could still be in the area.

Don't miss
Falling for His Suspect *by Tara Taylor Quinn,*
available July 2021 wherever
Harlequin Romantic Suspense
books and ebooks are sold.

Harlequin.com

HRSEXP0621